STEEL GODDESSES

by

Ann C. Brandt

ISBN-13: 978-15-39-76715-2
ISBN-10: 1-5397671-5-9

For more information:
AnnBrandtWrites.wordpress.com
AnnCBrandt.Author@gmail.com

Cover photo: © Photoeuphoria | Dreamstime.com

"Don't write in starlight, for the words may come out real."

~ Ronnie James Dio, Don't Talk to Strangers

"Good girls go to Heaven; Bad girls go backstage"

~ seen on a Rock Angels t-shirt

Chapter 1

New York City, 1985

Toni knew she looked good. Guys stared as she swayed past, drinking in the skin-tight black spandex catsuit hugging her curves and accentuating her long legs. The four-inch red stilettos on her feet added height to her 5'7" frame. She took her time threading through the crowd, shoulders thrown back, a well-practiced half smile on full lips that glistened with cherry red gloss. A halo of carefully teased, white-blonde hair framed an angelic face and fell past her shoulders. Baby blue eyes, ringed with electric blue eyeliner, completed the picture of lazy sensuality.

Toni had made an art out of entering nightclubs and tonight was no exception. She heard one guy moan as she brushed past him and smiled knowingly, letting her fingers trail along his thigh, laughing as he turned crimson and spun away from her. Spotting her friends at the bar, Toni increased her stride, motioning for the girl next to her to keep up. She noticed Maria had already ordered her a drink; she could spot the signature pink umbrella floating atop the orange concoction. She tried to catch Maria's eye, but her friend was staring quizzically at Toni's companion.

She had every right to stare. Kris was not the type of woman Toni usually chose to hang out with. She was drab, her long auburn hair loosely framing a heart-shaped face.

She wore no makeup and was dressed in a pair of jeans, Black Flag t-shirt, and sneakers. However, the toned down look only accentuated her emerald eyes, which were wide with wonder as she gazed around the slowly filling nightclub. Toni had cringed at Kris' outfit, but, Kris was Toni's new challenge, and if there's one thing Toni enjoyed, it was a challenge.

Her other project stood next to Maria. Rusty was tall and very busty, and the lace top she wore was wrong for her body. It looked a half size too small and flattened her boobs, making her look chubby rather than stacked. She had paired the pink top with a red polyester miniskirt, making her look like a porn cheerleader. Her teased, fried blonde hair only added to the silly picture. She looked as though she was trying too hard to fit in, but had fallen way short of the mark. Toni started to roll her eyes but stopped in the nick of time; Rusty had just turned to smile brightly at her.

Sighing inwardly, Toni introduced Kris to the others, finding comfort in the fact that Maria, at least, didn't look like a complete moron, even if she did look a bit morose. Maria was dressed in all black, from the leather jacket zipped nearly to her chin, skintight jeans, and boots. Her closely cropped hair was dyed white and shaped into small spikes what reached for the ceiling. Her brown eyes were violently rings in black; her pale face, white. She'd look dead had it not been for her blood red lips. Toni sighed again. At least Maria pulled her weight backstage and that's all that mattered.

Toni turned back to her drink and noticed the nearest bartender watching her, enthralled. She slowly fished the cherry out of her drink with her tongue, bit down and smiled. He grabbed the nearest glass and began wiping

6

furiously, obviously trying to keep himself in check. She laughed and winked at the bartender, then turned back to the girls. Kris was staring around the club, a look of wonder in her emerald eyes. Toni followed her gaze, taking in the wild mix of men and women as Crazy Train by Ozzy Osbourne pumped through the sound system.

Toni tried to place herself in Kris' shoes; tried to remember what it had felt like the first time she'd ventured onto the metal scene. Try as she might, she couldn't remember. It was as though she'd always been here, sharing her wares with countless musicians. Some had gone on to superstardom; others had gone straight to the gutter. The one thing everyone had in common: they'd never forgotten her.

She was so deep in her reverie; she didn't notice a pair of arms encircling her waist from behind. By the time she realized what was happening, a pair of lips were pressed against her ear.

"Hey, baby."

Toni pulled away and turned to face the speaker. Vinnie Tedesco, the bassist for Torpedo, grinned and tried to pull her closer. She hadn't known they were back in town. They were supposed to be on the road with Deep Purple.

"Vinnie!" she exclaimed, injecting a note of false cheer into her voice. She gently pushed him away from her. "I thought you were in Cincinnati."

His grin widened, showing uneven teeth. "The band and I had a little disagreement, so I'm back home for a while."

This news didn't surprise Toni. Vinnie had an ego that was much bigger than his talent... and his dick, for that matter.

Toni slid out of his grip and smoothed the puckers out of her spandex tights. Reaching up to check her hair, she said in a cooler tone, "Well, Vin, it's nice to see you, but I've got other plans tonight."

Vinnie's face fell; even his large, aquiline nose seemed to sag with disappointment. He began to turn away, then noticed Rusty. Toni caught the split second of interest that registered on his face.

"Vinnie! Let me introduce you to my good friend Rusty!"

She took his arm and led him over to Rusty, who knocked over her nearly full glass of rum and coke in nervousness. Rusty obviously knew who Vinnie Tedesco was and was anxious to make a good impression. Toni ordered another rum and coke for Rusty and a shot of Jack Daniels for Vinnie. Nothing like a drink to loosen things up. Toni caught Maria's eye and winked, but Maria didn't crack a smile. She just stared at Rusty and Vinnie, her brows wrinkled in annoyance. Could she be jealous? Maria had never expressed an interest in Vinnie or any of the guys she'd gone with, for that matter. She usually went about her business in, well, a businesslike way. Maybe there was more to her tall, gloomy friend than Toni realized.

She filed that thought away for future reference, before turning her attention back to Rusty and Vinnie. They were standing very close to each other and Vinnie's hand was snaking around Rusty's waist. Toni smiled knowingly. She knew where this night would end.

Toni sipped her drink, thinking just how well the night was progressing so far. She had one recruit a step closer to sealing her first deal. Now, she could focus on the other new girl. Kris was still staring around the club, but her head was bobbing in time to the music now. Toni recognized the song as Night Blindness by Black Gallows. She'd learned Kris was a big Black Gallows fan earlier that week, when Kris walked into Toni's record store, Metal Vinyl. Toni prided herself in stocking all the latest releases and keeping tabs on which imports would sell, too. Kris had come in looking for Black Gallows' new album. Toni had dug a cassette out of the shipping box, listening to Kris go on about the singer, Marty Brinkman. This had surprised her, because Kris had been dressed from head to toe in an outfit that screamed "Conservative!" Her auburn hair had been pulled into a severe bun, the look completed with a pair of tweed slacks, white silk blouse and a gold chain with a tiny heart pendant dangling at her collarbone.

But as they'd talked, Toni had discovered Kris was quite the metal head. She worked at a midtown law firm (which explained the outfit!) and had moved into the City six months ago from the Jersey shore, harboring the dream of writing for one of the dozens of heavy metal magazines that had seemingly sprung up overnight. As soon as Kris mentioned that, the wheels began turning in Toni's head. Kris possessed the kind of naive enthusiasm that would turn some guys on, and she knew she had to somehow recruit her for Marius' harem. Kris' face had lit up when Toni mentioned her connections in the scene, and had practically turned cartwheels when Toni had invited her to tonight's Hardwire show at L'Amour. Taking in Kris' boring outfit again, Toni knew she had her work cut out for her.

Chapter 2

Kris stared around her, trying to take in all the sights and sounds at once. This club looked more like a heavy metal fashion show - women were dressed in every conceivable combination of skin-hugging fabrics and nearly every guy looked as though he played in a band. Long hair, tight leather pants or ripped jeans were the norm for the men and no one looked remotely abashed at walking around in pants that outlined their crotches so noticeably.

Kris thought the women looked glamorous with their hair teased to perfection and makeup that accentuated eyes and lips. Their hands were tipped with long fingernails painted with bright colors that made even holding a cigarette look fashionable.

Cigarette smoke mixed with fog pumping in from the ceiling, giving the cavernous room a hazy glow. A steady stream of heavy metal music pounded from the speakers. The deejay mixed old Led Zeppelin and Black Sabbath with newer bands like Ozzy Osbourne's solo stuff, and her favorite, Black Gallows.

Kris was vaguely aware she was horribly underdressed for tonight's outing, but she didn't own any of the flashy clothes the other women were wearing. She wasn't even sure she'd like wearing any of that stuff. She'd just started dressing up in suits and heel for work, and hated them. She was much more comfortable in what she wore now: jeans, t-shirts, and sneakers.

Kris caught Toni looking at her and smiled. She didn't want her new friend to see that the simple act of coming to a huge rock club overwhelmed her, but there was no other way to describe her feelings of awe at standing here. She'd read about L'Amour in several magazines but had never ventured out to Brooklyn, even though she'd grown up down the Garden State Parkway on the Jersey shore. Truth be told, she'd left Point Pleasant just once in her life, to intern at the Asbury Park Press newspaper.

Moving to New York City six months ago had felt like moving to another country. Kris knew deep down she'd be fine. After all, this was what she'd wanted for so long. Exploring her new neighborhood on the Upper West Side had been a great adventure. Each weekend, she'd ventured farther and farther from her street. Last weekend, she'd ridden the subway to Greenwich Village and wandered around, exploring the shops and cafes.

She'd written about each journey afterward, trying to be as descriptive as she could, then mailed each story to her sister Kim, who lived with their mother in Point Pleasant. Kim was 15, but already a high school senior and two inches taller than Kris. She was as dark as Kris was fair, and wielded a pen in a different way, drawing lines instead of writing them. As an apartment warming present, Kim had drawn a beautiful portrait of Marty Brinkman, Black Gallows' lead singer, and framed it. The portrait hung next to Kris' bedroom window, so she should see it every night before she went to sleep and every morning when she awoke.

The sound of Black Gallows' latest hit, Night Blindness, shook Kris out of her thoughts. She noticed a tall, dark haired man talking to Toni and recognized him as the bass player from the band Torpedo. She saw Toni laugh and lead him over to Rusty, a tiny but busty women who worked for Toni's dentist. Rusty had been very friendly and drawn Kris into conversation as soon as they were introduced. Kris noticed Rusty seemed very uncomfortable in her outfit, as she alternately tugged at her miniskirt and crossed her arms over her revealing lace top.

Maria, on the other hand, had looked down her nose at Kris. The tall woman looked like a vampire, with her white face, red lips and black outfit. The shock of short, white hair stood up like an exclamation point. She exuded an air of gloominess that screamed, "Stay away!"

Kris had lucked out when she'd met Toni at the record store near her apartment. Toni seemed to know a lot about the heavy metal bands out right now, from major acts to local bands looking to make a splash. She had seemed interested in Kris' desire to write for a heavy metal magazine and had offered to help her build contacts. In the six months she'd worked in New York, she hadn't made any friends, except for a couple of women at the law firm who had taken her under their wing. They were much older than her and not remotely interested in her type of music.

Kris felt a thrill of excitement as she took in the crowded club. It was filling up and the music seemed to be competing with the dull roar of conversation. She recognized her favorite Dark Disciple song blasting from the speakers, and saw a group of rowdy guys near her shout the chorus along with the recording, heads bobbing up and down as the guitars wailed. She hadn't heard much about Hardwire, the band playing tonight. She knew they were from Brooklyn and knew the owners of L'Amour, so they played here a lot. Toni had blasted their cassette all the way to Bay Ridge from Manhattan. Her car had a booming sound system and she had turned up the volume so high, Kris was sure cars speeding along next to them could hear Hardwire, too.

When they'd reached L'Amour, Toni had parked her candy apple red Camaro in a special lot behind the club. She'd told Kris the lot was reserved for a select number of people. She'd tipped the parking lot watchman a $20 and tickled his chin. He'd flashed a toothless grin in return. They'd also bypassed the long line snaking around the club. The doorman had taken one look at Toni and unhooked the velvet rope, letting Toni and Kris in before snapping it shut and glaring at a girl who'd tried to slip in behind them. Kris grew more impressed. Toni certainly did have connections at this major nightclub.

Now, they were at the bar, waiting for the band to take the stage. Kris couldn't believe her luck. She'd read all about L'Amour in the Aquarian Weekly, the regional rock newspaper. She'd also seen the club mentioned in several major magazines, including her favorite, Metal Countdown. She knew the editor, David MacGregor, was Scottish and great friends with Marty Brinkman. David's articles in Metal Countdown were witty and down to earth, peppered with terms she didn't quite understand. Toni had mentioned she knew an editor for one of the magazines, and hoped fervently that it was David, and that Toni would introduce them soon.

Kris watched Toni down her drink, then motion for the others to follow her as she cut a path toward the left side of the stage. Kris trailed behind, looking warily at the stack of Marshall amps looming closer. Surely they weren't going to park themselves in front of that.

They were.

Kris tried to position herself as far away from the wall of speakers as possible. The overhead lights dimmed and bright spotlights began crisscrossing the stage. A disembodied voice boomed over the speakers: "Now! Back by popular demand! HARD-WIIIIIIRE!" An ear-splitting guitar riff sliced through the air and with a crash of cymbals, the band took the stage. Kris cringed at the decibels that ripped through her head and body. She looked at the others and saw they were banging their heads in time with the beat, hair whipping back and forth with each snap of the neck. Someone crashed into her from behind and she stumbled into Rusty, nearly knocking the petite woman over. Regaining her balance, Kris spun around angrily, then was jostled again as the crowd around her moved, swayed and jumped to the music pounding out of the amps, fists pumping furiously into the air.

Kris turned back to the stage in time to see the singer thrust his hips in her direction, leering as he growled into the microphone. A wild tangle of blond curls obscured his face; all she could see were the tip of his nose and his mouth, open in a throaty howl. The black spandex tights he wore left nothing to the imagination. She glanced at Toni and did a double take. Toni was gesturing at the singer, her hand pumping up and down. He gyrated toward her, reaching down to cup himself. He pointed to Toni, who slowly licked her lips at him.

A wave of embarrassment engulfed Kris. She felt as though she had intruded on a very private moment, but it was out there for all to see. Kris saw several women turn and glare at Toni, but her friend seemed oblivious to the hostility bubbling up around her. Maybe the singer was her boyfriend. She'd never mentioned it, but they hadn't talked much about their personal lives. Kris tried to focus on the

14

band again, but the music was just too loud. She wished they could stand farther back.

Chapter 3

Toni could tell Kris wasn't enjoying herself. She seemed dazed by the experience and cringed every time a guitar pealed. Not a good sign. Toni sighed. She knew Kris would be a challenge, but now she wondered whether it would be worth the trouble. This girl was GREEN. Toni wondered idly whether Kris was still a virgin, then snorted. She couldn't be. Kris had to be 21 or 22. No one was a virgin by that age anymore.

Then again...

Toni's eyes narrowed shrewdly. A 21-year-old virgin would certainly up the ante in Marius' circles. The man had built a reputation for gathering a groupie harem that could cater to any sexual taste, and a virgin would be a hot commodity. Making a mental note to learn more about Kris' sexual history, she turned her attention to Rusty.

Rusty seemed to be faring a bit better. Vinnie was glued to her side as they banged their heads to the music, one arm wrapped possessively around her shoulders. Toni noticed Hardwire's guitarist, a tall, lanky guy with a mop of shocking red hair and blue eyes, making eyes at Rusty. More specifically, he seemed to be transfixed by Rusty's breasts, which bounced wildly as she jumped up and down.

Toni smiled smugly and turned back to the stage in time to see Bobby, Hardwire's singer, shoot her a lusty look. She locked eyes with him and made jerking motions with her hand. His eyes grew wide and he gyrated in her direction, pointing at her and cupping himself. She smiled and slowly traced her lips with her tongue. He grinned, mouthed "later," and turned back to the screaming crowd.

Maria leaned in close and yelled, "Dimitri and I are meeting after the show!" Dimitri was the band's bassist; a short, swarthy man with shaggy black hair, black eyes, and oversized lips. Toni didn't care for him. He had horrible body odor and constantly scratched himself. He'd nearly raped Toni backstage once, after she told him she'd only give him a hand job. Bobby had come along just in time to pull Dimitri off her, and she'd shown him her appreciation, using her mouth and hands. Even though she'd warned Bobby she'd never fuck him, that all he'd get were blow jobs, he'd hooked up with her every time Hardwire played L'Amour.

A guy had to be special to get into her pants. The only exceptions were the men Marius set up for her, but those were just business; as well as Marius, himself, because she worked for him and it was his right. She didn't care who she blew, though. It was just her mouth and she had a reputation for being the best. She flicked Dimitri a dismissive glance and turned away. Let Maria deal with him. *She* had bigger fish to fry.

Toni closed her eyes and an image filled her mind: a tall man with blond hair cascading down his back in soft waves, a dreamy expression in his sky-blue eyes. Don Lyden was Toni's ultimate fantasy. He was lead guitarist for Lizard Lust, an up and coming headliner. The band might be new, but Don was big time. He had worked his way from a tiny backwater town in Alabama to the stages of the world, and was as hard to get as he was handsome. Not even Toni's reputation could get her access to his backstage lair.

Luckily, he was good friends with Marius, who had just as good as promised a dalliance, as soon as she helped build up his special harem. Maria was already working on her backstage rep. Rusty was next, then hopefully, Kris.

Rusty should be no trouble, Toni thought. She wanted to meet guys in bands and seemed so desperate for action, Toni knew she'd give them exactly what they wanted. Kris was another story. Toni didn't know how far Kris would go to get printed in a major magazine. They'd find out soon enough.

Chapter 4

All in all, the music hadn't been bad, Kris thought. It was just a bit too guttural for her taste. She preferred singers who could *sing*. But, she conceded, this growling man could be considered sexy in some obscure way. Too bad he sounded like a troll.

Hardwire finished its set and strutted offstage. People immediately lined up, trying to talk their way backstage. Toni marched to the front of the line, Maria, Rusty, and Kris trailing behind her. The same man who'd let Toni and Kris into the club now blocked the hallway leading to the dressing room. As soon as he saw Toni, he stepped aside to let them pass before resuming his post, arms crossed over his beefy chest.

The dressing room was smaller than Kris had imagined. There was barely enough room for twenty people, yet nearly twice as many were crammed inside. The overpowering smell of body odor mingled with perfume in the humid room. A cracked mirror hung lopsided on one wall, reflecting the jostling crowd. The other walls were covered with scrawled writing; messages from members of the many bands who had passed through.

Hardwire sat on the only chairs in the room, smiling as men and women pushed their way forward, looking for the chance to say hello. Kris became separated from the others, and she glanced around for several minutes before spotting Rusty. The petite woman was chatting with one of the guitarists, a tall, lanky man with red hair. Vinnie Tedesco was nowhere in sight. She watched as the guitarist ran his hand down Rusty's back and pull her close to him. Rusty giggled and murmured something in his ear. He laughed loudly and pulled her out into the hallway.

Kris found an empty space along the wall and leaned against it, looking for Toni and Maria. The only band member in the room now was the drummer. Kris wondered where the others had gone. She took in snatches of conversation around her and heard one woman mutter, "I'll bet Toni snagged him first, the whore!"

Kris craned her neck, trying to spot the woman who had spoken. Just then, a door on the other side of the room opened and Toni sauntered out, patting her well-teased hair. Behind her came the singer, lazily zipping his pants. He slapped Toni lightly on the ass and headed to the center of the room, where he could hold court with fans.

Toni made her way toward Kris, pausing only to spray breath freshener into her mouth. They stood together, not speaking. A few minutes later, Maria stormed out of the back room, Dimitri hot on her heels. He tried to grab her around the waist but she shook him off angrily.

"That's all you get, pervert!" she shouted, and stomped out of the room. Dimitri looked livid. He quickly grabbed another woman and nearly dragged her to the back room, slamming the door behind him. Kris gasped, astonished, and quickly turned to get Toni's reaction. Her friend looked annoyed, and when she spoke, her tone was brisk.

"I need to take you home. I've got plans."

They left the dressing room and passed Rusty in the hallway, who waved cheerfully at them before turning back to the guitarist. Kris was quiet on the drive home, although her mind churned with questions. Toni cranked Hardwire and tapped her fingers on the steering wheel as she drove. She barely said goodbye as she dropped Kris in front of her apartment building and pealed out as soon as Kris slammed the car door shut. Shaking her head in annoyance, Kris let herself into her building and smiled at the night watchman as she headed to the elevators. Once upstairs in her apartment, she poured a glass of water and sat at her tiny kitchen table, mulling over the night's events. Toni had certainly was treated like a VIP at the club, but Kris pondered what had happened backstage, as well as the hostility she'd heard aimed at Toni. Kris admitted to herself that the experience had been jarring, but the evening had also excited her. She couldn't wait to go back to Brooklyn.

Chapter 5

Toni sat on her bed, wiping makeup off her face. She winced as she touched her jaw. Bobby had needed a lot of attention before he'd finally calmed down. Being onstage seemed to give him a perpetual erection, one that could only be appeased by a good, long fuck. But Toni had laid the ground rules. He'd only get her mouth. If he wanted sex, he'd have to find someone else. Bobby had taken it in stride, though, and kept coming back to her. He was nice, so she didn't mind the extra work it sometimes took to get him off. He was also one of the few musicians who returned the favor, and she had to admit, his mouth was as talented as hers.

The phone rang and she picked it up, holding it away from her jaw. Only one person called her this late, but she played dumb anyway.

"Hello?"

"Hello, doll face." Marius Mann's deep rumble filled her ear. "And how was your night?"

"Oh, not bad," she replied, massaging her jaw with her free hand.

"I heard Mr. Bobby Bright was quite demanding." He chuckled. Toni wasn't surprised he knew. Nothing seemed to escape his attention.

"How did Maria do tonight?" he asked.

Toni paused, knowing he already knew the answer to this question.

"Not too well," she finally admitted. "She stormed out on Dimitri.

The silence on the other end grew taut.

"That's two strikes against Miss Maria," he finally murmured. "One more and she's out. And that puts *you* behind in your quest for Mr. Lyden." He spoke the words lightly, but Toni knew he was not pleased.

"Rusty's off to a decent start," she jumped in. "She went right off with the other guitarist, Mark. And Vinnie Tedesco was interested in her, as well."

"Rusty is nowhere near ready to join," Marius said, dismissively. "She needs lots of work. It doesn't matter that she's eager to put out. The way she is now, she's nothing more than a garden variety groupie and we can't have that, can we?" Toni didn't miss the threatening note in his pleasant voice.

"No matter. I'm sure Miss Rusty can be transformed," he said, breezily. "Now, tell me about the new one."

"Kris? I don't know whether she's cut out for this. She's very green."

"I'll raise your allowance to cover the cost of grooming both girls." Marius sounded bored now. "Progress, Toni, progress. Only through progress, will you pro-*gress*. Remember that." He chuckled deeply and hung up before she had a chance to reply.

Toni sank back onto her bed, clutching the receiver. She needed to have a serious talk with Maria. If she screwed up one more time, Toni's chances of meeting Don Lyden could move out of reach. She rolled onto her stomach and hung up the phone, frowning. Upstairs, she heard the floorboards creak and a few minutes later, the pipes clanked as a shower was turned on.

Toni glanced at the clock. It was already five in the morning. Her younger sister was up and getting ready for work. Her eyes went to a photo on the dresser. She could barely see it among the makeup and jewelry cluttering the dresser top. Two young girls, grinning with their arms around each other. They wore matching Holly Hobby dresses and pigtails. It seemed a lifetime ago that Angie and she could talk to each other.

But as they grew older, their dad took more to her brainy younger sister, and beamed with pride as she graduated summa cum laude from Harvard, aced law school, and became the youngest partner at the midtown law firm that had hired her five years ago.

Angela and Antoinette. Her father called them Heaven and Hell, nicknames that grew stronger over time, as Toni showed no sign of giving up "that street whoring life" and find a real job. "You're not getting any younger, my girl," her father had sneered, the night Angela's longtime boyfriend had asked permission to propose to Angie.

Thinking about her sister made Toni's head hurt. It wouldn't have been so bad had Ang been the way she was when they were kids, carefree and nonjudgmental. But, with each successful step in her life, she'd grown more sanctimonious, looking down at Toni and her way of life. Their mom treated them equally, but Toni knew she also preferred her straitlaced sister to her. Mom tried to understand Toni, but it was difficult to do when Toni didn't understand herself.

She had fallen into the metal scene in high school. She had been unnoticed, until she began wearing spandex and hanging out with the kids who skipped class to hang out in the park, smoking, drinking, and cranking Black Sabbath and Deep Purple. She'd given her first blow job in that

24

park… how many years ago? The boy had been wary of the braces on her teeth, but she'd learned quickly how to give pleasure. More importantly, she learned how this small act could give her so much power. He'd wanted to go all the way, but she'd refused. She wasn't on birth control and didn't want to end up pregnant. Plus, the rush she felt as he begged on his knees to get into her pants was unlike any feeling she'd ever experienced.

Back at school, word had spread quickly about Toni and her talented mouth, and she'd become one of the most popular girls. Guys learned if they wanted time with her, they'd have to pay up, in cash, records, or whatever Toni fancied at the time. She remembered the day she and Angie's relationship splintered. Toni had been going down on one of the football players in a deserted hallway after school. As he neared orgasm, the boy had begun grunting and moaning loudly. Angie heard the noise down the hallway and rushed over to see whether he was hurt and needed help. As she rounded the corner, she yelped in surprise at the sight. A startled Toni had pulled away from the boy just as he came, spraying all over her face and neck. She'd never forget the look of horror on her sister's face as she stood frozen for a moment, then fled, footsteps pounding down the hall. Toni had cleaned herself up the best she could. The boy had been no help. He'd quickly zipped up his pants, run a hand through his hair, then taken off in the opposite direction from Angie.

Toni's face burned as she relived the memory. Angie had not spoken to her for a week, and Toni walked on eggshells, waiting for the explosion that would come from her father when Angie ratted her out. That explosion had not come. The following weekend, Toni had been in the kitchen, drinking coffee and reading the paper, when Angie walked in the back door. Their mom was out in their tiny backyard, trying to coax some life into her prized rose bush, and their dad was down at the pub, watching the ball game. Angie had stopped when she'd seen Toni. A look of hesitation had briefly crossed her face before she braced herself and walked over to where Toni sat, her expression a mixture of embarrassment and disgust. Toni had warily watched her approach.

"What's up," she drawled, trying to appear relaxed and unconcerned.

"I've been hearing a lot of things about you at school. None of them good." Angie's back stiffened.

"Yeah, well. I found out I'm pretty good at something."

Angie pulled out a chair and sat down.

"How can you do something so disgusting with boys you hardly know?" she burst out.

Toni shrugged. "Don't knock it till you try it," she replied, casually. Inside, her stomach churned. Would their mother walk in on this conversation and demand to know what was going on? Toni closed the paper and stood.

"You telling on me?" she asked, eyeing her sister shrewdly.

Angie met her glance, held it for a few seconds, then looked down at the table.

"I'm not telling them because it would break their hearts."

Toni had left the kitchen then.

Angie had been true to her word, Toni thought now. She left for Harvard two years later. By that time, Toni had graduated (barely), and taken a job waitressing at the pub her dad frequented. Even there, she got no peace from him, but she learned to thicken her skin against the insults and sly comments he tossed her way as she passed him with a loaded tray. Each evening, he'd demanded to know how much she'd made in tips and ordered her to hand the money over.

"You're a working girl now. You're paying rent," he'd stated, over her mother's muttered objections.

Toni had begun stashing half of her tips inside her bra. Otherwise, she'd have no spending money.

That summer, she'd been at L'Amour to see Metallica when she met Marius Mann. He'd been lounging at the bar, sitting on a barstool, his long legs stretched out before him, a cowboy hat slung low over his face, casting a shadow over his eyes. Even the most casual fan could recognize him, however. His height and notoriety preceded him into every nightclub and restaurant in the five boroughs. On this night, he was surrounded by gorgeous women vying for a glance, a touch, a kiss. Toni had seen him on several previous occasions, including once at Charlotte's Harlots, the well-known metal clothing store in the Village. He had been leaving as she arrived, and she'd watched as he'd gripped Charlotte's chin and forced it up to kiss her. He'd chuckled deeply and lumbered out, holding the door open for Toni. She'd walked in to find Charlotte rubbing her chin, then wiping her lips with her sleeve, looking disgusted. She'd spotted Toni and her expression had changed with lightning speed into a wide, welcoming smile. Toni had wondered what was going on between the two, then had forgotten about it as they dove into Charlotte's newest styles.

A few weeks after that first encounter, she'd walked into L'Amour to find him at the bar. She'd approached from the other side to order a drink and had remained at the bar, stirring her Mai Tai with the paper umbrella. Finding his watchful gaze upon her, she'd removed the umbrella from the glass and licked it, suggestively, letting her eyes flicker over his briefly, before turning her back to him.

All evening, she'd felt his eyes on her as she stood with Maria while White Lion played, then as Metallica took the stage. Halfway through their set, she'd felt him standing behind her. He'd taken her by the arm and gently (but firmly) led her away from the stage to a booth at the back of the club. There, he'd asked her to demonstrate the talented mouth he'd heard so much about.

"Right here?" she'd asked, stalling.

He'd grinned widely. "Where else? No one is watching."

So, she'd climbed under the table, unzipped his jeans and gasped as the biggest, longest dick she'd ever seen sprang out, fully erect. She'd licked her lips nervously, not knowing whether she could take all of him into her mouth. His large hand had grasped her by the back of the head and firmly pushed her face closer to his monstrous erection, and somehow, she'd managed to take all of him, deep throating for the first time. She'd thought she'd choke, but had quickly learned to breathe through her nose, and let nature take the rest. When he'd finally let go, she thought she'd drown in all the cum that jetted down her throat.

She'd remained under the table, regaining her composure as he zipped up and handed her a napkin. She'd wiped her mouth and chin, then gratefully accepted the drink he'd handed down to her. He'd been gone when she'd crawled out from under the table. She'd found a hundred-dollar bill wrapped around a scrap of paper. Unfolding it, she'd read: "Call me tomorrow at noon" along with a phone number. She'd spent the rest of the night in a daze, and called him the next day. He'd told her about his "entertainment" business and wanted to recruit her for his special harem. Her performance under the table at L'Amour had been an audition, and he'd said she'd passed with flying colors. He quoted her a weekly salary that she knew rivaled her sister's, and she'd hesitated for just a fraction of a second before saying yes.

Now, here she was, five years (and many men) later. She still enjoyed the feeling of power over the men she serviced, but a tiny part of her longed for something more. She ignored that longing, feeding it instead with a steady diet of drugs, alcohol and metal.

Shaking her head vigorously, as if to wipe out the cobwebs, Toni headed to her bathroom and a hot shower.

Chapter 6

Dear Kim,

What a wild night! We went to see this band called Hardwire. I think they're from Brooklyn. The club is huge - much larger than I imagined. The front half has the stage and a dance floor dotted with little round tables. The back half has bigger tables and chairs, like a little restaurant. Don't get any fancy ideas. The place is pretty basic, just like the food, from what I saw.

The ladies' room has an attendant, though! This little old woman sits by the door, making sure there are enough paper towels. She also keeps a supply of deodorant, gum, and hair spray, if you can believe it!

Toni, the woman I told you about last time, invited me to the show and introduced me to two of her friends, Maria and Rusty. Maria's kind of stuck up and gloomy. I don't think she smiled once and she was dressed in all black. Ugh. Rusty's bubbly and nice. I think you'd like her.

The band was okay. The singer growls too much for my taste. You know I prefer bands with great singers, like Black Gallows. I think this singer is Toni's boyfriend, based on something I saw backstage. I won't go into detail here. Just remind me to tell you about it when I come down to visit. It was intense!

Speaking of backstage, the dressing room is kinda small, but you should have seen all the people crammed inside. It was worse than a subway car during rush hour and even smellier! Rusty hit it off with this guy from that band Torpedo. They seemed to like each other. Then, after the show, I saw her leave with Hardwire's guitarist. Weird. Maria had a fight with the bass player and ran out of the room. He was ugly, smelly, and reminded me of an angry gorilla.

Well, see you this weekend. I can't wait to check out your latest artwork and get an update on where you've decided to go to college. My sister, graduating high school at 15! I always knew you were the brains in our family.

I hope you and Mom are having fun.

Love, Kris. Xo

Kris sealed the letter and addressed it to her sister, then sat back and thought about what she'd written. Maybe she shouldn't mail it out. Better to wait until she went home for the weekend. Kris ripped up the envelope and threw the pieces away, then pulled her old typewriter out of the closet and set it on the small kitchen table. She loaded a sheet of paper and opened her notebook, where she'd scribbled a brief review of the Hardwire show. She typed it out, then stored the review in a folder.

That Friday, Kris sat on the train, staring out the window as it snaked its way down the New Jersey coast. She pressed her headphones closer to her ears and cranked the volume on her Walkman. The frantic guitars and thunderous rhythm of Black Gallows filled her ears.

She leaned back in her seat and closed her eyes, absorbing the wails of singer Marty Brinkman. Now, *this* was a man who knew how to use his voice! She dreamed of interviewing him. Every article and interview she'd read showed him to be witty, garrulous, and friendly. It didn't hurt that he was good looking, too.

She pictured him now: soft brown hair hanging halfway down his back, framing a firm face with liquid brown eyes, a nose that looked as though it had been broken a few times, and lips that looked as though...

Kris shook her head violently to erase the images that had just popped into her mind. There was absolutely no way she'd ever meet Marty. And even if the stars aligned and placed him in her path, she had zero chance of catching his eye. He was a world-renowned rock star, handsome and sexy, with his pick of any woman out there. She'd seen what girls who got band members looked like, and she could never hope to compete. Nor would she want to, Kris thought firmly, remembering the backstage scene at the Hardwire show. She tried to picture herself in the outfit Toni had worn. On Toni, the spandex looked sleek and glamorous. On her... no way.

When the train rolled into Point Pleasant, Kris hopped off and walked the ten blocks to the cottage where she'd grown up with her mother and sister. She still marveled at her mother's strength. Elaine Lindsey had raised her two daughters on her own after her husband walked out, saying he hadn't seen enough of the world and couldn't stand being a "family man." He'd left just after Kim had been born. Kris had been six and barely remembered her dad. Even though he never called or wrote, Elaine never uttered a word against him. Instead, she'd tell her daughters he gave her two beautiful treasures before he left.

Kris thought of her mother, old fashioned and strict, yet loving and supportive of everything she and Kim had ever wanted to try. Elaine had been there when Kris won an award for running her high school newspaper, and had ferried her to and from a summer job as a paid intern at the Asbury Park Press during her junior year. She had understood when Kris decided to forego her second year at Monmouth College and use her savings to move to New York City and pursue her dream of becoming a rock journalist.

The metal scene was teeming right now and Kris wanted to dive in. So far, 1985 was a magical year for metal, and new magazines were popping up all over the place to fulfill the needs of frenzied fans. Kris was sure if she could meet just one contact, her writing would do the rest. She had explained this to her mother and whether Elaine approved or not, she understood her daughter's passion and fully supported it. She and Kim had helped Kris move her meager belongings to a small apartment near Lincoln Center, in an old but tidy building complete with daytime doorman; an elderly Englishman named Henry. Kris had lucked out here, too, subletting the apartment for two years from an attorney at the law firm who was on sabbatical in Europe and Asia. He had moved his things into storage so Kris could have room for her furniture. Kris, Kim and their mother had a great time flitting from yard sale to yard sale, finding bookshelves and knick-knacks. Kim had visited twice since Kris had moved to the City, and enjoyed the hustle and bustle.

Kris spent a relaxing weekend helping her mother clear boxes from the attic and walking on the beach, even though it was the middle of winter and bitterly cold. She loved the wild way the waves crashed to shore under a dark and roiling sky.

Kim showed Kris her latest piece of art; a realistic ink drawing of Lizard Lust guitarist Don Lyden. Kim's talent had grown tremendously over the last year and the teen confided that she'd already been accepted to RISD - the Rhode Island School of Design. She would take advantage of the school's early entry program and move to Providence in August. Kris felt a pang at this news. Kim would be four hours away at school, far from Kris and even farther from their mother. Even though Kim was six years younger, the sisters were very close.

"Hey, we'll still keep in touch!" Kim insisted. "You can write me longer letters and reviews of all the shows you go to. You can write personalized articles just for me! Plus, I'll be right up I-95. You can come up on weekends and we can check out shows in Providence.

Kris smiled at her sister, younger but more mature in so many ways. Kim's amber eyes even seemed wiser than Kris' clear emerald gaze.

"You're right," Kris agreed, linking her arm through Kim's. "Let's go see what Mom's baking. It's making me drool!"

Kim hesitated. "Seriously. I need a favor."

Kris shot a worried look at her sister. "Oh, it's not bad!" Kim laughed. "I just want to say... if you ever get to meet Don Lyden, will you give him this drawing for me?" She held out the portrait Kris had admired.

"You bet." Kris took the drawing and carefully rolled it into a tube.

After dinner, the sisters walked on the beach again and Kim begged for more details about the Hardwire show. She giggled at Kris' descriptions of Tony, Maria, and Rusty; a teenager once more. Her eyes grew wide as Kris recounted the backstage shenanigans she'd witnessed.

"You know..." Kim said slowly, as they ventured out onto a windy jetty. "You could write about this stuff. It's much more interesting than concert reviews."

Kris snorted with disgust. "No one wants to read about that garbage! Besides, I don't know if I'll get backstage again. Toni seemed a bit annoyed when she dropped me off, although I don't know why." She caught her sister's eye and smiled reassuringly. "Not a bad idea, though," she said, more to ease the frown on Kim's face. She'd forgotten that her sister was still naive about certain things.

After Sunday dinner, Elaine drove Kris to the train station, even though Kris protested that she could use the walk. As Kris hugged her mother goodbye, she felt a wad of bills being stuffed into her hand. Kris tried to give it back, insisting she had enough money, but Elaine wouldn't take it.

"Put it aside for an emergency, then," she said, reaching up to cup her daughter's face. She gazed into the green eyes that mirrored her own and smiled proudly. They hugged again as the train clattered into the station. Once aboard, Kris waved as the train began moving, until she could no longer see her mom from the window.

Chapter 7

Marius sat in an overstuffed chair, his long legs crossed at the ankles, a glass of brandy on the table beside him. He sipped, set the glass down, and picked up the photos lying next to it. The first showed a young woman with auburn hair tied at the nape, dressed conservatively in black slacks and a white silk blouse tucked in a belted at the waist. A fragile gold chain encircled her throat and tiny gold hoops pierced delicate earlobes. Her head was slightly tilted as she read the track listing on the back of a cassette tape. Her lips were slightly parted, as though she'd been reading a title aloud. Toni had managed to take the photo without Kris being any the wiser.

He felt a stirring as he gazed at this photo and put it aside almost regretfully to look at the next one. This photo showed Kris, her auburn hair loose and flowing around her shoulders, emerald eyes sparkling, mouth open in laughter at something Rusty must have said or done. This shot only showed her from the waist up, so he couldn't see how her ass and legs looked in a pair of faded Levis. The Sex Pistols t-shirt she wore bagged out, showing nothing of the lithe body he knew was underneath. Even so, this shot was more enticing than the other, and he found himself gazing at it long after his brandy had vanished.

He had to see her in person. Toni had told him Kris had accepted an invitation to see Blinding Fire at L'Amour that coming weekend. Maybe it was time for an outing. He hadn't set foot in the Brooklyn club in years, preferring the soirees he held at his mansion. But… he had new demands to meet; musicians and high-powered men with tastes only his girls could fill. Marius gazed at the photo again. She looked innocent, untried. Don Lyden was clamoring for a young girl. He wondered whether this one would fit the bill. Granted, she was a bit older than the teens Don preferred, but she looked the part, didn't she? Toni thought she might even be a virgin. That thought made him swell slightly. It had been years since he'd savored a virgin.

He leaned back in his chair and idly stroked the face in the photo. Yes, there was something about her. He'd have to check her out in person.

Chapter 8

Kris brushed her hair and shook it out, letting her naturally wavy curls settle on her shoulders, then looked at the clock. She had to leave in a few minutes to catch the train to Queens. She was meeting Toni at her house. They'd drive to the Blinding Fire show from there.

Toni lived in a three-story brownstone on a tree-lined street. A petite, dark-haired woman opened the door to her knock. Toni's mother had an ageless face, free from lines, save a generous smattering of laugh lines around the eyes. The aroma of tomato sauce wafted down from the kitchen, and to Kris' embarrassment, her stomach growled in response. Toni's mom laughed and held the door open for her to enter.

"We've got plenty of ziti, if you want to join us for dinner before you girls go out," she said in a warm voice.

She led Kris down a short hallway to the kitchen, a large, warm, and roomy space. A heavy, round wooden table anchored the center of the room, four chairs space around it. The table was set for three people. Toni's mom pulled out the fourth chair and invited her to sit, then called up the stairs to Toni.

Several moments later, a door slammed upstairs and Toni clattered down the stairs in her trademark red stilettos. She sauntered into the kitchen and Kris saw Toni's mom avert her eyes slightly at her daughter's outfit: leather mini skirt, red bustier, fishnet stockings. A cropped leather jacket was slung over one shoulder.

"You ready to go?" Toni asked Kris.

Toni's mom made a sound of protest.

"Eat something before you go!" she urged. "You're too thin."

"Street whores don't eat!" bellowed a deep male voice from the next room, and a tall, wide-shouldered man lumbered into the kitchen, a newspaper clutched in one meaty hand. He threw the paper down onto the table, pulled out a chair, and sat down heavily. Kris could tell he had been handsome once, but weight and alcohol had taken their toll on his face and body. Toni's dad still exuded an air of menace, and Kris found herself standing and slowly backing away from the table. He glared from Toni to Kris, then back at his daughter's outfit. He made a sound of disgust.

"You won't make much in that outfit, my girl," he sneered. "You're showing too much. Guys'll know just what they're getting - not much." He turned jet black eyes on Kris.

"And who's this? Your newest disciple?"

Toni didn't reply. She just turned and clattered down the hallway, her steps measured. Kris half-waved at Toni's mom and hurried to catch up.

Neither spoke on the drive to Brooklyn. Toni blasted a Lizard Lust cassette and Kris stared out the window, trying to forget the scene she'd witnessed. She felt a burst of sympathy for Toni, and wondered what had happened to her friend. She knew she'd never dare ask. Toni was prickly about the most basic of questions. In fact, in the handful of times they'd hung out, Kris had done most of the talking. She didn't even know how old Toni was, and wouldn't hazard a guess. From a distance, Toni looked to be in her twenties, but up close, she looked older. Her face wasn't lined, but it was hard. Her baby blue eyes looked more calculating than compassionate, and Kris wondered whether Toni had ever had a truly close friend. Kris hadn't had many friends growing up, but she never missed it because she and her sister were so close. She closed her eyes and fought off the headache that was slowly building behind her eyes.

Blinding Fire turned out to be very good. The singer had a strong voice but Kris didn't think he was too good looking. He was very short and reminded her of a bowling ball. The fact that he was bald only added to the image. His size clashed with the rest of the band members, who all stood over six feet tall and sported the long hair so popular with metal bands, although no one was in very good shape.

After the show, they got backstage right away and once again, Toni disappeared - with Blinding Fire's singer! Kris watched them head to the back room, an odd couple if there ever was one.

Kris saw Maria sidle up to the band's drummer, the only handsome one of the bunch. His hair was a shaggy caramel mane; his eyes, a vivid blue. He insolently looked Maria up and down then turned away, bending his head to a petite blonde girl whose red rubber dress left nothing to the imagination. Maria's eyes darkened with anger and she stormed out of the dressing room. Rusty rolled her eyes at Kris, grinning, before getting drawn into conversation with the bassist, a tall but chubby man with long curly brown hair. He was dressed rather unwisely in a pair of purple spandex tights. His bare stomach flopped over the waistband and his sparse chest hair clung damply to his skin.

Kris hovered near Rusty in case the other woman wanted a quick escape, but to her surprise, Rusty giggled and let the man lead her out of the dressing room. Before the door swung closed, Kris saw them duck down the back hallway.

She leaned against the wall, idly watching the interactions play out before her. She wasn't paying attention to anyone in particular and jumped when a hand touched her arm. She looked up to see one of the band's guitarists standing next to her.

"Hello!" he smiled. "I saw you standing over here by yourself and thought I'd come over. I'm Chad. I've seen you here before and you definitely don't look like any of them." He waved a hand to indicate the crowded room.

"This is just my second time to this club and my first seeing your band. I'm Kris." She held out her hand and he shook it.

Within minutes, they were chatting amiably, about Blinding Fire's beginnings in southern New Jersey, the band's climb up the local metal charts and a promising future with a small, but growing record label. They talked for nearly half an hour, Chad pausing only to sign autographs and pose for pictures. Kris finally saw Toni come out of the back room, Blinding Fire's singer scurrying to keep up with her. Chad followed Kris' gaze and an awkward silence fell. Kris broke it as she stepped away from the wall.

"Well, it was great chatting, but I've got to go."

He held out a hand to stop her. "I really enjoyed talking to you, too. Why don't you come back to our hotel so we can... talk some more?" Chad moved his fingers lightly up and down Kris' arm. She fought an overwhelming urge to yank it out of reach.

"Um... I don't think so." Kris moved away from him. "Look, I really like talking to you, but that's all I want to do. I'm sure you can find a nice girl to take back to your hotel." She started to walk away, but Chad blocked her path.

"Do you really mean that?" he demanded, with a look of disbelief.

She frowned. "Of course I do! Now please let me by." She pushed past him. This time, he let her go.

"What happened?" Toni asked as Kris reached her. "It looked like you guys were really getting along."

"He wanted me to go back to his hotel," Kris answered, uncomfortably.

Toni laughed. "That's great!" she exclaimed. "Getting invited to the hotel is a big step, Kris. You should go. He's not that bad looking," she murmured, checking Chad out. He was staring their way.

Kris bit back a wave of disgust. "I don't even know him!"

Toni rolled her eyes. "What's there to know? You go, make him happy, and you start to make a name for yourself. You get free tickets to their next show, more backstage privileges. Before you know it, other guys are requesting you. Bigger and better bands want to spend time with you."

Kris stared incredulously at Toni. "No, thank you!" she said firmly, reaching for the door.

"Suit yourself," Toni said coolly. "Oh - and you're going to have to find your own way home. I have plans."

Kris didn't respond. She strode through the club to the entrance, then stood on the sidewalk, seething. What Toni had suggested was so revolting. A taxi pulled up and she climbed in. She gave the driver her address and leaned back into the cracked faux leather seat, trying to put the night behind her.

Chapter 9

Toni sat in her car, fuming. Marius had been at the show, spying on her! She hadn't seen him in the crowd. He must have stayed well-hidden, as he was very easy to spot, standing nearly 6'6" tall with a mane of shaggy black hair, to boot. How had she missed him?

She knew he'd been there because he left a souvenir on her windshield; a scrap of gold fabric. Toni fingered the material, frowning. He must have come to check Kris out. He'd seemed pleased with the photos she'd given him, though, so why show up?

Sighing in frustration, Toni jammed the key into the ignition and started the car. The engine roared to life and the sensuous strains of Lizard Lust blared from the six speakers placed strategically in her Camaro. She knew she'd better head home. If Marius Mann had been there, he'd know all about Maria's latest fuck up. He might even know that Kris had turned down Blinding Fire's guitarist. Toni stared into space, overcome by the feeling that her chances of snagging Don Lyden were slipping farther away. She knew she could count on a call from Marius. The thought brought a tingle of fear. She had never gotten on his bad side and she didn't want to start now.

Toni spotted Maria trudging through the parking lot, heading for either the subway or a taxi stand. Gunning the engine, she pulled up next to Maria, pushing the button to lower the passenger-side window. It was time for a preventative measure.

"Get in," she barked, as Maria looked her way.

Maria paused, then stuck her chin out defiantly. "I'm good."

"Get your fucking ass in this car," Toni repeated, leaning over to swing the door open.

Maria glared at her, then plopped into the seat. Toni pealed out of the parking lot before Maria could close the door.

"What the FUCK happened back there?" Toni demanded, after several moments of tense silence.

Maria glared out the window. "None of the guys interested me," she muttered.

"I know you went for the drummer." Tony felt her anger rise. "I know you made a scene and stormed out of the dressing room."

"I did NOT make a scene," Maria retorted. "So I walked quickly from the room. Of course, it's going to look like I stormed out, as tall as I am!"

"That's not the point," Toni spat out. "Marius was there tonight. He knows."

At the mention of his name, Maria's spine stiffened. "What was he doing here?" Her voice remained defiant, but Toni detected a tinge of nervousness creeping in.

"I have no fucking clue," Toni shot back, although she knew damn well what he'd been doing at the club. "The point is, he knows. He told me last time you were on your third strike." She nosed the Camaro onto the Brooklyn-Queens Expressway and sighed dramatically.

"I have no choice, Maria. I Have to take you to him."

Maria definitely looked nervous now. She didn't speak for several minutes, then asked, with a quaver in her voice, 'What do you think he'll do?"

Toni shrugged, unconcerned. "Whatever he does, you know you'll have to take it. He's got those photos of you, remember?"

Maria blanched. "I forgot about those. My parents can't see those, Tone. They'd never understand!"

"Well, then, you know what you've got to do," Toni replied, drawing out the sentence. She stepped on the gas. "You're gonna have to apologize to him in person. Now."

Maria looked sick. "I can't do him, Toni. I just can't!"

"There's no other way, Mare." Toni worked hard to swallow the malicious grin threatening to spread across her face.

"Do you know what he's like?" Maria's normally icy brown eyes were wide with fear.

Toni was silent. She knew damn well what Marius Mann was like, but she wasn't about to share that with Maria. For Marius, fear was as much a turn-on as anticipation.

"Just prepare yourself for anything," she said finally. She cranked the volume and the sounds of Lizard Lust filled the car again. The throb of music and the hum of her car's powerful engine combined in a strangely erotic way that nearly had Toni panting for the real thing. She stepped on the gas and they sped faster toward the twinkling lights of Manhattan and Marius Mann's waiting libido.

Chapter 10

Kris spent two weeks wondering whether she'd pissed Toni off by not going to the hotel with that guitarist. Toni hadn't called and the record store had been closed every time Kris passed by. But as Kris resigned herself to the fact that she'd blown it, Toni called, acting as though no time had passed, and invited her to another show at L'Amour. Kris accepted eagerly.

This time, only Rusty joined them at the bar. Toni vaguely explained that Maria was "under the weather." Kris was secretly glad Maria hadn't shown up. The tall woman looked down her sloping nose at Kris, never spoke, and generally exuded such an air of negativity that Kris didn't care to hang out with her.

Rusty was much more fun. Her outfits were mismatched; too clingy in the wrong places, her makeup stark on her pale face. But she was so bubbly, it was hard not to have a good time when Rusty was around.

That weekend's band, Meteor, played to several beats - all at the same time. Kris had a hard time keeping up. The singer had a hard time, too. He was always a phrase behind, and kept glaring at the guitarist, who glared at the drummer, who seemed oblivious to the animosity bubbling up around him as he kept his gaze turned to the ceiling while hammering his way through the set.

Backstage, the air was tense with anger. The singer and drummer nearly came to blows. Toni stepped between them just in time. She took the singer by the arm and motioned for Rusty to take hold of the drummer. All four disappeared into the back room, leaving Kris staring after them.

Rusty and the drummer came out first, the drummer looking embarrassed and Rusty looking a bit disgusted. She strolled over to Kris and asked whether she had any gum or mints. Kris dug a roll of Certs out of her pocket out of her pocket and handed it over. Rusty popped three into her mouth and sucked on them as they leaned against the wall and watched the drummer gather up his things and stalk out of the dressing room.

"Fucking two-minute Charlie," Rusty muttered under her breath as he passed. Then she grinned at Kris. "At least it was over quickly," she said brightly.

"Why did you go with him?" Kris asked. It was obvious Rusty hadn't enjoyed whatever had happened.

Rusty shrugged.

"You've got to if you want to become one of the elite girls. It's not so bad. I just hate swallowing, if you know what I mean."

She flipped her long blonde hair over her shoulder and grinned again. "I see the guitarist is looking a little lonely. I'll see you later."

With a wave, she walked off, just as Toni came out of the back room with the singer. The singer looked happier than the drummer had. Toni looked bored as she joined Kris. If she was annoyed that Kris wasn't talking to any of the band members, she didn't show it.

They left Rusty with the guitarist and headed out of the club. Toni drove Kris home and invited her to see Hardwire play the following weekend.

"Oh, you're dating the singer, aren't you?" Kris asked.

Toni snorted. "I guess you could call it that," she said snidely.

Kris could see her laughing as she drove away.

Chapter 11

Toni lounged behind the counter at the record store, her mind racing. Marius had told her Maria had paid her penance, but would no longer be going to the club.

"I have found a special... need for her," he said, cryptically.

Toni was dying to ask what had happened, but knew better. There was a line one didn't cross with Marius Mann. Instead, she asked whether Maria was all right.

He chuckled. "She's being ministered to, here at my place. She is under excellent care."

Toni could just imagine the "care" Maria was getting. She remained silent.

"Which means, you must find someone to take Maria's place." His voice was dangerously silky. "You're a girl short. But I know you'll come through for me. You always do."

Toni leaned back in her chair, thinking hard, but even as the wheels turned, she felt a flash of annoyance. In the past week, Toni had serviced three of Marius' "friends;" a rich businessman from Turkey, a Swiss scientist with a penchant for hot wax, and an Appeals Court judge who put some high-profile criminals to shame. She winced as she remembered their "session." Her breasts still hurt from the clamps he'd placed on them. She'd rather limit her liaisons to rock stars, but Marius called the shots and she was his best girl.

She was a girl short and that meant she'd have to get going on Kris. Rusty was eager for action; she just needed grooming. Kris, however, was still an unknown quantity. Toni wondered what it would take to get Kris to cross the line. She also needed to find out whether Kris was still a virgin. A virginal Kris was worth two Marias.

Chapter 12

Toni asks the strangest questions, Kris thought, as they lounged backstage at L'Amour. Toni hadn't shown the slightest interest in the band, whose name Kris couldn't remember. Rusty was in the back room with the guitarist and bassist. Toni's eyes had gleamed as they'd closed the door behind them. She had stuck by Kris, pointing out hairstyles and outfits she thought would look good on Kris. Then she'd asked, conspiratorially, the wildest place Kris had ever had sex.

"For me," Toni confided, leaning closer, "it was behind the counter at the record store, while customers were milling around. I can't believe they didn't know what was going on. It wasn't as if we'd tried to keep quiet!"

She stared shrewdly at Kris. "What about you?"

Kris thought back to her few meager relationships. Her first time had been on a stretch of beach behind the boardwalk at Seaside Heights. She'd thought it would be romantic, but it had turned out to be uncomfortable and painful; the sand, cold and gritty. To make things worse, the guy she'd given her virginity to had stopped calling the following day, leaving Kris upset and feeling humiliated over her bad judgement.

Her second try hadn't been as dismal as the first, but it had been lackluster. That relationship had barely lasted three months. All in all, Kris thought, she didn't have anything to crow about.

She noticed Toni looking at her and shrugged.

"No place special," she replied. "Nothing as exciting as yours."

"But you have…?" Toni let the question dangle.

Kris frowned in annoyance. "Well, of course I have! I'm 21, for God's sake, not some 16-year-old virgin!"

Toni looked taken aback, but Kris didn't feel a bit sorry. She fixed Toni with a steady stare and said, "Just because I don't go running to that back room with every guy who crooks his finger, doesn't mean I'm a virgin. I just haven't met someone I liked well enough. Standing around here, making small talk, hardly gives you the opportunity to get to know someone."

Toni let out a bark of laughter.

"You know, you're worse than a virgin. You're a prude!" she chortled. "I have so much to teach you. Lesson number one: RELAX!"

She took Kris by the arm and led her out of the dressing room to the bar. There, she ordered two Mai Tais and handed one to Kris.

"Drink," she ordered, clinking her glass with Kris'.

Kris sipped her drink. It was fruity, but she could feel the alcohol burn a trail to her stomach. She had to admit, it was pretty tasty. At Toni's urging, she drained it and set the glass on the counter. She felt light headed; she had downed it too quickly. She blinked her eyes hard, refocused, and found Toni grinning at her.

"You really ARE green," she said. Taking Kris' arm again, she led her out of the club. "Lesson one is over. Time to get you home."

Kris went to a few more shows with Toni and Rusty. Maria seemed to have dropped off the face of the earth.

Rusty confided that Maria had fallen from favor, but Kris had no clue what that meant.

The only thing Toni insisted Kris do at each show was to have a drink and finish it. So far, she'd had another Mai Tai, a rum and coke, and a drink with vodka, orange juice, and cranberry juice. She found the vodka drink easiest to handle and stuck with that.

Kris noticed that Rusty went to the back room every time, sometimes with Toni, sometimes on her own with a band member. Each time, she came out looking slightly sick, stopping only to pop a handful of mints into her mouth.

After one outing, she'd asked Kris to go to a nearby all-night diner for a meal.

"I didn't eat any dinner. That was a bad idea," she groaned, holding her stomach.

Stopping only to tell Toni they were leaving, Rusty and Kris walked to the diner around the corner from the club and ordered breakfast. As they ate, Rusty told Kris about Toni's obsession with Don Lyden, the flamboyant guitarist for Lizard Lust. Kris told Rusty about her sister's crush on Don as well, and about the beautiful portrait Kim had drawn.

Rusty grinned and said, "Your sister's crush is nothing compared to what Toni wants to do with him. She says the stuff she's doing now is to work her way up to him. She says the more guys I go with, the more I can help her reach her goal, and find a boyfriend for myself, too."

"That's the dumbest thing I've ever heard!" Kris exclaimed. "Why screw around if you have your eye on someone? Why not just go after him?"

Rusty shook her head. "You don't understand the groupie scene, Kris," she said, shoveling a forkful of scrambled eggs into her mouth. "This is how you build up your name, your reputation. Guys talk to each other. You get known, you get in with bigger bands, until you're like, elite. Toni's almost there. Don is supposed to be her big payoff."

Kris tried to take it all in, but it still made no sense. A groupie hierarchy? Was there such a thing?

When they finished eating, they walked to a nearby subway station and took a train to Times Square. There, Rusty got off to switch to a train to Queens, while Kris continued uptown. She spent the time thinking of everything Rusty had told her.

Chapter 13

"Rusty's really coming along," Toni said, with an earnest tone in her voice.

"She's still pudgy. What are you doing to help her lose weight?" Marius' voice sounded pleasant, as always, but Toni heard the hard edge beneath the silkiness.

"I'm working on it. She doesn't like the speed I gave her. Says it makes her too jittery."

"Well, try something else."

"Can you help me get some coke? I think I can get her to do that. She'll do anything she thinks rock stars like. I'll tell her all the top stars do coke, and she wouldn't want to look like an amateur in front of them."

Marius chuckled. "You have all the answers. I'll see what I can do."

He paused. "Lizard Lust is playing Philly next weekend. I got you tickets to the show."

"Did you get backstage passes, too?" Toni asked, excitedly.

"One thing at a time, doll face. You have tickets to the show and rooms at the same hotel. That's as far as I'm getting you. Maybe being in such close proximity to your dreamy Mr. Lyden will help you focus on your priorities."

Toni's mood took a dive. He sensed it and chuckled again.

"Consider it a reward for Maria not turning out to be a complete failure, and for working hard on Rusty."

She remained silent.

"Ah, you're sulking. What do you expect, an engraved invitation to his hotel room? I thought I was being generous." He spoke the last words sternly.

Toni jumped. "Of course, you're generous! Thank you!" she added, injecting a smile into her voice.

"Take the filly with you. The new one. Take Rusty, too. Maybe a weekend in a posh hotel will help put stars in their eyes."

Toni snorted. "Rusty doesn't need any persuading. She's already got stars in her eyes. But Kris... all she wants to do is see her name in a metal magazine. She doesn't seem interested in dating musicians. I couldn't get her interested in any of the bands we want to see."

"Every woman has her dream... and her price," Marius said, sagely. "We shall find Miss Kris' weakness. I confess, I find her highly arousing. I like that freshness. I may just save her for myself."

Toni laughed in disbelief. He didn't join in. Her laugh trailed into awkward silence.

"Tell Kris to write a review of the show and give it to you. Tell her you've set it up with Annie. Maybe I can arrange for her to go to the show, too," he mused.

"She's in L.A. all month," Toni reminded him.

"Ah, yes. No matter. I'm sure you can make it happen." The phone clicked softly in her ear.

Chapter 14

So, she didn't want to put out. She had principles, this one. If he got her published, she would be grateful. But how would she repay him? He leaned back, his mind wandering to the other new girl, Rusty. She'd had no trouble servicing band members. She wasn't elegant, though. She was clumsy, and enthusiasm would only take her so far. The way she was right now - no, she'd never set foot in any of his private parties or even move up to the next tier. He sighed. He'd finally gotten the cocaine Toni had asked for. Let's see if this helps Rusty slim down. He gazed at her photo again. She needed new hair; this fried blonde mop just wouldn't do. In fact, she needed new everything - clothes, body, personality.

He turned his attention back to Kris. Toni had supplied more photos, but he had her image firmly etched in his mind. He remembered the way she'd looked and moved that night at L'Amour, when he had hidden and watched them. Her innocent air made her even more desirable. Toni had said she wasn't a virgin. It didn't matter. Her inexperience shone like a beacon. The more he learned about Kris, the more he realized he wanted her for himself, and he stiffened at the thought. It had been so long since a filly had attracted him.

Lightly, he traced a finger down her body in the newest photo. He imagined her gratitude and how he could turn it to his advantage, and his erection became almost unbearable. He rang a bell sitting on the table next to him. Almost immediately, the door opened and a woman walked, dressed in a filmy golden robe. She stopped only to unfasten the clasp and let it slip to the floor, revealing her naked, lithe body. She moved gracefully toward him and dropped to her knees. Unbuckling his belt and pulling the zipper down, she let her mouth do the rest.

Chapter 15

Kris surveyed her closet excitedly. She was going to Philadelphia to review a band! And not just any band - she was going to review Lizard Lust! When she got the call, she thought Toni was pulling her leg.

"Why the hell would I joke about something like that?" Toni had snapped, irritated. "You keep talking about wanting to write for a magazine. Well, here's your chance."

Toni had ended the conversation abruptly by telling Kris to be ready to leave Friday evening. They'd see Saturday's show and come back Sunday, which was perfect, Kris thought. That way, she wouldn't miss any work.

Kris packed hurriedly, then threw a handful of note pads on top of her clothes before zipping the bag shut. She was waiting outside her building when Toni pulled up in her Camaro, Rusty waving from the passenger seat. She got out to let Kris slide into the back seat, her bag next to her. Henry, the doorman, waved jovially as they pealed out, shaking his head slightly at the noise.

Toni blasted Lizard Lust all the way to Philadelphia. By the time they reached the hotel, Kris was quite sick of the band. As they checked in, Kris learned both Lizard Lust and Hardwire were staying at the same hotel. She stared around the marble lobby, taking in the dark wood accents and gold fixtures, wondering how Toni could afford such luxury. She had insisted on paying for the room.

Their room was one floor below Lizard Lust's bank of rooms. It was massive, containing two large beds with plush bedding, a refrigerator and mini-bar, several closets, a large desk and several easy chairs. The bathroom boasted a large, jetted marble tub with an array of scented bubble baths lining one side.

Toni ordered a feast from room service and cheerfully signed the slip when the food arrived. After she ate, Toni vanished into the bathroom and stayed there for two hours. When she reemerged, the scent of roses wafted out behind her.

Rusty marveled at the luxury. She wrapped herself in a thick cotton bathrobe, admiring the gold hotel crest embroidered on the front, and squealed in delight when Toni told her to keep it. The coffee service included a selection of flavored coffees and creams. The mini-bar was just as fully stocked, but they decided to go downstairs for drinks, Toni scanning the lobby for any sign of Don Lyden or anyone from Lizard Lust.

They lounged in the hotel bar until it closed, with only the bartender for company. As the bartender brought their bill, they heard a commotion by the elevators. Toni rushed to pay, then ran out to the lobby, only to see a couple of roadies heading out for a late-night meal. One of the men ran his eyes up and down her spandex-clad body, before meeting her eyes with a suggestive glance.

"In your dreams," she purred, motioning to Rusty and Kris as she sashayed toward the elevator.

The next morning, Kris awoke feeling groggy and stiff. Rusty had tossed and turned, taking all the blankets, so Kris had finally moved to one of the chairs. Unfortunately, it wasn't as comfy as it looked. A hot shower worked the kinks out of her body and a cup of hot coffee helped perk up her mind.

She dressed quickly and decided to wait for the others in the lobby. Toni and Rusty appeared half an hour later. They were standing by the registration desk, discussing how to while away the hours until the show, when the elevator doors dinged open and Don Lyden sauntered out, blonde hair flowing silkily down his back. He was dressed in a pair of tight jeans and an equally tight Lizard Lust t-shirt. A group of giggling women immediately flocked around him, holding out photos, record sleeves, and slips of paper. Smiling indulgently, Don paused to sign autographs and take pictures, thanking each woman for dropping by.

Toni took one look at him and scurried in the other direction, toward the ladies' room. Kris and Rusty followed, and found her leaning against one of the sinks, looking furious.

"Why did you run away?" Rusty asked, puzzled. "I thought you wanted to meet him?"

Toni shook her head angrily.

"I don't want to be lumped in with those garden-variety groupies out there!" she spat. "When Don meets me, I want to be the only one he sees."

Kris stared at her. In her red spandex catsuit, black mini-skirt, four-inch heeled boots and leather jacket, she looked just like the girls out in the lobby. Yet, here she was, calling *them* garden-variety groupies! When they returned to the lobby a few minutes later, Don was gone. Only the women remained, giggling and chatting about their brief encounter with him.

They didn't get the chance to meet Don or anyone else from Lizard Lust that weekend. In fact, the only time they saw the band was when Lizard Lust performed Saturday night. Kris spent most of the show scribbling furiously in her notebook, while Rusty jumped up and down in time with the music, while Toni shot nasty looks at them.

After the show ended, Toni didn't even try to get backstage. She rushed them back to the hotel, sure the band would return for a party on their floor. She jumped up when the elevator doors dinged open, but instead of the band, several crew members came out, each lugging two suitcases. They told Toni and Rusty that the band had gone to a private party after the show. The tour bus would pick them up there the next morning.

The news sent Toni over the edge. After a frustrated rant in the lobby, she spotted Bobby, Hardwire's singer, walk in. She grabbed him by the hand, pulled him into an empty storage closet, and went down on him so furiously, he tried to tug her off him.

"Hey, easy," he moaned. "It's about the come off!"

She lightened her movements, but only a fraction. He didn't last long after that and as soon as he came, she stood and walked out of the room, leaving him staring dazedly after her, his pants still down around his knees.

When Toni walked off with Bobby, Kris and Rusty headed back to their room, ordered a pot of coffee and chatted. Rusty confessed she didn't want to go with guys in bands, but felt she had no choice. She looked up to Toni, envied her glamorous lifestyle, and wanted terribly to fit in. In order to do that, she had to do her share of putting out.

"I'm sure you'll have to, too, sooner or later," she remarked, eyeing Kris over the rim of her coffee cup.

The thought was disgusting. "Put out to hang out? No thanks!"

"It's something all the girls do," Rusty said. "All the girls who hang out with Toni, that is. She says that's how we end up landing rich rock stars to take care of us. That's what she's doing to build up to Don Lyden. And you know what, even though she didn't get him tonight, I think she'll land him in the end. She's very determined."

She stopped speaking as they heard a key in the door. Toni strode in, still looking angry.

"I'm taking a bath," she snapped and stormed into the bathroom. Seconds later, they heard water running.

Rusty shrugged at Kris and poured them each more coffee.

"Why do you hang out, if you're not going to go with any guys?" she asked.

Kris explained that Toni had offered to help her get published in a metal magazine. In fact, Toni had promised to give Kris' review of Lizard Lust to a friend who edited a magazine. Kris said the only reason she'd come to Philly was to write the review, but she was having second thoughts about going to any more shows with Toni.

"Oh, please don't stop hanging out!" cried Rusty earnestly. "I don't know what I would do if I only had Toni to hang out with!"

Kris' heart softened as she took in Rusty's open, trusting face. She promised to think about it.

The drive back to New York the next day seemed to take forever. Toni, dejected and annoyed, didn't speak. Instead, she blasted Lizard Lust music so loudly, Kris and Rusty couldn't talk, either.

When she finally pulled up outside Kris' apartment building, Toni barely gave her enough time to jump out before pealing away from the curb, leaving a startled Kris and an angry doorman staring after her.

Chapter 16

Kris read and reread all the "reviews" she'd written, and waited to hear back from Toni's editor friend. The last time she'd asked Toni about it, she'd gotten a curt reply, so she stopped asking. Toni had also claimed to be too busy to hang out, so Kris had taken to visiting a cafe around the corner of her building, jotting notes about the backstage shenanigans she'd witnessed so far. The more she wrote, the more she warmed to her sister Kim's idea of turning this into a book.

Kris tried to remember the conversations she'd overheard and the actions she'd seen, and recounted all the chats she'd had with Toni and Rusty about bands and sex. She elaborated on Toni's obsession with Don Lyden and her failed attempt to meet him in Philadelphia.

Several weeks went by, and Kris had nearly put Toni behind her, thinking their brief friendship was finally over, when Toni called, excited.

"Black Gallows is coming to New York for an entire week of shows!" she exclaimed over the phone. "A friend of mine found out where they're staying. I've booked two rooms in the same hotel!"

"When are they coming?" Kris asked, heart pounding in her throat. "And why two rooms? Are we getting our own rooms?"

Toni laughed. "One room to prepare in - the other, in case we hook up and need some privacy." As usual, she'd thought of everything.

"That sounds great!" said Kris. She hesitated, then asked, "Have you heard anything about my review?"

"Sorry," Toni replied, not sounding sorry at all. "She just couldn't fit it into this issue. I'm sure you'll get another chance. Well, gotta go. I need to call Rusty." Toni hung up without waiting for Kris to say goodbye.

As the day of Black Gallows' arrival drew closer, Kris grew more excited. She really did want to meet Marty Brinkman. Maybe, just maybe, she'd get the chance. She'd just read that he was crazy about baseball and wanted to be the first heavy metal front man to at least try out for a major-league team. He seemed very jovial in the interview. She hoped he was the same in person.

They checked into the hotel the day before the first show. It was as luxurious as the one in Philadelphia, and Kris wondered again how Toni could afford not one, but two rooms. Since the shows ran Wednesday through Sunday, Kris would go to work from the hotel. They had tickets for every show - another gift from Toni.

Kris was first to the room and was busy unpacking when a woman swept into the room. She had cascading golden-red hair, intense blue eyes, and a stunning figure on her statuesque frame.

"Hello," she purred. "I'm Francine, a friend of Toni's."

Kris introduced herself and Rusty, who had just flounced into the room. Francine explained that she wasn't staying in the room with them. She was dating Black Gallows' bassist Andy Spate, and that Toni had invited her to wait in their room until he checked in. She told them Toni sometimes "dated" one of the guitarists, Billy Williams, and that she might also disappear for rest of the week.

Toni arrived, lugging several large suitcases. Kris looked at her own overnight bag filled with several pairs of jeans and t-shirts that could be mixed and matched for each show, and the separate garment bag that held outfits for work, then gawked at Toni's luggage. She watched curiously as Toni unpacked. One suitcases contained countless pieces of lingerie ("We have to dress to fit the occasion," Toni explained). Another opened to reveal an array of spandex, leather, lace, and rubber outfits ("Again, better to be prepared."). The third held enough makeup to service an entire Broadway cast.

Francine helped Toni hang up her clothes and arrange lingerie in a drawer. A soft knock at the door revealed Andy, a pleasant but plain looking man with shoulder length brown hair and kind, hazel eyes that brought to mind a puppy dog. He smiled at everyone, but Francine led him out without introducing him to anyone. As they walked out, he turned his head toward Toni and opened his mouth to speak, then closed it again. Kris thought he looked a bit sheepish.

The evening of the first show was spent inside the hotel room. Toni made Kris and Rusty get ready in the second room, as they had fewer belongings. That suited them just fine. They dressed quickly; Rusty taking a little longer with her makeup, then went down to the lobby to wait for Toni.

As they sat in the bar, sipping coffee, a tall man with long, dark hair ambled in, a pretty brunette by his side. They ordered beers and sat at a small table. Rusty grabbed Kris' arm and squeezed.

"Oh, God! That's Brian Hart!" she whispered excitedly. "He plays guitar for Black Gallows!"

Kris looked up and saw the man and woman staring back at them. Even though Rusty had whispered, they seem to have heard her. She gathered up her courage and walked over to their table.

"Hi, my name is Kris. My friend Rusty and I enjoy your music and we're looking forward to tonight's show."

Brian shook Kris' hand and introduced his wife Linda in a soft voice, his English accent pronounced. Linda also smiled and shook hands. Kris waved Rusty over and introduced her. As they stood to leave, Brian asked Kris if she and Rusty would like backstage passes. Thinking Toni had already taken care of this, Kris said no. That drew looks of surprise from Brian and Linda, who smiled more genuinely and wished them the best.

Toni arrived as Brian and Linda were leaving. She made a beeline for Kris and Rusty. When Kris told her she'd turned down backstage passes, Toni erupted in fury.

"I thought you were getting passes from your boyfriend," Kris tried to explain.

"That fucker hasn't even called. I don't think their manager told him I'm here." Toni's face was white with anger, her blush standing out in two bright red stripes.

"Uh…" Rusty interrupted. "Isn't that him right there?"

They swung around to see a tall blonde man amble by. Toni hurried after him. The others watched him hug her with one arm then release her quickly. As they talked, an equally tall blonde woman, dressed in tight faded jeans and a beaded halter top, joined them. He draped one arm around her shoulders and seemed to be introducing her to Toni. He then turned and walked away with the woman, while Toni stalked back to Kris and Rusty.

"Who was that?" Kris asked.

"New girlfriend," Toni fumed. "I can't believe he's got the balls to bring a girlfriend on tour. What a fucking idiot!"

"I thought you were his girlfriend," Kris said.

Toni threw her a scathing look. "Oh, grow up, for fuck's sake!" she snapped.

"Brian Hart has his wife with him," Rusty volunteered.

Toni snorted. "He's always got that ball and chain with him. You can't get near him!"

She stalked up to the bar, ordered a drink, and downed it right there. Slamming the glass on the bar, she stalked back to Kris and Rusty.

"Let's go," she said shortly.

They ran into Francine and Andy in the lobby. Toni pulled Francine aside for a hushed but heated discussion. Francine then pulled Andy into their conversation, murmuring in his ear. He reached into his jacket pocket and pulled out a handful of stickers. Francine handed them to Toni, then caught up to Andy as he walked toward the front doors. Toni doled the stickers out. Kris looked at the one in her hand. It was an "all access" backstage pass. The others tucked their passes into their purses, so she stuck hers in her pockets, as she carried no purse.

The last time Kris had visited Radio City Music Hall; it had been to see the Rockettes Christmas special with her mom and Kim. Now, the building was packed with men, women, and teenagers decked out in a variety of outfits; hair teased or loose; women's faces bright with makeup. Kris glanced around the cavernous hall; every seat was taken and an expectant buzz filled the air.

The opening band took the stage first, to little fanfare. They were an up and coming band from Tennessee whose name Kris had forgotten. They were very energetic and she was sure she'd have liked them anywhere else, but she was anxious to see Black Gallows, so she waited impatiently for the band to finish its set and get off the stage.

During the brief intermission, Kris and Rusty talked excitedly about Black Gallows.

"I have a confession to make," Kris said.

Rusty's eyes widened. "Oh, do tell!" she urged.

Kris blushed, then confided, "I've had a crush on Marty Brinkman for the last three years."

Rusty laughed, "Oh, is that all?" She waved her hand airily. "I thought you were going to confess some deep, dark, sordid secret!"

Kris smiled ruefully. "I guess that sounds awfully dull and immature, doesn't it? Having a 'crush.'"

Rusty gazed at Kris. "Crushes are good. Fantasies are better. And don't tell me you've never fantasized about what it would be like to bang Marty Brinkman, because I can see it in your eyes."

Kris blinked, then blushed as Rusty laughed again. Okay, so she *had* fantasized about Marty's generous lips, about his broad hands, which looked as though they could easily cup her breasts. A tingle ran through her as she imagined this and she shook her head, trying to clear the image. Rusty grinned at her and playfully punched her arm, then motioned toward Toni and Francine, who were huddled together, locked in a furious conversation. Kris wondered what they were talking about, then turned abruptly back toward the stage as the lights suddenly dimmed.

Funereal music poured from the speakers. A green mist enveloped the stage and the music swelled louder and louder until, in a flash of smoke and a thunderous bang, Black Gallows hit the stage and launched into their hit song, "Execution." The music slammed into the crowd like a sledgehammer. Marty Brinkman did more than jump around the stage. He leaped, twisted, and crouched, energy erupting from his compact body, his long brown hair whipping wildly around his head. The rest of the band played furiously, keeping up the breakneck pace of the show.

Black Gallows performed two encores before the lights finally came up for good. Kris felt as though she'd just run a marathon. She grinned at Rusty, who grinned back, eyes sparkling. Toni and Francine, on the other hand, looked as though they'd just stepped out of the pages of a heavy metal fashion magazine; not one hair out of place and makeup intact, right down to the glossy red lipstick. They stuck their passes onto their jackets and motioned for Kris and Rusty to do the same.

The four joined the crowd making its way backstage. A burly man waved them through, smiling at Francine and smirking at Toni. He didn't give Rusty or Kris a second glance. Once backstage, they got lost in the crowd. There were so many people milling about, looking for any Black Gallows members. Kris spotted Brian Hart's wife Linda standing near the cold cut tray and made her way over to say hello. Linda looked at her coldly and walked away. Rusty gave Kris a questioning look. Kris shrugged and moved closer to the wall. She spotted Francine and Andy in a corner, surrounded by gushing fans. Francine gently pushed Andy into the crowd, handing him a pen. He signed autographs, looking embarrassed by the attention.

Another movement caught Kris' eye. Toni was trying to slip through a door at the far side of the room, only to be rebuffed by a beefy man with thinning blond hair and a very red face. The two began to argue.

"I think your friend is having a spot of trouble," sneered a voice. Kris turned to see Linda standing next to her.

"Her trouble is not my trouble," Kris said quietly.

"No? I thought you lot stuck together."

"Then you thought wrong. We're not the same at all." Kris stared evenly at Linda, then walked away, motioning for Rusty to follow her.

The found an urn filled with hot, strong coffee and each poured a cup, before sitting at an empty table, away from the hubbub. Rusty slipped off to the cold cut table and returned with a plate laden with goodies. Kris refilled their coffees and they sat in a comfortable silence.

Toni had disappeared. The florid-faced man stood angrily in front of the door she had tried to slip through. Another girl approached the door tentatively, but he crossed his arms in front of him and shook his head firmly. Kris figured Toni must have somehow gotten through. She was so engrossed in what Toni might be doing, she jumped when a hand touched her elbow, nearly spilling her coffee in the process. Linda Hart was standing next to the table; an apologetic look on her face.

"Mind if I join you? It's a madhouse over there."

Kris scooted over to make room.

"We've stolen some food. Would you like some?" Rusty offered up the plate.

Linda smiled and took a browning. As she chewed, she gazed thoughtfully at Rusty and Kris.

"I've been watching you. You're not part of his madness."

Kris shrugged and sipped her coffee. "We're not into this. We're with our friends who are."

"Your blonde friend is going to get hurt," Linda said solemnly. "I remember her from last tour. Billy liked having her around quite a lot. But this time, he's got a new girlfriend and she's very no-nonsense.

She jerked her head toward the door. Billy's girlfriend was arguing with the red-faced man. He seemed to be trying to keep her from going through the door. Suddenly, she shoved him out of the way and yanked it open. There was no one on the other side. She yelled something at the man and stormed off.

Linda chuckled wryly. "Lucky escape this time."

They sat in silence for a few minutes, eating, before Kris asked Linda how she dealt with the shenanigans her husband faced on the road. Linda shrugged.

"You have to trust... and you have to look the other way. The most important thing to remember is why you got together in the first place. If you can and you still feel the same, you stay together. If you can't..." she trailed off, shrugged again, then smiled at someone behind Kris.

"Hullo, Nate!" she exclaimed, as Kris and Rusty turned to look. Nate Brandon, Black Gallows' drummer, stood there, towel draped over his shoulders and a beer in one hand. "This is... I'm sorry, luvs. I've forgotten you names."

Kris and Rusty introduced themselves. Nate shook their hands, grinning, as Linda pulled an empty chair around. He plopped into it with a groan, stretching his long legs out before him.

"You must be all right," he drawled, after taking a long pull from his beer. He had the same thick accent as Linda. "Linda never hangs out with groupies."

Linda slapped his arm and laughed.

"Och, these two seem to have their heads on straight."

The four chatted amiably and Nate signed a backstage pass for Kris to take home to Kim. An hour later, Toni strutted up, flicked a cursory glance at Linda and Nate before announcing, "We're leaving now."

Kris stared at her coolly. "We're enjoying ourselves," she replied. "We'll walk back to the hotel, thanks."

Rusty gaped at Kris, aghast to hear her speak to Toni this way.

"I'll go with you," she stammered, squeezing out of her seat.

"Well, come on then," Toni snapped at Rusty. To Kris, she said, "You may not have a room to sleep in tonight."

"Big loss," Kris answered, unconcerned.

She watched Rusty flounce off after Toni and shook her head sadly. Linda gave her a quizzical look.

"Why didn't you go?"

"I'm not a dog on a leash," Kris replied, shortly. "But, it *is* getting late. I think I'll just head home."

Linda smiled. "Will I see you tomorrow?"

Kris smiled back. "I have tickets for the entire run. I really *am* a fan. I just don't take my interest past the music." With a wave at Linda and Nate, she left.

Toni called the next day.

"You're forgiven for last night's transgression," she announced. "It never occurred to me that you might be trying to hook up with Nate."

"I wasn't. And what makes you think I need forgiveness?" Kris snapped.

"No matter," Toni said, expansively. "You may actually be onto something. Make friends with the women and you find another way in. Easier access to the band if the wives like you, and Linda is a tough nut to crack. You seem to have done it and that's saying something." Toni paused, then laughed at something in the background.

"Are you coming tonight?"

At Kris' assent, she said briskly, "Good. We'll meet you here at the hotel at 6:30. And *please* try to dress up a little. I have a surprise for us tonight."

Kris hung up, fuming at Toni's nerve. She had absolutely no desire to hang out with her, but... she did want the chance to meet Marty Brinkman. She was also curious about Toni's "surprise." She dressed carefully for the show. She wanted to be hip, but not slutty. Black denim jeans, a red tank top and her black leather jacket seemed to do the trick. She shook out her thick auburn hair so it fell in soft waves past her shoulders and applied enough makeup to accentuate her emerald eye, not realizing how striking she already looked.

She met the others in the hotel lobby and did a double-take. They looked like models for a Frederick's of Hollywood catalog! Francine was dressed in some type of merry widow getup, with thigh-high black patent leather boots. Her reddish-gold curls tumbled wildly down her back, and her makeup made her look like a Greek goddess.

Toni was sleek in a full-body catsuit made of shiny red rubber, four-inch spike heels and a peek-a-boo lace top. Her white blonde hair was carefully disheveled, brilliant blue shadow ringed her eyes, and her lips shone with cherry red gloss.

Rusty had made a valiant effort to fit in, but seemed to just miss the mark. Her red miniskirt was a tad too clingy, her shimmering silver blouses a notch too loud. A black jeweled bra and candy apple red pumps completed the mismatched outfit. Her long black hair was teased to within an inch of its life and her makeup looked as though Francine had applied it.

Kris sighed inwardly and suppressed a grin as Toni eyed her critically.

"I thought I told you to dress *up*." Her voice betrayed her annoyance. "Maybe Francine can touch up your eyes."

Kris backed away. "I like my makeup just fine," she said firmly.

Toni arched one perfectly penciled eyebrow.

"Whatever." She spun and marched to the bar. "One quick drink and then we head to the show. I have a surprise tonight."

The surprise manifested at the hotel entrance. A shiny black limousine idled at the curb. The doorman held the door open to let them slide onto the plush leather seats.

Once inside, Toni opened the mini-fridge and pulled out a bottle of Dom Perignon. Rusty goggled at the label.

"A treat, for us," she announced, "from a very important person."

She exchanged a knowing look with Francine and popped the cork as Francine pulled out crystal champagne flutes. When everyone had a glass, Toni raised hers.

"To us... and our dreams," she said loftily. "May we all get what we truly deserve."

They clinked glasses. Rusty drank hers so quickly, a few drops of champagne spilled onto her blouse. She frantically wiped at the stain with her hand as Toni cast her a disgusted look.

Kris looked around at the others before taking a tentative sip. There was an ominous ring to Toni's words, and she wasn't sure she wanted to drink to such a wish.

The ride to Radio City Music Hall took just minutes. This time, even Kris thrilled to the reaction they received when the chauffeur opened the door and helped them out, one by one. Toni smirked as she sashayed up to the doors, basking in the attention. The line of fans waiting to get in gawked at them; men in awe, women in envy. The ticket takers, thinking them famous, let them cut in line. Rusty squeezed Kris' hand in excitement, shivering with glee.

That night's show as good as the first. As Black Gallows launched into their last song, Toni started looking up and down the aisle. Halfway through the song, a disheveled looking man sidled up and handed her a stack of passes. She briskly handed them out and waved at the others to follow her. This time, they took a different route backstage and ended up in a swanky, dimly-lit room furnished with deep red velvet furniture; the walls a sea of glossy black. A man stood discreetly in the corner behind a fully-stocked bar.

Toni glanced around the room, spotted someone, then turned to the others.

"Have a drink if you want, then wait for me over there." She pointed to a dark corner in the back. She ran her hands over her hips, making sure there were no lumps in her rubber catsuit, then looked at Francine, who nodded and gave her a thumbs up. Toni nodded back, then strutted toward a group of men lounging on sofas. The others watched as she leaned in to kiss one of them. He grabbed her ass and pulled her onto his lap. Kris squinted in the dim light to get a better look. The man had bushy black hair and she could tell he was tall; his long legs stretched out in front of him. She saw Toni whisper something in his ear and pull him to his feet. He motioned for two other men to get up. They all disappeared through a black door near the bar.

Francine broke the silence. "I'm getting a drink. Any other takers?" Without waiting for an answer, she clattered toward the bar.

Rusty looked at Kris.

"You drinking?"

"Not sure," Kris replied, taking in the room again. She unzipped a jacket pocket and pulled out a small notebook and pen. Flipping it open, she leaned against the wall and began jotting some notes. Rusty sighed and joined Francine at the bar.

Kris wrote, lost in thought, and jumped when a masculine hand closed over hers, causing her pen to mark a jagged line across the page.

"What the hell..." she spluttered, whipping her head up to see who had so rudely interrupted her, then blanched.

Marty Brinkman grinned at her, long brown hair wet from a shower, face shining with the exertion of his performance, warm brown eyes twinkling in amusement.

"Taking notes on all of us, luv?" he drawled, releasing her hand and grabbing the notebook instead. He propped himself against the wall with one hand as his eyes flicked over what she'd written. He smiled again.

"Ah, the makings of an article on tonight's show. Love your description of me: 'front man Marty Brinkman bounced around the stage, reminding one of a cross between a hyperactive child and a court jester on speed.'"

He gently placed the notebook back in Kris' hand and traced a line down her cheek with one finger. She shivered under his light touch.

"Ah, an aspiring journalist," he murmured. "But just how far will the lady writer go to get an exclusive with Marty Brinkman, one wonders?"

He pushed himself away from the wall and held out his hand.

"This bloke is willing to go *in depth* and *under cover* to get the answer."

Kris stared at Marty in horror and revulsion. He placed a hand on her shoulder and she violently shook it off.

"Is THAT what you want from me?" she burst out. "I thought you'd be a fun, interesting *conversation!*"

He laughed again, his tone sarcastic now.

"Ah, cut the crap, lass." He put his hands on his hips. "You birds start out all the same: 'I just want to *talk*.'" He thrust his hips to one side. "'I just want to know what makes you *tick*.'" He thrust his hips to the other side. "Then…" he thrust his hips forward. "You're in my bed, letting me do whatever I want to you, so you can pride yourself in having had the great Marty Brinkman. So, let's just cut the crap." He looked her up and down.

"You want me. I don't think you're half bad. A bit stiff, but I think I can loosen you up." He held out his hand again. "Coming, luv?" He stepped toward the door that Toni had disappeared through. "There's a nice, cushy couch waiting for us through that door. Or… we can go back to my hotel room. I think I can give you the full-service treatment."

Kris' look of revulsion melted into a look of deep sadness.

"I truly thought you were different." Somehow, she managed to keep her voice even. "Your interviews are so interesting. I thought you could have a decent conversation and not make it about sex. I see I was wrong and that's a great disappointment." She pointed to Francine and Rusty. "I'm sure you'll have better luck over there."

Pocketing her notebook and pen, she walked away, willing herself not to burst into tears until she was safely out of the room.

Kris hailed a cab back to the hotel and thought about getting her things from the room and just going home. Forget the rest of the shows! She didn't fit into Toni's group and never would. She decided to stop in the bar for a drink first, to calm her nerves. The others wouldn't be back for hours. She'd have time to get her things together and leave before they returned to the hotel.

She ordered an Irish coffee and found a secluded table. Pulling out her notebook, she continued to write, pausing only to pay and thank the waitress who delivered her drink. She was so focused on her writing, she didn't hear someone pull up a chair, and flinched when a voice spoke.

"I looked for you backstage. Your friends are stirring up quite a scene back there."

Kris looked up to see Linda Hart smiling at her.

"I didn't feel like hanging out with them, so I came back here."

"We got tired of the madhouse, too, so we thought we'd have a wee nightcap here." Linda gestured toward the bar, where Brian was buying drinks, then glanced curiously at Kris' notebook.

"What are you writing?"

Kris blushed. "Oh, nothing." She flipped her notebook closed. "Well, actually, I was writing a review of tonight's show. I'd like to write for a music magazine, so I've been practicing a bit, writing reviews of the shows I see."

"May I?" Linda asked, holding out her hand. Kris blushed again, but slid the notebook across the table.

Linda was immersed in the article when Brian arrived at the table with two beers. He smiled warmly at Kris and pulled out a chair next to his wife.

"What are you reading?" he asked softly.

Linda handed him the notebook. "You should read this. It's quite good." Looking quickly at Kris, she added, "You don't mind, do you?"

Kris did mind, but she shook her head, suddenly feeling very nervous. She gulped her coffee, not even feeling the whiskey's effects, letting Linda draw her into conversation as Brian read. After a few minutes, he looked up.

"I agree with Linda, this is good. You need to submit this."

"Thanks." Brian's compliment lifted her spirits. "I just wish I knew someone to send it to," she sighed, pocketing the notebook and pen.

Then she grinned. "Enough about me, let's talk about you!"

They spent the next hour talking about Brian and Linda's lives with Black Gallows and about their lives back in England. They had no children, kept a small house in Coventry and spent their time off leisurely exploring countries they'd only glimpsed from tour bus windows.

Her drink long drained, Kris finally stood.

"It's been great getting to know you," she said. "I probably won't see you again. I'm not going to the other shows."

Linda asked why, but Kris was vague. She didn't want to complain about Marty and she had no desire to run into him again, backstage or anywhere else for that matter. As she turned to leave, Linda asked for her address and phone numbers.

"I'd like to keep in touch with you," she said. "It's nice to meet decent folk. You don't often get to, in this life."

Kris was flattered. She and Linda exchanged information. Then, Linda did something surprising; she hugged Kris.

"You take care and don't give up your dream!" she said fiercely. "And don't let the others change you."

Kris hugged her back, waved to Brian, and went up to the room she shared with the others, and gathered her things. As she turned her key in at the registration desk,

Marty Brinkman sauntered in, alone. He spotted her and walked over, grinning.

"Change your mind about me, luv?" he called out. "You don't need to try to get my room number. You can just go up with me."

Kris glared at him.

"I wasn't trying to get your room number," she spat. "What I said before, stands. I don't want to be anywhere near you!" Turning on her heel, she grabbed her bags and stalked out, not seeing Brian and Linda standing there, stunned looks on their faces.

Chapter 17

Marty turned and watched the lass storm off, then shot a bewildered look at Brian and Linda.

"Was it something I said?" he asked, his hands held out in a "who, me?" gesture.

Linda flashed him a stern look.

"You two had a run in before, from the sounds of her. What did you do?" she said sharply.

Marty snorted. "I just called her on her game. Pretending to be a 'journalist.' Said she just wanted to *talk*. She should know that's one of the oldest ploys in the book! And then she played hard to get! All I have to do is crook my finger and the birds come running. I've no use for the likes of her!"

Linda bristled. "For your information, Mr. Sex God, that lass is trying to be a journalist. She has no use for the backstage games you lot love to play. If she said she just wanted to talk, that's all she wanted, you prat!"

Marty crossed his arms over his chest, but the defiant act was somehow muted by the look of uncertainty that crossed his face.

"She didn't want to just hop in the sack? Then what was she doing in the hotel?"

"Did it ever occur to you, my testosterone-packed friend, that she might have been staying here, too?" Linda's voice dripped mock sweetness.

Marty faltered, then hitched a sneer back onto his face. "Why would the lass want to stay here, when she lives here? Aaah, try to explain *that*, Mrs. Know-It-All!"

"Oh, come on!" Linda burst out impatiently. She forced a calm tone. "Look, Brian and I have had a chance to talk with the lass. She's not a bad sort. It seems to be that she's hooked up with an... interesting... lot. I know she hasn't lived here very long. She told me she moved to New York to try to crack into writing for magazines. And she's not bad, either. Brian and I have had a look at her article. It's quite good, isn't it, luv?" She turned to Brian, who nodded.

"Aye, it is."

Marty ran a hand through his long brown hair, twisting the ends around his fingers in agitation.

"So, I just up and chased off the first real lass I've had the good grace to meet in years. Is that what you're telling me?"

Linda threw her hands up. "Give the chap a pint and call him a winner!"

"That's not a bad idea," Marty muttered, making for the bar. Linda and Brian joined him as he popped into a chair, spilling a bit of his beer. He downed half the contents in one long gulp. By the time he met Linda's gaze again, he saw she was smiling gently.

"Rattled you, that one has," she said sagely. "I doubt you'll see her again, though. She told Bri and me she's not coming to the rest of the shows."

"Why not?" he demanded.

"Probably because of your pig-headed self." Though she spoke the words kindly, he winced.

"Ouch, that hurts."

"Serves you right, mate!" Brian grinned and raised his half-empty glass. "To Marty Brinkman, King of Pigs!"

"Up yours," grumbled Marty, but he clinked his glass and drank just the same, thinking about the auburn-haired woman who had made him twitch with excitement, even as she'd told him to bugger off.

Chapter 18

Kris called in sick and spent the day cleaning her apartment, reliving every second of her disastrous encounter with Marty. When every appliance sparkled and every piece of furniture gleamed, she grabbed her notebook and walked to the cafe. There, she finished her article on Black Gallows and reread it critically. It *was* good. If only she had someone to send it to! She thought again of Toni's editor friend. Kris wondered if this woman even existed. She had heard nothing about her Lizard Lust review. Sighing, she closed her notebook, drained the dregs of her cold cappuccino, and headed home.

She was walking down the hall toward her apartment when she spotted something on the floor in front of her door. She stopped in surprise, taking in the beautiful bouquet of flowers. Glancing down the empty hallway, she picked up the flowers and noticed a small envelope addressed to her. Her curiosity piqued, she let herself into her apartment, set the arrangement on the table, and pulled out the card. It read: *So sorry for misunderstanding you. I've been set straight. Please have dinner with me - Marty x*

She reread the card, puzzled. Set straight? Who had set him straight? And how did he know where she lived? She thought back to the confrontation of the night before. Who else had been in the lobby to witness it? Something clicked into place. Brian and Linda! Had they still been at the bar?

She had been so angry, she hadn't bothered to keep her voice down. She set the card down next to the flowers. It made sense. Linda knew where she lived; Kris had given her the address.

Flustered now, she wandered into the kitchen and brewed a pot of coffee, even though she'd just had a cappuccino. She needed caffeine; she needed to think. Marty wanted to have dinner with her. Just the thought made her stomach flutter, even though he had been such a conceited ass. She pictured again his cocky grin as he'd swept his long hair over his shoulder and held out his hand. She couldn't deny it. As stunned as she'd been, a part of her had wanted to take his hand and throw caution to the wind.

Idiot girl, chided a voice in her head. *All he wanted was a one night stand. You would have been just a nameless, faceless fuck.* Kris shook her head vigorously to clear the voice. Didn't she know that already? She was no fool. But... a tiny part of her dreamed of day when Marty would fall in love with her and sweep her away. Didn't everyone have a dream like that? She knew she was no different from countless other women who fantasized about celebrities. Her eyes flicked to the card. Maybe there was still a chance.

Kris poured a large mug of coffee and sat, gazing at the flowers. He had thought enough to send her flowers. Or, had Linda made him? She frowned slightly as she fingered the yellow and pink roses. The petals felt like silk in her hands. She imagined Marty' skin under her fingertips, then shook her head again. That was dangerous territory. She picked up her coffee and marched into the living room, determined to put Marty out of her mind, at least for the night. Maybe her favorite comedy show could distract her for a while.

The show was just wrapping up when the phone rang. Thinking it was Toni demanding to know where she was, she let the machine answer, then started as a husky male voice came over the speaker, his brogue pronounced.

"Hello, I'm looking for Kris. This is Marty. I wanted to make sure you got my apology. I truly am sorry and want to take you to dinner. Please call me at the hotel. I'm in room 1609."

Kris froze, listening to the message, resisting the urge to pick up the phone. She waited for the click signifying that he'd hung up, then replayed the message, savoring his smooth tenor voice. She wanted to go to dinner with him, but what did that make her? She knew what he wanted, even though he was suddenly being so nice. Would going out to dinner send him the message that she wanted it, too? That she was like the other girls he'd talked about the night before, who came across as innocent - then jumped in the sack? Because, as much as she denied it, she did want him. But, surely she was strong enough to survive dinner without making a fool of herself? Would he show her to side of him reserved for friends and family?

Curiosity got the best of her and she had just decided to call him back when the phone rang again. Thinking it was Marty, she snatched up the phone.

"Hello?"

"Where the HELL are you?" Toni's voice was icy.

"Oh, it's you." Kris' tone grew cool as well. "Sorry. I've got things to do. Can't waste time hanging around a hotel all week."

"Marty Brinkman's been looking all over for you. I promised him I'd deliver you to him tonight. You *are* going to dinner with him, aren't you?"

The words slammed into Kris like a punch. Toni had promised to "deliver" her to Marty? Was she the one who had given him her address?

"I wouldn't go out with Marty Brinkman if he was the last man on earth," she said, her voice deadly quiet.

There was a pause, then Toni drawled, "Have it your way, darling. See how far you get."

Kris heard a click as Toni hung up. Tears stung her eyes and a wave of humiliation burned in her stomach. She had nearly convinced herself that he could be nice; that he was sincere in his apology. She pulled on a pair of jeans and a t-shirt, grabbed her notebook and stormed out of her apartment. She ended up back at the cafe, where she downed three more coffees and write angrily for three hours. She wrote about Marty, Toni, and the whole scene. If she had to be like Toni to get ahead in this business, she didn't need it. She'd have to give up her dream of writing for rock magazines, because she certainly wasn't getting anywhere.

These thoughts filled her head as she made the short walk back to her building, and she was still preoccupied as she rode the elevator to her floor. As she started down the hall to her apartment, she saw something that stopped her in her tracks. For the second time that day, something was in front of her door. Or rather, *someone*. The figure spotted her and stood, shaking long brown hair out of his liquid brown eyes.

"I was wondering if you'd like to have dinner," Marty said, a sheepish smile on his face.

Kris' eyes flashed with anger.

"I don't know what kind of shit Toni's been feeding you, but I don't get 'delivered' up to anyone!" she said hotly. "Now, get the hell away from my door!"

Marty flinched.

"That's not what I'm here for," he sputtered. "Linda told me you were a good 'un, not like those flashy birds you hang with. It's been such a long time since a lass had just wanted conversation with me… I guess I'm a bit jaded by it all." He pulled his hand out of his pocket and held it out to her.

"Truce?"

Kris stared at his outstretched hand, uncertain.

"Linda told you where to find me?" she finally asked.

He nodded, grinning now.

"Linda let me have it with both barrels for the way I treated you in the lobby last night. She and Brian heard everything. She was spitting, she was so mad. She probably would have beaten me, had she gotten close enough."

Kris tried to picture such a scene in her head and fought a smile. Instead, she shook his hand tentatively. His grin grew more confident and he gave her hand a little squeeze.

"I'm glad you've decided to give me a chance," he said. "I'm really not so bad." He jammed his hands in his pockets. "Now, is there a place nearby that serves food this late?"

She took him to a diner a few blocks from her apartment, and quickly learned she wasn't the only one who liked breakfast, day and night. Marty ordered eggs, sausage, toast, baked beans and fries. Kris stared quizzically at him, as did the waitress.

"If that's what you want," the waitress said, dubiously.

Marty grinned in anticipation. "I always have beans and chips with my eggs."

He fell silent as Kris ordered, asking, "What's corned beef hash?"

Kris thought a moment, then answered, "I don't know, but it's pretty good, especially when it's overcooked."

They made small talk as they waited for their food. The waitress dropped a carafe of coffee at their table. "That way, I don't hafta keep botherin' you," she explained.

Kris made Marty taste the corned beef once it came. He made a face and said, "It tastes like salt!"

She shrugged and dipped a piece of her toasted bagel into the golden egg yolk.

"At least I'm not eating baked beans with my breakfast. And what's with the fries?"

"I'll have you know, this is a normal breakfast in England!" He dug into his food with gusto.

They ate in silence for several moments, the silence between them more comfortable than before. Kris watched Marty mop up the baked beans with fries, then toast. At this moment, he wasn't a rock star. He was just a guy eating breakfast for dinner, like her. She wondered what else they had in common.

He caught her looking, swallowed, and smiled.

"What's on your mind, luv?" he asked.

She blushed slightly and turned her attention back to her coffee.

"Nothing," she said. She busied herself with the carafe, filling their cups. He kept his eyes on her the entire time. Finally, she spoke.

"I was just wondering about your background, your family and such. I haven't met anyone who likes to eat breakfast for dinner, like me. I was wondering what else we may have in common."

He leaned back in his seat and stretched.

"Well, if you've been raised by a headstrong mum who took a family of seven in hand after your dad left when you were two years old, then we've got more in common than our taste in meals."

Kris stared at him. "My mother raised my sister and me, too. My dad left when I was six, saying he hadn't seen enough of the world and wasn't ready to be a dad. He never came back or kept in touch."

He studied her. "Your mum seems to have done a great job," he said softly.

She blushed again. "She's been wonderful. I wouldn't trade her for all the dads in the world."

He nodded in agreement. "Me, too. My mum raised six girls and me. I'm the youngest and the biggest handful, according to her." He drank more coffee. "She kept me out of trouble. I was more afraid of her than the local thugs."

He grinned at the memory. "When I made my first batch of money, I made sure Mum was taken care of. She deserves so much."

At Kris' urging, Marty told her more about his childhood in Liverpool, growing up in the shadow of the Beatles. All his friends had wanted to play in bands and get famous like the Fab Four.

"Brian and I started our first incarnation of this band when we were about twelve. I think we called ourselves Hemlock. Brian was very into Socrates at the time. You should hear tome of the songs we came up with, even then!"

Kris talked about her writing, about starting the first newspaper at her elementary school, the internship at the Asbury Park Press, and her decision to leave college to pursue a career as a rock journalist.

"Linda told me you weren't handing me a line," he said. "She said your writing is very good."

"I don't think it's too shabby." She smiled, a bit shyly. "This business seems to be so hard to break into, though, for the magazines that are out there right now." She sighed wistfully and poured more coffee. The clock caught her eye.

"It's three in the morning!" she exclaimed, jumping up. "I have to get up in a couple of hours to get ready for work!"

Marty paid the check and walked her back to her apartment building. He didn't ask to come up, and she didn't invite him.

"Will you come to the show tomorrow - I mean, tonight?" he asked.

"I don't know," she replied, honestly. She wasn't too keen to see Toni just yet.

"Fair enough," he said, lightly. He turned to go, then turned back again.

"I would like to see you again before we leave town." He bent and kissed her cheek, his lips softly brushing her skin. The gentle touch felt electric - and she fought an insane urge to grab him and kiss him properly.

He whispered something that sounded like "thank you" before he walked away. Kris watched him go, trying to quell the butterflies in her stomach. She heard someone cough behind her and saw Henry, her elderly doorman, holding the door open for her.

"Thanks, Henry," she smiled.

"Nice young man, he seems," said Henry, blue eyes twinkling. "Sounds like a fine English lad."

"We'll see," she replied, heading for the elevator.

Chapter 19

Toni paced the hotel room, seething. She could never remember being so angry. Billy was spending time with his fucking bimbo. Francine and Andy were wrapped up in each other like a sickening, heavy metal version of "Ozzie and Harriet." Rusty was completely useless. She had tried to pick up the drummer from the opening band, but he had been more interested in the statuesque redhead who was standing nearby. None of the others in the opening band seemed interested in Rusty, either, and Black Gallows was way out her league.

Toni plunked down on the edge of the bed. Her best bet had been Kris. Marty was panting after her like a dog in heat. If Kris would just go with him, Toni would move closer to landing Don Lyden. But Kris had refused to consider it, had even sounded offended by his interest! Toni scowled as she remembered their conversation. Kris had sounded like a fucking nun.

Toni stood and began to pace again. She knew women who would pay for the chance to spend five minutes with Marty Brinkman. For one, he was famous... with a capital F. Two, he was reportedly very well endowed. Toni regretted not having gotten the chance to do him, but she had already hooked up with Billy, who wasn't too shabby when it came to size. Toni had a hard and fast rule: she never did two guys from the same band unless she was doing them both at the same time.

She heard a key in the door and looked up as Rusty stumbled into the room, obviously drunk. She stopped short as she saw Toni, swaying slightly.

"Oh, hey," she slurred. "I ran into the guitarist for the opening band and he's looking for you. He wants us to go party in the singer's room."

"Both of us?" Toni asked skeptically.

Rusty nodded vigorously, black hair flopping into her yes. "They've got the bassist with him and were wondering if we knew any other girls. They bought me shots downstairs and send me looking for you. They've heard all about you." Rusty's eyes shone as she collapsed onto the bed. "Toni, the girl so talented, she only needs one name."

Toni stood and smoothed her spandex mini skirt.

"Well, why not?" she said to one in particular. She reapplied her lip gloss and strode to the door.

"Let's go," she commanded, then stopped. "Wait," she amended, seeing how disheveled Rusty looked. "Straighten yourself out, first."

She tapped her foot impatiently as Rusty wiped smudges from under her eyes, shakily applied new lipstick, and clumsily finger-combed her heavily sprayed hair, which lurched dangerously to one side.

The singer's room was two floors below theirs. By the time they reached it, the was plowed and the other two were hopped up on coke. Toni noticed a mountain of white powder piled on the dresser, a razor blade lying nearby, along with a rolled-up dollar bill. Rusty collapsed next to the singer and the two of them burst into fits of giggles. The bassist and guitarist crowded around Toni, each trying to kiss her and grab her breasts. She reached down and felt them both. They were limp, which she found odd. Cocaine usually made a guy so hard, he couldn't get off.

"What else have you taken?" she demanded, pushing them both away. They guys looked at each other and shrugged, trying to remember. Toni noticed a bottle next to the mountain of coke, picked it up and glanced at the label. Valium. Lovely. These two wouldn't be good for anything.

The guitarist tried to kiss her again. She pushed him away impatiently and watched him fall, almost in slow motion, onto the second bed. He didn't get up. She bent toward the dresser and scraped together two lines of coke. Deftly, she snorted a line up each nostril, tossing her head back as she did so. Turning back to the others, she snapped, "you're pathetic!" and stormed out the door.

She made her way down to the bar, thinking a couple of Mai Tais might dull her anger a bit. Heads turned as she strolled through the lobby; men staring lustfully, women with disgust. Toni didn't pay attention to anyone. Once in the bar, she spotted a familiar face, partially hidden in the semi-darkness of a booth. Her stomach lurched as he beckoned to her, but she gave herself a mental slap and smiled as she slid into the booth across from him.

"Thanks again for the treat," she purred, grazing his arm with scarlet-tipped nails.

"You already thanked me backstage, and very nicely, too." he drawled, with a bawdy wink. He shook his glass, ice tinkling, then drained his drink.

"Now, where are the new girls? Busy, I hope."

Toni didn't meet his eyes.

"Rusty is upstairs with the singer from the opening band," she said smoothly. "And I'm working on getting Kris together with Marty. He wants her badly."

Marius' black eyes narrowed.

"Brinkman?" he spat. "She's too good for him." He leaned back in his seat, stretching his long legs out before him. "Keep her away from Brinkman. He'll only sully her. In fact, I want you to save her for me."

Toni started to scowl, but quickly hid it.

"I don't know why you want Kris," she said, a little peevishly. "She's not a virgin, like I originally thought, but I do think she's frigid. She's definitely very uptight."

Marius Mann chuckled, his deep bass voice rumbling with mirth.

"Oh, she's not frigid. She just needs the right touch." His black eyes twinkled as he beckoned to the waitress for another drink. The waitress hurried over with a bourbon on the rocks, then looked questioningly at Toni.

"A Mai Tai," she said with a dismissive wave. She felt a stab of annoyance at Marius. The more she got to know Kris, the more boring she considered her to be. How could he want her?

He seemed to read her mind.

"Kris is rare. She hasn't been jaded by the business, not yet. She'll still got a sweetness about her. Something I don't think you would understand. You've always been a go-getter, even when I met you all those years ago."

Marius finished his drink and heaved himself out of the booth.

"Your new mission for Miss Kris - get her ready for me, doll face." Cupping her face with a large hand, he squeezed, hard, then caressed her skin gently. With a sardonic wave, he left the bar.

Toni sipped her drink, mind working furiously. She had to work quickly. First order of business: get back into Kris' good graces. That meant playing Kris' game, for a while, at least. She'd call Annie and make her print Kris' article, no matter how bad it was. She had never given Annie Kris' Lizard Lust review, even though Marius had told her to.

Luckily, Annie had been out of the country so she couldn't rat Toni out. She'd just let Marius believe things had been too hectic and he'd let the matter drop. Of course, he'd been busy setting up that party for the Japanese businessmen, so he hadn't had time to investigate Toni's story more thoroughly. But now, Toni had to go through with it. Annie would publish this article. She had no choice. And Toni would convince Kris Marius was behind it, that he wanted to be her benefactor, and prepare her for a meeting. Wondering what the hell Kris had that she didn't, Toni made her way back up to her room.

Chapter 20

Kris enjoyed her second dinner with Marty as much as the first. He was as animated and interesting as she had originally hoped he'd be. He talked about going to school in England and how that differed from her experience in New Jersey.

"We stay at school for practically the entire year," he explained. "We only go home for the winter and summer holidays."

She stared incredulously at him. "How could you stand being away from your family that long?"

Marty shrugged. "It was a good education. Mum saved every penny to make sure I went to a good school. I wasn't going to grumble. Of course, he added, smiling wryly, "I could have applied myself and gotten better grades, but that was when I realized I wanted to be a rock singer. Maths and science didn't matter to me."

"Did you wear a uniform?" Kris asked, curious. She tried to picture a miniature Marty in a school uniform. The only uniform that came to mind was one she knew the kids who went to St. Agnes Catholic School near her house wore: blue and green plaid tie, white shirt, navy pants, and shiny black shoes. Mini-Marty in blue and green plaid just didn't work. She giggled softly.

"What's funny?" he demanded, playfully. "Trying to picture me as a lad in uniform?"

When she nodded, he said, "Okay, then. Picture this: gray pants, white shirt, gray tie, and blue sweater. Oh, and black trainers on my feet."

"Trainers?" she repeated.

His brow furrowed. "Trainers. You know." He looked around the diner, then at her feet. He brightened and pointed to her sneakers. "Live you've got on, but black."

She looked down. "Oh, sneakers."

It was his turn to laugh. "Sneakers? Why do you call them sneakers? You can't sneak up on anyone wearing those bloody things. They squeak and give you away!"

She laughed. "That's just what they are," she insisted. "I didn't name them."

They talked about his six sisters, who all still lived in Liverpool near their mother. Three were married; two had children. Marty had set up trust funds for the kids. He lived in a small apartment in London; a "flat," he called it, preferring to save his money instead of spending it on a lavish home he'd never see. His apartment was empty, too, save for a collection of baseball bats signed by various Major League players.

"I'm crazy about baseball," he confessed. "The blokes in the band take the piss out of me about that. They're all football nutters."

Kris said, "there's nothing wrong with football. I'm a huge Giants fan."

Marty chuckled. "Football in England is soccer here."

"Oh," said Kris quietly. "Um… what do you mean by 'take the piss'?"

He laughed. "That means teasing. Take the piss or take the mickey, if you want to be more polite."

She shook her head. "We speak the same language, yet we don't."

"It's not so bad," he grinned. "So, tell me, do you like baseball?"

"Oh, yes," she replied enthusiastically. "My mother's uncle played for the Yankees in the 1930s. We'll all Yankees fans, of course."

He backed away in mock horror. "I'm a Red Sox fan, meself." That makes us mortal enemies!" He brandished a piece of garlic toast at her.

She burst out laughing and his grin widened, his eyes crinkling with mirth.

Marty had never had a serious girlfriend. He said his schedule didn't allow for full-time relationships. He leaned back in his seat and said, wistfully, "I wouldn't mind a young 'un of my own, one day."

"Do you ever wonder whether you're a father now?" Kris asked, quietly.

He looked startled. "I never considered that," he mused. "Do you think I could have a wee one out there somewhere?"

Kris stared at him incredulously. "You mean, you never thought about that, all the women you've had, around the world?"

He smiled ruefully. "I must confess, at the time I wasn't really thinking about babies, if you know what I mean."

She reached for her latte, shaking her head sadly. "I'll never understand it."

"Understand what, luv?"

"The allure of all those one night stands. I just can't imagine being with someone whose you-know-who has been who knows where." Kris kept her gaze firmly locked on her mug, avoiding his gaze. She was afraid she'd gone too far.

He was silent for a moment, then let out a bark of laughter.

"Oh, you are the end!" he chortled. 'You should be sitting across from me wearing a high collar, hair pulled back in a painful, tight bun." His eyes flickered over her and his tone softened. "You shouldn't be sitting here, your soft hair framing those innocent green eyes, that poet shirt hiding all your secrets, tantalizing me."

Kris stiffened under his gaze, which had darkened. She felt as though all the air had gone from the room. Her heart thudded painfully and butterflies took flight in her stomach. Her body was responding to his words. Had they been in her apartment, she had no doubt she would have taken him to her bed. She gave herself a mental shake and saw Marty was smiling gently at her.

"A change of topic for the lady, methinks," he announced, and launched into a diatribe about the Red Sox and the curse of the Bambino. He waved his garlic bread at her again.

"It's you Yankee lot's fault that the Red Sox are cursed, you know!" he stated.

"No, don't hang that on us!" she protested. "It's not our fault Babe Ruth played better in New York than in Boston!"

They argued amiably about baseball through dessert. Again, he walked her home but did not ask to come up. He brushed his lips to her cheek again, one hand lightly on her waist, and murmured in her ear. "Maybe one day I can try to explain the allure to you. All I can say now is that being here with you like this is more alluring than any one night stand I've ever had." He ran his hand lightly from her waist to her back, before releasing her.

With a jovial wave at Henry, Marty turned and sauntered down the street, long brown hair swinging with each step. Kris stared after him, trembling from his touch and words. She let herself into her apartment several minutes later, mind whirling with thoughts she didn't want to consider. Just now, she wanted him to crush her to him, to feel his hard body as those sensuous lips claimed hers. She shook her head furiously, hair whipping about her face.

The band was leaving after the next show. She was just a harmless little dalliance during his time in New York; a novelty because she wouldn't jump in the sack with him. In a way, she was glad he was leaving, because the more time she spent with him, the more she wanted him. He pushed all the right buttons. All he had to do was look at her with that smoldering gaze and she melted.

Kris squared her shoulders. She had to stand up to her feelings and resist them. He'd been with hundreds of women and hadn't given them a second thought. Hell, he hadn't even considered the possibility he might have children out there. Resolutely, she put him out of her mind. She was about to collapse onto her couch when she noticed the answering machine's message light blinking. She pushed "play" and Toni's voice filled the room.

"Hey, I've been hard on you. I'm sorry. I know you're different and I…. well, I know I need to respect that." A pause. "Look, my friend Annie is coming to tomorrow's show. She wants an article on Black Gallows and I talked her into looking at your stuff. I promise she'll publish it this time. Call me at the hotel. I don't care how late it is. I'll be up."

Kris stared at the machine, puzzled. Where had that come from? Did Toni mean it? She grabbed her notebook and scanned her recent article. She liked it and thought she'd captured the excitement and intensity of the show. She called the hotel. Toni answered on the second ring.

Although she did sound as though the phone had woken her up, she greeted Kris warmly.

"Do you have an article for Annie?" she asked.

"Yes, but I don't understand why you're doing this now," said Kris, suspicion creeping into her voice.

"Well, I told you. I feel bad about the way I've been treating you. I've been pushing you to be someone you're not. I know Annie flaked out about your Lizard Lust review, but she really does want to see another article from you." Toni's tone was sincere.

"I don't know," Kris hedged.

Toni cut her off. "Oh, come on!" she snapped. "Take it for what it is, an opportunity for you to get your foot in the door. Isn't that why you started hanging out with me in the first place - for my contacts?" She sighed loudly. "Stop acting like such a good girl, Kris, because we both know that deep down, you're not."

Her tone grew brisk. "Come to the hotel before the show. Bring the article. I'll introduce you Annie and you guys can take it from there."

Kris agreed to meet Toni and the girls in the lobby at six, then hung up and excitedly called Marty. He sounded pleased to hear her voice, even though he had just left her. She told him about Toni's offer. He sounded happy for her.

"What's the magazine called, luv?"

"I don't know, but the editor's name is Annie," she related. "She's one of Toni's friends."

There was a long silence at the other end. Then Marty said, haltingly, "I'm not sure that's such a good idea."

His response stunned Kris.

"Why not?" she demanded, a little defiantly.

"Annie's not very nice," he said, cryptically. "In fact, if you think Toni is a barracuda with the guys, Annie is a great white shark."

"It sounds like you know her," Kris said, surprised.

"Let's just say we're... acquainted."

"Did she interview you?"

"Er... not exactly."

It took a moment for his words to sink in.

"Oh," was all she could muster.

"Yeah, well... it was a long time ago."

He brusquely changed the subject. "About the show. It's our last one here. Are you going?"

When she said yes, he asked, "Fancy a meal afterward?"

"Yes, please," she replied, secretly pleased to spend one more night in his company.

"It's a date," he said, and they rang off.

Kris was tired, but also excited. She pulled out her typewriter and typed out the article, then slid the pages into a manila envelope. Humming to herself, she went to bed.

Chapter 21

Kris arrived at the hotel a few minutes early and paced nervously in the lobby. The concierge finally came over and asked, in a tone of frosty politeness, whether he could help her. She shook her head and found an empty chair. Sinking into it, she closed her eyes, resting the envelope on her lap, trying to quell her nervousness.

A hand closed over her hers, making her jump. She opened her eyes to see Marty smiling down at her.

"Thought I'd find you here," he said. He turned serious. "Look, I need to talk to you before you meet Annie."

"Forget it," she said, a blush creeping up her neck.

"No, not that," he said. "I really need to talk to you. Please come up to my room for a minute."

At her look of hesitance, he said impatiently, "I'm not going to lay a hand on you! Just come with me. I can't talk about it here and they'll be down any minute."

He stood and held out his hand, his gaze intense and urgent. She hesitated another second then placed her hand in his and let him pull her to her feet. They rode the elevator in silence. He didn't speak again until they were inside his room. He sat heavily on his bed, motioning her to a chair by the window. She sat and waited for him to speak.

"Look. I hope you don't mind, but I called a mate of mine who publishes a magazine. I'd like to read your article and see if he'll publish it. No strings," he quickly added, holding his hands up.

"Why are you doing this?" Kris asked, confused.

He stood and paced for a moment, before turning to face her.

"I just don't like the idea of you being beholden to Toni for anything."

"What are you not telling me?" she demanded, catching the evasive tone in his voice.

He frowned. "Nothing concrete," he finally replied. "Just a feeling she's setting you up for something."

He crossed to her and held out his hand. "May I read it? Please?"

Silently, she handed him the envelope, then sat nervously as he read it. He looked up, smiling.

"This is quite good," he said. "I especially like that you left in that daft description of me."

He leaned over and picked up the phone. He punched in a number and Kris heard it ring on the other end before a booming voice answered.

"Yeah, hey, MacGregor! It's Brinko again." The male voice said something. Marty chuckled. "Yes, I've read it. It's quite good." He paused. "Yes, I'll send it over tomorrow before I leave." Another pause. "Yes, I'll make sure her contact information's included." He paused, then chuckled again. "No, nothing like that." He winked at Kris. "She fancies me anyway." He said goodbye and hung up.

"I'll keep this and send it off to MacGregor tomorrow."

She gulped. "MacGregor? As in DAVID MacGregor? As in Metal Countdown?"

Marty laughed again. "Yeah, MacGregor's a mate of mine from Scotland. He came here to make his fortune ten years ago and found it in his wee magazine."

"Scotland?" Kris was confused again. "I thought the magazine was published here."

Marty nodded absently. "Yes, it's based here in New York because Davey likes it here."

Panic filled her. "Marty, I'm not sure my article is of that caliber!"

He waved her off. "If I say it's good, then it's bloody good. I've seen my share of articles. I think I can judge what's rubbish and what's not." He smiled at her again. "We should probably head downstairs. I've got to get over to the Hall."

He pulled her out of her chair and wrapped his arms around her, holding her close. She tensed, then relaxed, breathing in his scent - a mix of sandalwood soap and musk. She closed her eyes, intently aware of how she was affecting him. He groaned softly and gently pushed away from her.

"I'm not going to take advantage of you here. I won't do anything until you're absolutely ready." His brown eyes darkened as they held her gaze. "I do have to do this, though," he murmured, leaning forward. His pressed his lips to hers, keeping the kiss soft. Her eyes fluttered closed and she savored the gentle pressure of his mouth on hers.

"Mmmm... sweet," he whispered against her lips.

Her body ached and she longed for him to deepen the kiss. Instead, he turned away and she stared after him, her vision blurred. She reached out a hand to steady herself. He took it and led her to the door.

"It's time to go, luv," he said softly, and they rode the elevator back to the lobby in silence, fingers intertwined.

When they reached the lobby, the girls were waiting. They goggled at her and Marty. Toni recovered first as she glanced toward the elevators and back at Kris.

"So..." she drew out the word. "Interesting turn of events." She raised one perfectly penciled eyebrow. Rusty gaped at her, open-mouthed. A shorter, blonde-haired woman gazed at her with frank curiosity. Toni noticed and stepped forward.

"Kris, this is Annie White, editor of 'Metal Maven' magazine. Annie, this is Kris Lindsey, the writer I told you about."

Annie looked Kris up and down before sliding her eyes over to Marty.

"Well, Marty Brinkman, as I live and breathe," she said, her voice low and husky.

He flicked a dismissive glance her way, tightening his arm around Kris. He kissed her and said, "See you later, luv," then walked toward the lobby.

Chapter 22

Toni threaded her arm through Kris' and led her toward the bar.

"You've got to fill us in," she said, working to keep her voice light.

"There's really nothing to tell," Kris protested.

"Bullshit," said Toni, forcefully. "Two nights ago, you couldn't be bothered with Marty Brinkman. Now you're coming down the elevator from his room, holding hands with him?"

She pushed Kris into a chair and snapped her fingers at the waitress, calling, "A round of Mai Tais!" She took the chair next to Kris and said quietly, "I told you, you weren't a good girl deep down, and I was right."

Kris didn't reply.

Rusty and Annie joined them, Rusty still staring avidly at Kris.

"How did it happen, Kris? You landed a huge rock star on your first try!" Toni heard the awed tone in Rusty's voice, and frowned.

"It's not like that," Kris began, but Toni cut her off.

"What I want to know, is he as big as they say?"

"I told you, he's hung like a fucking horse," snapped Annie. Toni ignored her. Kris blushed, and Toni took that as a "yes."

Annie said, more loudly," I'll bet he was a fucking animal. He likes it rough."

Kris flared with anger. "You couldn't be more wrong," she said shortly. "Marty is very tender."

Annie snorted. "I don't know who you fucked last night, but *Marty Brinkman* is anything but tender."

She rummaged through her purse, pulled out a pack of cigarettes, and lit one. Blowing out a stream of smoke, she said, "So, what about this article?"

"I don't have it," Kris replied, and Toni saw the look of annoyance cross her face.

Annie exchanged a significant look with Toni, then said, "Suit yourself." To Toni, she said, "I've gotta run, hun. Got two interviews before the show. The opening band's drummer and singer. At the same time." She raised her eyebrows meaningfully, and Toni grinned knowingly.

"Keep 'em away from the Valium or they'll be useless," she said. With a sly wink, Annie tossed back her drink, then rummaged in her bag again. She handed Kris a business card.

"You decide you wanna get published, send your little story to this address. I'll make sure it gets published." With another look at Toni, she stalked off.

Toni watched Kris over the rim of her glass. This was not a good turn of events. Marius specifically wanted her saved for him, and *now* she turns up with Marty! Fuck! Toni took a closer look at Kris. She didn't look as though she'd spent the night getting banged by him. Maybe they hadn't sealed the deal yet. She needed to tell Marius, so he could call Marty off. Marty had no choice but to cooperate. If he didn't, well... Toni smirked. What Marius Mann knew about Marty could sink his career faster than a battleship. Marius knew secrets that could sink nearly every band out there right now. Toni watched Kris, now deep in conversation with Rusty, and smirked again.

Rusty. She'd have to work on her next. Oh, her enthusiasm was real enough, but her look sucked. Marius had said Rusty wasn't presentable enough, and Toni agreed. She needed a diet and a different wardrobe. He had extended her credit at Charlotte's Harlots, the rock clothing store in Greenwich Village, so Toni could take Rusty, and Kris, for that matter, shopping for suitable clothes. The store was named after a character in an Iron Maiden song - a hooker. Toni smiled at the irony. She also had accounts at the Silky lingerie shop on Fifth Avenue, and the Frederick's of Hollywood store on Broadway. Rusty caught Toni's glance and smiled eagerly. Toni allowed a faint smile to cross her face, then looked away. What she saw surprised her. Billy was loping toward their table.

"Hey, girls. Hey, Toni," he called genially.

Toni eyed him coolly. "What do you want?"

"To talk to you," he replied, his grin widening.

"Where's your bitch?" She injected ice into her voice.

"Shopping," he said, dismissively.

"Don't you have to get over to the Hall?"

"Five minutes," he urged, blue eyes twinkling under his mop of blonde hair.

She eyed him for a long moment, then shrugged.

"Five minutes," she agreed, and followed him out of the bar. He led her down a hallway and through a door marked "Storage."

"What the hell is this?" she said furiously as he locked the door, then gasped as he grabbed her and spun her around. He bent her over a stack of boxes and pushed her mini skirt up to her waist.

"Hey!" she cried angrily. "What the fuck do you think you're doing?"

"What you want me to," he growled as he yanked her stockings and panties down with one pull.

She struggled, but he was too strong. He held her down with one hand and unzipped his pants with the other. She bit her lips as he took her forcefully, grunting with each thrust. If she wasn't so angry, she'd have enjoyed this. How dare he try to control the situation! Try? He *was* controlling the situation!

Toni closed her eyes and willed him to finish quickly. He did, and released her so suddenly, she fell to the floor. By the time she'd pulled herself up, he had zipped up his pants and smoothed his hair. Smiling sardonically, he said, "Thanks, luv. I needed that." He unlocked the door and ambled out, whistling tunelessly.

Trembling with rage, Toni stood on shaky legs and pulled her panties and hose back up. She noticed a rip in one stocking, and swore. She'd have to go back upstairs and change. She ran her fingers under her eyes, and was surprised to find tears on her face. Angrily, she wiped them away, smoothed her smudged eyeliner, and opened the door. She glanced down the hall to the lobby, then hurried to the service elevator in the opposite direction.

Five minutes later, she was on her way back to the bar, having changed into fresh underwear and stockings. She seethed inwardly. They had played out that fantasy many times, but this time, he'd given her no warning. Did she think she wouldn't have gone along with it? Girlfriend or no girlfriend, all he had to do was beckon and she would have gone with him willingly. If she wasn't so bent on getting Don Lyden, she would have fought a little more for Billy's attention. But now, he was going to pay. No one took her by surprise and got away with it.

Chapter 23

Marty paced his dressing room, trying to work out the jitters. If he was honest with himself, he knew it wasn't just the show getting him all worked up. His mind replayed the phone call from Marius Mann, telling him to lay off Kris. Had she been anyone else, he would have been able to do it. But Kris Lindsey had gotten under his skin. It had been a long time since he'd met a girl he could imagine having a serious relationship with. The fact that she didn't want to jump into bed with him right away, made her all the more desirable. She sincerely wanted to get to know Marty the man, and not bang Marty, the rock star.

He lunged, stretching out his hamstrings, then straightened. Oh, there was no doubt Kris was attracted to him. He'd felt her respond when he'd pulled her close and kissed her up in his hotel room. Another night, and he probably could talk her into bed. But, he thought as he lunged again, he didn't want to rush her into sex. That was odd. Normally, he couldn't go two days without getting laid. This time, he'd gone nearly a week, and although he ached for her, he felt a satisfaction in holding back.

He stood on his hands, feeling the blood rush to his head. As he balanced upside-down, he thought again about Marius Mann's call. He righted himself and shook his head firmly. There was no way he was going to give Kris up to that pervert. Pulling on his boxing shoes, Marty knew what he had to do. He had to tell her everything.

Chapter 24

Toni was distracted at the show, her mind working furiously on revenge. After the show, they joined the throngs of fans heading backstage. Once they got through, Toni noticed Kris leave the group and make a beeline for Linda Hart. Saw Linda greeting Kris warmly. Toni's eyes narrowed as she watched Linda and Kris get coffee and sit at a table.

A few minutes later, she heard a commotion and swung around. Marty had appeared out of the dressing room and was surrounded by fans. Toni watched him sign autographs and pose for pictures, his eyes scanning the crowd. She saw him disentangle himself from a group of scantily-clad women and amble across the room to Kris and Linda. Brian Hart joined them a few minutes later.

Toni frowned. It didn't look as though Marty had any intention of leaving Kris alone. She knew Marius had called him. Marius had told her so.

Someone called her name. She turned to see the guitarist from the opening band making his way toward her. He was tall and lanky, with untidy blonde hair and laughing blue eyes. He reminded her of a younger Billy.

"Hi," he said breathlessly, stopping in front of her. "Can I have another chance? I'm sober. No booze, no coke, no nothing." He smiled beseechingly at her.

Toni scanned the room and saw Billy holding court in a corner, his bimbo by his side. He met her glance and raised one eyebrow, smirking. She whipped back to the guitarist.

"Why not?" she said, her eyes over bright. "We go to your room, though, and it had better be clean," she warned. She looked back again and spotted Rusty, leaning against a far wall, looking the other way. Sighing inwardly, Toni wound her arm through the guitarist's and said, "Well, shall we?"

Chapter 25

Kris sat, watching Marty and Brian banter. Linda sat across from her, smiling and nodding. Kris could feel Marty's arm around her chair, his hand reaching out to rub her back or play with her hair. Each touch sent electricity coursing through her. She steeled herself against feeling anything for him, but knew she was fighting a losing battle. He was leaving tomorrow. She'd probably never see him again.

Kris noticed Toni eyeing her shrewdly and leaned back into Marty's arm. He tightened his grip on her and squeezed her shoulder. She smiled and absorbed his embrace, as well as the shivers it sent down her spine. She tried to refocus on what Linda was saying, noting the subtle romantic nuances between husband and wife; the light touches, the twining of fingers, the gentle smiles.

Out of the corner of her eye, Kris saw Toni leave with the tall blonde guitarist from the opening band. She looked around for Rusty, but didn't spot her immediately. A few minutes later, she saw Rusty emerge from the ladies' room, looking pale and very upset.

Kris excused herself and hurried over to Rusty, who was now hunched in a corner, wiping her eyes with a soggy napkin.

"Rusty, what's wrong?" Kris asked.

Rusty sniffed and breathed deeply, trying to pull herself together.

"It's... it's nothing," she stammered.

"No, really." Kris led Rusty to an empty chair. "Something's happened and I want to help." She kneeled beside Rusty's chair.

Rusty gazed at her through red-rimmed eyes. "Thank you," she said tremulously. "Maybe I'm just too thin-skinned for this." She sniffed again.

Kris rubbed her back. "Do you want me to take you back to the hotel, or would you like to come home with me?"

Rusty shook her head wildly. "I d-don't want to mess up your groove. Toni would be very upset." She looked over to where Marty sat with Brian and Linda. All three were looking their way.

Anger flared in Kris. "I could care less about Toni. You're the one I'm worried about. And don't worry about messing up my groove. There isn't any groove to mess up."

Kris waved Marty over. With a word to Brian and Linda, he strode over to them.

"What's up, luv?" he asked, kneeling beside her.

"I need to get Rusty out of here. I'm taking her to my place."

Rusty tried, but couldn't hold back a fresh stream of tears.

Marty put his arm around her and made soothing noises.

"I'll come with you," he said.

"No," Kris said firmly. "I think I should take Rusty home myself." Pulling Marty aside, she said in a low voice, "I'm not sure what happened, but I have an idea, and it would be best if you're not there."

Marty looked crestfallen, but nodded. "Okay, I understand. At least let me help you get a taxi."

"Okay, she said, and together they helped Rusty stand. A security guard led them out a back exit and waved down a passing taxi. Marty helped Rusty inside, then turned to Kris.

"I want to see you before I go," he said, pulling her close.

"I'm not sure I can," she replied, glancing at Rusty, who sat hunched inside the taxi.

"Well, I'll call you, at least." He kissed her softly, then deepened the contact. Her mouth automatically opened under his and her heart pounded like a jackhammer has heat rushed through her. She felt his breath catch as he crushed her to him, then push her way with regret.

"I'll call you later," he said, as she fought to regain her balance. Swinging the door open, he helped her inside. With a last, lingering caress of her arm, he slammed the door and slapped the hood to tell the drive to get going.

The taxi pulled up in front of Kris' apartment building a few minutes later. Henry hurried over to help them out. He glanced curiously at Rusty, but didn't say anything - just smiled kindly at Kris over Rusty's head.

Once inside the apartment, Rusty asked if she could take a shower.

"Of course!" Kris exclaimed. She showed Rusty to the bathroom and laid out some sweats she thought might fit the smaller girl.

She had a fresh pot of coffee brewing when Rusty appeared in the kitchen, hair in a ponytail, her face scrubbed pink. Kris filled two mugs and led Rusty to the living room. They sat in silence for a while, then Kris asked gently, "What happened tonight?"

Rusty took a deep breath and told her. She had gone backstage with the others. Kris had gone to sit with Linda. Toni had gone another way, leaving Rusty alone in the middle of the room. She had moved over to the wall, watching everyone, when a burly man approached her. He told her he worked for Black Gallows and asked her for a blow job. When Rusty told him she only went with musicians, he had snorted sardonically.

"You ain't got what it takes to land a top-notch musician," he'd sneered. "Do you see any rock stars heading your way? I'm the best you're gonna get tonight, but if you're good to me, I can swing you to one of the big guys."

Rusty had gone off with him and he had totally degraded her.

"I kept telling him to stop!" she sobbed. "He fucked me everywhere and held me down so I couldn't get away!" She buried her face in her hands. "He even took me... back there. No one's ever done that!"

With those words, Rusty broke down completely. Kris put her arms around her friend and let her cry. When only dry sobs wracked her body, Kris made Rusty lie down on the couch and covered her with a blanket. She brought Rusty a sleeping pill and made her take it. Several minutes later, Rusty's eyes dropped, then closed as she fell asleep.

Kris cleared away the mugs, enraged at the way the roadie had treated Rusty. She jumped when the phone rang and sprang to answer it quickly.

"Hello, luv." Marty's voice filled her ear. "How's Rusty?"

Anger flared again. In a cold voice, she told Marty just what had happened. He remained silent until she finished.

Then he asked quietly, "Did she tell you the bastard's name?"

"No, and she's sleeping now, so I'm not going to wake her to ask."

"When you find out, call me. I don't care what time it is." His voice was deadly quiet. "I want to deal with him myself."

Kris promised to find out and hung up.

Rusty woke up several hours later, a little groggy but calmer. She ate the soup Kris gave her and leaned back into the couch, smiling weakly. Under Kris' gentle questioning, she remembered the man's name: Jimmy. He had thinning brown hair and body odor. He said he was a sound tech for Black Gallows. Kris made a mental note to call Marty, then spent the next hour trying to distract Rusty from her ordeal. They watched TV and opened a bottle of wine. They drank, not talking, then Rusty asked for another sleeping pill.

As soon as Kris was sure Rusty was asleep, she called Marty and told him what she'd learned about the man who'd raped Rusty. Marty said he knew exactly who she was talking about, and promised to take care of things. Then, his voice husky, Marty asked Kris to slip away for a late dinner.

"I can't," Kris said, regret in her voice. "I need to be here in case Rusty wakes up."

He sighed. "You've really grown on me, Kris Lindsey," he said softly. "And if I may be so bold, I think I've grown on you, too."

She didn't reply.

"Can I ring you from the road?"

"Yes," she whispered.

"Good," he said, his voice still husky. "Please keep an open mind about me, luv. I'm really not that bad."

"I'll try," she replied softly, and hung up.

Chapter 26

Rusty stayed the entire weekend. They lounged around, ordered Chinese takeout talked. Despite the rape, Rusty was still desperate to fit in and still looked to Toni for guidance.

"She's going to help me lose weight and change my look," she confided. "We're supposed to go shopping next week."

Kris stared at her in surprise. "After all this, you still want to hang out with rock bands?"

Rusty thought for a moment, then nodded. "It makes me feel glamorous to dress up and go to shows," she said, sighing wistfully. "My biggest dream is to have a famous rock star fall in love with me and take care of me forever."

"You don't really mean that!" Kris burst out. "There's got to be something else you want to do, to make your life worthwhile."

Rusty shook her head. "Oh, no," she said, with a small laugh. "I'm not really good at anything. Even my job at the dentist's office. I'm just the receptionist there and I screw up at least a couple of appointments a day." She leaned back and stretched her arms in front of her. "No, being a rock star's girlfriend is all I've dreamed about. Just look at Billy's girlfriend. She looks like a model and spends most of her time shopping. Then, she spends nights hanging off his arm. That's the life for me!"

Kris refused to give up.

"What do you like to do in your spare time? What are your hobbies?" she persisted.

Rusty laughed again. "Honestly, I don't do anything. I don't have a passion to write, like you do. I don't even clean house that well. My dad's always telling me how useless I am; that I'm not even good enough to be someone's wife."

"And what does your mother think?" Kris burst out angrily.

Rusty's smile faded. "I haven't seen my mom since I was ten years old. She left and took my younger sister with her. She said my dad could have me."

Kris' heart went out to her friend. "Oh, Rusty, I'm so sorry!" She reached out and clasped Rusty's hand.

The other girl shrugged. "I got used to it. Mom's sister took care of me for a while, then something happened and she stopped coming around. I think Dad made a pass at her or something. After that, I had a string of 'babysitters.' Funny, they always ended up sleeping in my dad's room." Rusty shrugged again and pulled at a loose thread on her sleeve. Kris could see she was on the verge of tears, so she stood and started clearing away the dishes, motioning for Rusty to remain seated.

Rusty didn't bring up her family again, and Kris didn't push. Instead, they walked to the cafe where Kris did most of her writing. Kris had fun introducing Rusty to the different ways people drink coffee. Rusty decided she liked the French cafe au lait, with lots of sugar and cinnamon. She grimaced a Kris' favorite, a double cappuccino.

"Ooh, it's so strong! I don't know how you stand it!" she exclaimed, pushing the cup back toward Kris.

She read all of Kris' articles and pronounced her an "amazing writer."

"I wish I was good at something," she murmured, almost to herself.

Kris felt tears prickle her eyes as she took in Rusty's forlorn expression and on impulse, threw her arms around her friend. "Let's find you something fun!"

Rusty's expression cleared. "I have found something! I will be a rich rock star's girlfriend by the time this year is over, just you wait!" She linked her arm through Kris' as they walked up the street.

"We'll have so much fun! You can come visit me in my penthouse apartment and we'll have amazing shopping trips because my credit cards will have no limit!" She smiled toward the sky and Kris saw the rapturous expression on her face. This dream was like the golden ring for her, the only thing that kept her going. As they wandered up the street, Kris hoped, not for the last time, that Toni didn't do anything to hurt Rusty, to make the light go out of her sparkling blue eyes.

Marty called over the weekend. The band was in Boston, playing two shows before heading to Canada. They chatted for half an hour while Rusty watched TV. Marty said he and Brian fired Jimmy before they left New York. Jimmy was very angry at losing the Black Gallows gig. Marty warned Kris to be careful. He also told her he'd given her article to his friend David, and to expect a call from him in the next few days.

"Davo really liked your article," Marty said. "It's running in the next issue."

Kris could hardly contain her excitement.

"The next time I see you, Mr. Brinkman, dinner is on me!"

"*On* you?" he asked, softly.

She blushed. "You know what I mean."

"I can hardly wait." His voice dropped another notch. "I miss you, luv."

With a promise to call from Canada, he rang off.

Chapter 27

Toni got busy grooming Rusty. She placed her on a strict diet and mild exercise program, to firm her muscles just slightly and give them definition. She warned Rusty not to get too muscular, because men liked softness and curves, not sinewy biceps.

Toni glanced at the clock over her bedroom door. It was nearly time to pick Rusty up and head into the City to try on the clothes they'd ordered from Charlotte's Harlots. She called Rusty and told her to be waiting outside, then headed downstairs.

Her mother was standing at the stove, stirring a big pot of spaghetti sauce. Her father sat at the table, reading the Post and snorting with disgust.

"More potholes in Queens than any other borough," he snarled, slapping the paper shut. "You need a goddamn investigation to figure that out? Just drive down the goddamn streets, you morons!" he shouted at the newspaper, slapping it again before throwing it aside.

"Useless," he grumbled, then spotted Toni rummaging in the refrigerator.

"Speaking of useless," he growled. "What the hell are you doing poking in my fridge? Do you ever contribute to the groceries? No! That's MY hard-earned money keeping this house in food!"

Toni ignored him, took out a tomato and a block of cheese, and carried them to the counter, where she sliced them for a sandwich.

"Leave her alone, Joe," said Toni's mother. "She contributes enough." To Toni, she said, "Are you sure you don't want any spaghetti, Antoinette, honey? Your sister will be home in a few minutes. We could all have dinner together, for once."

Toni flinched at her given name and mention of her younger, perfect sister, but kept her expression and voice bland.

"No thanks, Ma." She spread mayonnaise on her sandwich. "I've gotta pick Rusty up in fifteen minutes."

"Where are you going?" her father demanded. "And dressed like a street hooker! You can't be up to anything good!"

"Joseph!" her mother warned. "All her friends dress like this. They're just having fun." She patted Toni on the back. "Our Antoinette's a good girl. You leave her alone!" Toni's mother was tiny, but she stood up to her bear of a husband with no problem.

"Good girls don't dress like dime store whores! I've never seen Angela dressed like a streetwalker."

"Ang likes books more than boys," Toni muttered quietly, but her father heard, and rounded on her.

"Your sister works damn hard at that law office of hers. And she's got a great boyfriend! They're getting married in the fall. She's got her life on track! I can't say the same about you! You're just wasting your life, and my money!" He stood in a huff and left the kitchen.

Toni stood frozen, working to control her emotions. Deep inside, she knew her father was right; that she had wasted her life. But, she'd known no other life, and although she wasn't proud of the way she now lived, she had built a reputation for herself, and she was determined to live up to it. If she were truly honest with herself, her longings mirrored Rusty's. She wanted a powerful, respected rock star to fawn over her and make sure her needs were met. She dreamed that Don Lyden could be that man. She'd thought Billy might have been the one, but it was obvious he was like all the others who wanted one thing from her, without giving anything in return.

Toni kissed her mother goodbye and hurried out to her car, eating as she walked. Fifteen minutes later, she was outside Rusty's apartment, honking her horn. An old woman on the first floor glared out her window at the noise, but Toni ignored her and honked again, irritated. The door finally opened and Rusty tottered out in ugly, high-heeled red boots, tight, faded jeans, and a glossy, form-fitting yellow top that hugged the bulges at her waist. Toni cringed at the sight, glad they were heading straight to Charlotte's Harlots.

Rusty climbed into the car, apologizing for being late. Toni snapped, "Forget it," and hit the gas pedal.

They hit light traffic heading from Queens to Manhattan and found a parking space near the shop with no problem. Charlotte herself met them at the door, beaming enthusiastically.

"You're gonna love how the clothes came out!" she gushed, ushering Rusty into the dressing room. Toni endured the impromptu fashion show; Rusty acting as though Christmas and her birthday had come all at once; Charlotte, acting like a benevolent Santa Claus. As if she wasn't making a bundle on this pile of clothes, Toni thought, sourly.

After Rusty modeled her last outfit, a pair of form-fitting black leather pants with fishnet cutouts up the leg, a black leather bustier with a blood red satin blouse tied at the waist, and a pair of spike-heeled black leather ankle boots, Toni told her to keep the outfit on.

"What about the clothes I wore here?" Rusty asked.

"Trash them. You don't need them anymore," Toni said tersely, striding over to the cash register. She stood, tapping her fingers on the counter, her long nails making loud, clicking noises on the highly polished surface.

Rusty made her way over, walking unsteadily in her new boots. She looked worried.

"Uh, Charlotte," she stammered. "Do you have a payment plan? I don't have enough money to pay for all this today."

"Don't worry," said Toni, briskly. "This is taken care of. You don't owe a cent."

Rusty gaped at her.

"This must've cost a fortune!" she spluttered. "Who would pay for all this stuff, for someone they don't even know?"

"Let's just say someone really wants you to look your best when he meets you." Toni winked conspiratorially at Charlotte, who grinned slyly and she wrapped lingerie and lace in tissue paper, before placing them into a shiny black shopping bag bearing the store's logo - a woman's silhouette standing under a lamp post with a sparkly red light.

"Oh!" Rusty squealed. "Someone wants to meet me? Someone who can afford all these cool clothes?"

Toni smiled sardonically. "Yep," she answered, as they made their way back out into the street. "Now, let's do something about your hair."

Chapter 28

Marius smiled as he studied photos of Rusty's transformation. He liked the haircut. Gone was the shapeless mane teased within an inch of its life. In its place was a shorter, sassier 'do, dyed white blonde with slightly darker tips, styled in carefully disheveled spikes. Her clothing looked nice, too, but then again, Toni had good taste. She knew what to mix and match to achieve the look the men in his circles desired.

Rusty was still a little chunky, but he had faith in Toni's powers to help others lose weight. His black eyes crinkled as he chuckled. Better make that Toni's powers to help keep Rusty in a fresh supply of her favorite "diet" powder. Marius had hooked Toni up with his good friend Benny, who always got his hands on the best stuff this side of Colombia.

He gazed at Rusty's friendly, smiling face and felt a slight (very slight!) stab of regret. The rocker he had in mind for her required a woman with lots of stamina and a very low threshold for pain. He sometimes wondered why, since a woman with a high threshold for pain lasted longer, but... ah, well... who was he to question other people's appetites? Rusty would learn quickly how to give pleasure while enduring a lot of pain.

Marius tossed Rusty's photos aside and turned his attention to his own special girl, Kris. He lifted the latest photo Toni had snapped, frowning. Brinkman was in the shot, too, and they looked a little too cozy for comfort. He would have to have another little chat with Marty boy, remind him of how much he stood to lose if he pursued this filly. He set the photo down, then picked up the phone.

Chapter 29

Kris hung up the phone, reeling. David MacGregor wanted her to do an interview. He had called after reading the Black Gallows article Marty had sent him, told her the story would appear in the magazine's next issue, and how much she'd get paid.

The check had arrived two days later. Kris thought that would be the end of her contact with him. Now, a week later, he was calling again.

"Hey, Kris!" he barked, his Scottish brogue making "hey" sound like "hee." "I've got an assignment for ye, if ye want it."

He wanted her to interview Hardwire, who was playing that weekend at L'Amour, and follow that with a review of the show itself. He gave her the band manager's phone number and told her to set it up.

Kris sat for a moment, stunned by the turn of events. Then, her brain kicked into gear and she spent the next half hour outlining the interview itself, jotting questions in her notebook. She thought about the last time they'd played at L'Amour and realized, with a jolt, it had been her first rock show. Her stomach clenched as she remembered Toni's antics in the crowd, then watching her come out of the back room with the singer. She also remembered Toni yanking the singer into a storage closet at the hotel in Philadelphia, after she was thwarted in her efforts to meet Don Lyden.

The wave of embarrassment that engulfed Kris was quickly replaced by a surge of relief that she had not dallied with any of them.

She called Hardwire's manager. An assistant assured her she'd track the band down and have them call her. Fifteen minutes later, Bobby called. He told her they already had an interview lined up the night of the show with Metal Maven, but the band was available right now. Kris agreed to meet them at the downtown restaurant where they were having dinner.

The band greeted her jovially enough. She ordered a coffee, noting they all seemed to have had several drinks already.

"Have something stronger," Bobby urged.

"No thanks," she replied. "Gotta keep my head clear."

Bobby peered at her closely and said, "Hey, you look kinda familiar."

When she explained how she had been at their last two shows with Toni, he leaned back in his seat and smirked.

"Oh, Toni..." His sigh sounded almost like a groan. "That is one talented lady!"

The others sniggered. Bobby eyed her and looked around at his band mates. "So, who did you end up with that night?"

"No one," she said, curtly. "That's not my scene."

"Oh, it's like that," he jeered, elbowing the guy next to him, who grinned.

Kris slid her tape recorder back into her bag, slammed her notebook shut, and stood.

"Do you want to do this interview or not?" she asked, coolly. "It really doesn't matter to me. I'm sure Metal Countdown can find some other up and coming band to cover."

That shut them up. Bobby even managed to look slightly ashamed. "Sorry about that," he mumbled. "No disrespect intended."

She glared around the table, saw the others looking just as somber, and sat back down.

Once the interview got under way, the guys changed, becoming more professional. She could tell they wanted to make a good impression and were serious about their music and the future of the band. When she asked them what incident in their lives made the biggest impact in shaping who they are today, they looked blankly at each other.

"What does that have to do with our music?" the drummer asked.

Bobby looked at him, scathingly. "I see where she's going with this." He turned to Kris. "No one's ever asked us anything like that." He pondered a moment. "For me, I'd have to say, my grandmother dying. She raised me and my sister, see. She was about 70 and she still worked at the A&P and never bought anything for herself. Everything went to me and Bridget, so we could have clothes and food and stuff. But she never seemed bitter. She always told her, 'Bobby and Bree, don't ever let know one tell you youse can't do something. If it's in your heart, youse can make it happen." He paused again, and the other guys looked at him in wonder.

"Bobby, you never told us your Gramma said anything like that," said the guitarist.

"No, well, you'd just call me a pussy, would you, Joey?" Bobby retorted. He turned back to Kris. "Anyway, what she said always stayed with me. When I started my first band, we sucked big time, but Gran always told me to keep at it.

Said I had a magic voice and it would all come together when it was supposed to; that the faerie-folk would help."

He glared around the table, daring anyone to laugh. When they didn't he continued. "Gran was pretty superstitious. Came to Brooklyn straight from Ireland. Said there were two things you could always count on: potatoes with dinner, and help from the faerie-folk." He fell silent, then shrugged. "That's it for me."

Kris looked at Bobby, impressed. She had imagined him to be shallow and self-centered, based on his actions at L'Amour with Toni. But, he had revealed a more vulnerable side and hadn't seemed ashamed to talk about his grandmother.

After Bobby finished, the other guys chipped in with their own stories, which ranged from the drummer seeing his father get laid off after more than thirty years on the job. ("That's why I still work for the post office, even though I know the band will make it. I save and give half my pay to my mom, who's alone since Dad died two years ago."), to bassist Dimitri's experience as a refugee from Romania ("We didn't have a very good beginning here. My mother, father, and older sisters all worked and didn't go to school. Only I did. My father wanted me to become a doctor, but I didn't have good grades. He thinks I'm useless, but my mother, she says like Bobby's grandmother, that I can be whatever I want, as long as I don't forget where I came from.")

By the time Kris wrapped up the interview, she had gained new respect for the band and, judging by the looks they gave each other, she guessed they also had newfound respect for each other. As she stood to leave, Bobby spoke again.

"Hey, sorry again about before. We're really not that bad, once you get to know us."

She smiled. "I've heard that somewhere before," she murmured to herself. Waving to the guys, she went outside and flagged a taxi. When she got home, her answering machine was blinking.

"Hi, luv," Marty said cheerfully. "Saw your article in the magazine and wanted to say 'cheers' on a great job!"

Warmth spread through Kris at the sound of his voice. As he started to talk again, though, a woman giggled in the background. A muffled voice said, "shh!" Then, Marty's voice again: "Well, it's quite busy here, so I'll ring off. I just wanted to tell you I'm thinking about you." Another giggle. "Talk to you soon."

The happiness of hearing Marty's voice quickly became a block of ice which settled in her stomach. She didn't feel jealous. Instead, she felt empty. What had she expected? He wasn't her boyfriend; just a guy who had apparently eased his own guilty conscience by helping her get a story printed.

Anger flared. He'd probably also fed her the story about Annie and Toni trying to set her up. Maybe he thought he could scare her into bed. When that didn't happen, he had moved on to greener pastures. Or, the thought ripped savagely through her brain, he wanted to keep her away from Annie and the sordid stories she could tell about Marty.

Kris stabbed the 'erase' button and wiped out his voice. Then, she called Toni.

"Hey, I've got an assignment to review Hardwire at L'Amour this Saturday. Want to go? Tickets and backstage passes on me."

138

Toni sounded delighted to hear from Kris and agreed to meet her at the club.

Kris hung up and paced her living room. Jealousy now hit her fast and strong and she felt a stab of pain as she imagined Marty screwing his way through the tour. She had begun to think he was different and had fallen for him, hard. Hadn't he confessed he found one night stands alluring? She supposed a leopard couldn't change his spots.

Feeling trapped by her thoughts, she grabbed her notebook and headed to the cafe.

Chapter 30

Toni smiled in self-satisfaction. Kris was not only calling her again; she was offering up the tickets and backstage passes. Toni had heard Marty had given that stupid Black Gallows article to Dave over at Metal Countdown, to try to keep Kris away from Annie. Like that would work!

Toni snorted. As well he knew, Annie wasn't the one calling the shots. Marius had told her last night that Marty was well out of the picture now. He'd made sure of it.

All she had to do now was touch up Kris' look a little. Not much, Marius had warned. He wanted to keep her as natural as possible. What a waste. Kris was pretty plain without makeup, a new hairstyle and clothes, but she'd learned the hard way not to go against Marius' wishes.

With that, she reached down and opened a dresser drawer, pulling out a cigar box filled with photos of Don Lyden in nearly every pose imaginable. In most of the shots, his beautiful, pale face was upturned and stamped with a look of ecstasy, his soft blonde hair cascading off his shoulders. Toni imagined him wearing that look as he thrust deeply into her, and gasped at the thought. Not many men got to fuck her, but that didn't mean she didn't ache for it. She pulled one photo from the bunch and lay back on her bed. Marius had promised Don to her after she delivered Kris, but that was still months away. Until then, she'd have to please herself.

Chapter 31

Saturday's Hardwire show went well and Kris thought she had enough material for a good article. Toni was friendly, too. She had given Kris a pair of beautiful black lace, fingerless gloves. They looked delicate and Kris liked them. She thanked Toni warmly and bought her a Mai Tai, but ordered a Coke for herself. She was on assignment and would not drink while working. She noticed Toni glancing at the drink, but didn't care. She had to take this job seriously, so she could be taken seriously.

After the show, they lined up to go backstage. Kris flashed the badge Hardwire had given her and pointed to herself and Toni. The bouncer jerked his head toward the backstage door and let them pass. They ran into Bobby right away. He pulled Toni close and squeezed her ass, but greeted Kris more formally, and asked how she'd liked the show. When she told him she had the makings of a good article, he grinned, then turned to Toni and raised his eyebrows. Toni smiled back and shook her head.

"Just not in the mood tonight," she drawled, running her fingernails down his arm.

He chuckled and pulled her closer, whispering in her ear. She grinned wickedly and said, "Well… maybe that."

She looked at Kris, who said quickly, "Don't let me stop you! I'll sit here and work on the article." She motioned to a corner and pulled out her notebook.

Bobby hesitated. "Er... he said, awkwardly, "you won't write about... this stuff, will you? Cuz my girlfriend won't appreciate it."

She waved him away. "Don't worry. Your secret's safe with me."

Kris leaned against the wall and surveyed the room. It reeked of perfume, sweat, body odor, and... excitement. She watched band members check out the women who flowed into the room like a glittering tidal wave; watched the women preen and show their cleavage to their best advantage; saw the guys look them up and down, appraising them before making their selections with the flick of the head or hand.

Some couple disappeared into the back room, like Toni and Bobby. Others headed out into the dark hallway, or perhaps the tour bus. Kris knew some of these women would end up at the hotel, especially if they were very talented. Some guys emerged from a tryst with one girl, only to choose another and disappear again. The girls not picked for the first round primped, fluffed, and smoothed themselves, trying hard to look good enough to make it to Round 2.

Kris felt slightly queasy by the action, but also found herself growing oddly fascinated. She'd never seen the groupie dance in this way before. The thought struck her. That's exactly what this was: a dance. Excited now, she opened her notebook and started writing. She didn't know what she'd do with this information; she just wanted to get her thoughts on paper. Maybe it would help her understand the allure of the one night stand. Maybe it would help her understand Marty.

Chapter 32

Toni emerged from the bathroom feeling well-sated. Bobby had given as good as he'd gotten tonight - a rare treat for her. Most guys she serviced couldn't give a shit about her needs. It was all about getting their rocks off. Bobby caught her looking at him and grinned. He was immediately surrounded by girls, but Toni knew there would be no Round 2 for him tonight. She had further plans for him at the hotel.

Toni looked around the room and spotted Kris leaning against the same wall where they'd left her. She was hunched over her ever-present notebook, writing furiously. Toni took her time joining her.

"What are you writing, a book?" she asked loudly, when she reached Kris.

Kris jumped and looked up, closing the book quickly. "Just jotting a few notes," she replied, vaguely.

"Oh," Toni said, trying to sound interested. "Well, are you ready to go? I have an early day tomorrow."

Kris nodded and stowed her book in her pocket. She pulled out the lace gloves and tried them on, holder her hands out to Toni, fingers splayed.

"What do you think?" she asked.

Toni looked at her hands and nodded. "They're you,"

she agreed, then added causally, "Hey, I know a great store to visit, if you want to try on some more cool clothes."

"Really?" Kris asked, intrigued. "Maybe we can go there soon."

Chapter 33

The opportunity came the following week. Charlotte announced a weeklong sale and said she'd keep the store open until nine each night. Toni and Kris made plans to meet in the Village on Wednesday after work. Rusty was coming, too. Kris was happy to hear that; she hadn't seen or spoken to Rusty since the weekend following her rape. She hoped Rusty was doing better.

On Wednesday, she left work an hour early and stopped by the cafe to jot some notes about groupies: what she knew, what she suspected, and what she wanted to know. She made a mental note to remember everything about Charlotte's Harlots, the clothing store that catered to groupies and rock stars alike.

Kris took the subway to Greenwich Village and ran into Rusty on Bleecker Street.

"Kris!" Rusty exclaimed, throwing her arms around a visibly stunned Kris.

Rusty had lost at least twenty pounds, cut her hair into a short, fluffy 'do and dyed it platinum blonde. Her makeup accentuated her cat-like blue eyes and her outfit... well... Kris could only guess where the outfit had come from. Still, Rusty seemed happy, the same bubbly person Kris remembered from before this transformation. She linked her arm through Kris' and gushed about the clothes and how Toni had been instrumental in it all. She leaned forward and lowered her voice.

"A rich rock star wants to meet me," she confided, squirming with excitement.

Kris raised her eyebrows. "Do you know who it is?"

Rusty shook her head. "Not yet. But he paid for all my clothes, makeup and hair."

This puzzled Kris. Who would foot such a bill, she wondered? But she had no time to dwell on this because Rusty led her around the corner and up a short flight of stairs, stopping in front of a black door with an awning painted glittery gold with silver stars scattered all over it. Rusty pushed the door open and led Kris inside. Loud music drowned out the tinkling bell over the door. Kris recognized the song as Flying High Again, by Ozzy Osbourne.

Rusty waved gaily at a tall, slender woman with a long mane of red hair and very large breasts. The woman carefully hung up a leather bustier and hurried over.

"Rusty, darling!" she called over the music as she drew near. Rusty bent to hug her, then introduced her to Kris. "This is Charlotte, owner of Charlotte's Harlots and a rockin' designer!"

Charlotte nodded at Kris, then turned back to appraise Rusty, reaching into her pocket and pulling out a remote control. She lowered the volume on the music before speaking.

"I like this outfit on you," she said, surveying the white lace blouse covering a cherry red tank top and tight, dark blue jeans studded with rhinestones up the outside seams. She glanced down at the spike-heeled black leather ankle boots on Rusty's feet.

"Are you getting used to those yet?" she asked, gesturing to the boots.

Rusty followed her gaze. "A bit," she said ruefully. "They hurt like a mother, but I don't feel so much like a cripple anymore." She looked around for a chair, but found none.

Charlotte turned her focus to Kris, who felt as though she were being sized up, literally and figuratively. After a few uncomfortable moments, Charlotte turned and walked briskly toward a rack of clothes. She surveyed Kris again and began pulling items off the rack. When she had a sizeable pile, she carried them to the rear of the shop, where there was a curtained-off area next to a floor-to-ceiling mirror with an ornate gilt frame. Charlotte hung clothes on hooks, forming outfits as she went. Then, she turned back to Kris and waved her over.

"Come," she commanded. "Try these on."

Kris walked over slowly, taking in the outfits hanging on the wall. Rusty trotted after her.

"Ooh!" Rusty exclaimed. "Very nice!"

Kris stopped in front of the first outfit - a simple pair of very tapered black jeans. Charlotte had paired them with a form-fitting spandex tank top in deep blood red, with a very scooped neck, and a fitted black jacket made of soft, supple leather. The jacket mimicked the popular biker style, but designed to hug the figure in a very feminine way. Charlotte had added accessories to the ensemble - a pair of dangly rhinestone earrings and a necklace with a heart pendant made up of hundreds of tiny twinkling rhinestones.

Kris was impressed, in spite of herself. She gathered up the first outfit and stepped behind the curtain. When she emerged a few minutes later, Rusty gasped.

"You look great!"

The clothes, which looked so simple on the hangers, were transformed on Kris. They hugged her curves without looking obscene. The tapered jeans accentuated her long legs; the tank top clung to her small waist. The only drawback she noticed - the flimsy fabric outlined her breasts and nipples too clearly. She'd had to remove her bra to wear it and now felt very self-conscious. Kris slipped the leather jacket on and zipped it up, letting just the top of the tank peek through. The jacket molded to her figure, moving against her skin like a gentle caress.

Charlotte rushed over and set a pair of boots at Kris' feet, saying, "I forgot these."

She stepped back as Kris slid her feet into the boots. The heel was not as high as those on Rusty's boots and the leather felt as soft and supple as her jacket. She turned and looked at herself in the mirror. She had to admit it; the outfit looked good. The blood red tank top brought out the green of her eyes. She turned this way and that, letting the light catch the rhinestone earrings swinging from her ears.

They didn't hear the door open and turned only when they heard Toni call out, "Hey!" She strode up and surveyed Kris, walking around her slowly, studying the outfit. Kris caught her exchanging a look with Charlotte.

"What?" Kris asked.

"Nothing," Toni replied. You look… stunning. I never imagined."

She leaned forward and unzipped the jacket, letting it fall open. Kris made to zip it up again, but Toni stopped her.

"Leave it open."

"But my top's a bit… revealing," Kris protested.

Toni smirked. "Letting people get a glimpse is not a crime. Besides, if you're all zipped up, you look unfriendly, unapproachable. Exactly the opposite of how you want to look if you're looking to meet people to interview."

Toni eyed the other outfits Charlotte had assembled. She pulled one off the hook and handed it to Kris, saying, "Try this."

Kris took the hanger. On it hung a dress of white, stretchy lace with a tight-fitting bodice, flowing skirt and fitted sleeves that flared at the wrist. Charlotte had paired it with sheer stockings, a garter belt, and deep red pumps.

"I don't know," said Kris doubtfully. "This really isn't my style."

"Just try it on," said Toni impatiently. "You don't have to buy it!"

Kris nodded and slipped behind the curtain again. When she reemerged, everyone stared. Startled, Kris turned to the mirror. The woman who looked back was a vision in flowing white - innocent, yet sensual. The white lace clung to every curve. Her tousled auburn hair and wide emerald eyes heightened the outfit's allure.

Rusty sighed. "She looks like an elf queen, a princess or something. You know...." She broke off at a glare from Toni.

Kris stared at her reflection again, then pulled aside the curtain to change.

"Wait."

Kris stopped and looked at Toni questioningly. Toni started to say something, then stopped. She eyed Kris thoughtfully, then smiled.

"It really does look great on you," she said. "You should think about getting it."

Kris shrugged and stepped behind the curtain. She couldn't think of any reason to wear this dress. Why waste money buying it, only to let it hang in the closet? She did buy the jeans outfit and black leather jacket. She also bought a second pair of jeans in dark, distressed denim, several less-revealing tank tops, and the boots.

Charlotte brought the white dress over and looked crestfallen when Kris shook her head and said she didn't want to buy it.

"It fits like it was made for you," Charlotte protested. When Kris persisted, she sadly placed the dress back on the hanger and returned it to the rack.

Toni bought some lingerie and Rusty bought three bustiers in silver, black, and hot pink. They took their purchases and with cheery "good byes" to Charlotte, made their way across the street to a small cantina, where they had dinner and gossiped about bands and other girls.

Toni entertained Kris and Rusty with a story about Maria and a sleazy band called Beaver.

"Maria got all worked up because the drummer tried to trick her into anal sex. She freaked out and ran out of his room and into mine, stark naked. The problem was, I was in a, shall we say, delicate position with the singer at that moment. He was all for having her join us, but she ran out of our room, too. She nearly got arrested for indecent exposure."

Toni chuckled at the memory. "She complained for two weeks after that, kept going on about how a guy in a band called Beaver wanted ass. She even told him they should change their name to Back Door. Instead, they wrote a song with that title."

Toni drained her margarita, grimacing. "This tastes like shit. I don't know why they couldn't have just made me a fucking Mai Tai."

Kris sipped her margarita gingerly. She didn't drink much and found strong ones went straight to her head. She reached for a handful of chips and munched, waiting for

Toni to continue her tales from the road. Instead, Toni turned to Kris, her blue eyes twinkling mischievously.

"So," she drawled. "Has Marty tried to get in your back door yet?"

Kris choked on a mouthful of chips. She took a gulp from her drink, coughed, and stammered, "What did you say?"

"Your back door, Kris. Has Marty tried to get you to have anal sex with him?" Toni's eyes were gleaming now.

"No!" Kris nearly shouted the word. "Why would you even ask such a thing?"

"I heard that's how he likes it nowadays," Toni said casually.

A wave of revulsion swept over Kris, but she fought to keep her expression neutral. Before she could say anything, Rusty jumped in.

"How do you know? Did Annie tell you? Or have you been with him yourself?" she asked eagerly.

Kris' gaze sharpened on Toni. She hadn't considered that. Had Toni slept with Marty?

"On, no!" Toni chortled. "I had the chance to do Marty, years ago, but I was already with Billy then and I won't fuck two guys in the same band, unless we're having a threesome."

Rusty's eyes grew wide. "A threesome?"

"Well, I don't do them often. Too much work." Toni leaned back in her seat, clearly enjoying herself. She ordered another margarita and waited until the waitress brought it, before continuing.

"Do you know Charley, the hardcore chick who hangs out at L'Amour? She'll fuck anything with a dick and long hair."

Rusty and Kris looked at her blankly. They had no idea who she was talking about.

Toni noticed.

"Oh, you'll see her soon enough, if you keep hanging out with me." Toni sipped her drink, grimaced again, and continued.

"Like I said, she hangs out at L'Amour and travels with a lot of bands. She looks like a skank and never dresses up, but she must be pretty talented. Some bands even take her overseas with them. Well, she tried to hook up with Marty the last time Black Gallows was here - last year- but he found out she'd fucked every guy in the opening band that same day. Old Marty told her the only way she'd get him was if she let him put it up her ass." Toni's voice dropped a notch.

"So... Charley showed up at Marty's hotel room that night with a big jar of Vaseline!"

She leaned back again, enjoying the shocked look on Rusty's face, and the sick look on Kris'.

"Anyway," she continued, as though they were discussing the weather. "I heard ever since that night with Charley, Marty prefers the back door."

She looked at Kris. "Well, maybe not with you," she amended. "You haven't seen that much action, so you're not stretched out. You're still fresh."

Kris looked even sicker.

Toni turned her attention to Rusty. "Important advice: give blow jobs whenever you can. Be choosy about who you screw. It keeps you tighter than if you fuck everyone. Poor Charley, I don't think she feels anything anymore, unless the guy's hung like King Kong."

Kris fought back the urge to vomit and managed to stay at the table. Her head was swimming and she knew it wasn't just the alcohol, although she'd chugged the rest of her margarita. Rusty seemed to be taking mental notes on everything Toni had just said. Kris saw her mouth the words "blow job" to herself.

Kris tried to detach herself from what she'd just heard. A sudden, sharp image of Marty positioned behind a faceless woman sprang into her mind. She willed herself to erase that image, and gulped from her glass of water.

The rest of the conversation consisted of more of Charley's exploits; how she'd fucked her way to Germany with a band called Bad Habit, only to be dumped in Hamburg when it turned out she'd given the entire band crabs. She'd had to remain there until they'd cleared it up, then it took her another month to find a band that would let her fuck her way back home to New York.

Rusty soaked up every story, eyes round with astonishment.

"Why would a band want to be with someone like that?" she asked.

Toni looked scornfully over her glass at Rusty.

"It's because nothing is off limits to Charley. She's done some pretty sick things. And she never says no. Second bit of advice, Rusty: stick to your guns. Be choosy when you can. Always look your best. You want to be known for talent and glamour, not just that you'll do what classy girls won't. You'll get popular, but you'll get fucked out fast. And no rock star in his right mind will want you for a girlfriend. You'll just be the girl to fuck if a guy's desperate."

Kris stared from Toni to Rusty. Rusty was enthralled, while Toni looked smug. She pushed away from the table and stood. She could feel cold sweat beading her forehead.

"I've got to go," she said, trying to sound as normal as she could.

"I hope I didn't say anything to upset you," said Toni, trying to look concerned.

Kris shook her head. "I just have to go." She picked up her bag, waved, and forced herself to walk casually toward the exit. She wanted to sprint out of the restaurant and down the street. At the door, she turned and looked back at the table. Whatever Toni was saying, she had Rusty's undivided attention; an apt pupil soaking up her mentor's teachings.

The sun was setting as Kris reached Seventh Avenue. Thoughts and images whirled in her head as she walked north. The faceless girl who'd had anal sex with Marty. The woman who'd giggled in the background when Marty had called from Buffalo. The stuff Annie had said about him. Marty had asked her not to judge him, but how could she not? From everything she'd heard, Marty sounded like the animal Annie said he was. Had his tenderness for her just been an act? Had he just been playing a role to get her into bed?

Kris shook her head wildly to clear it. She hadn't thought it was an act. Marty had seemed genuine and sincere. His tenderness toward her had seemed natural, not contrived. When he'd pleaded with her to not judge him by what she heard, had he been acting?

A horn honked and Kris stopped short. She'd nearly walked into traffic. She looked up and noticed she was standing in front of the hotel where she, Toni and Rusty had stayed because the band was staying there. Unbidden, tears filled her eyes and spilled out as she remembered the flowers he'd sent and the lengths to which he'd gone, to show her he truly was a nice person.

It was pitch dark when Kris reached her apartment building. Henry held the door open and said, "You're out walking late, Miss Lindsey."

"Just doing some thinking, Henry."

His look of affection turned to one of concern as he studied her troubled face.

"Are you alright?" he asked gently. "You look like you've just lost your best friend."

Kris forced a smile.

"I misjudged someone," she answered, and continued to her apartment.

Once inside, Kris felt suffocated. She grabbed her notebook and headed to the cafe. She wrote down everything she remembered about the day, especially the conversations. As she recounted Rusty's words about the stranger who had paid for her clothes and makeup, she paused. Who would do that? She circled that section of notes and drew a big question mark next to it.

Kris wrote until the overhead music stopped. She was shocked to see she was the only one left in the cafe. She quickly gathered her things, paid the bartender, and went home.

Chapter 34

Toni knelt uncomfortably on the cold floor between Marius' spread knees. Every upward movement she made brought her head into sharp contact with the table she was under.

She heard him groaning softly above her, hands gripping the tabletop. Toni moved her head faster, willing him to come quickly. Her knees, back and head hurt. After a few more uncomfortable moments, she heard him mutter, "It's time," and was ready when he let go. She made sure not one drop spilled before pulling away from him. She straightened her hair, wiped her mouth using the napkin he handed down to her, then crawled out from under the table. The waitress, who has studiously avoided their table for the last few minutes, hurried over with a Mai Tai.

Toni took a healthy gulp, trying to wash away Marius' taste. He was nasty business, but business she had to endure if she wanted to stay on top. She applied a fresh layer of lip gloss, slathering it on slowly and sensuously, the way he liked her to, and smiled at him. He smiled back, indulgently.

"You really know how to use that pretty mouth of yours," he murmured.

She started to take another gulp of her drink, caught herself, and sipped instead. It wouldn't do to show him just how much he disgusted her. She smiled again.

"Now, to other business," he said briskly. "Are they ready?"

"Nearly," Toni answered, sipping more of her drink. I think Rusty's ready to move up to the next tier. I'm going to set her up solo with the singer from Hot Cat."

"And Kris?" His tone grew husky again, and Toni felt an odd stab of jealousy. She shook it off.

"Kris is back on track. She's done with Marty Brinkman. I helped make sure of that."

"Good," he rumbled, his bass voice deepening. "I'm getting the guest list ready." He signaled for another drink. "Are Annie and Francine available?"

Toni laughed. "Annie'll fuck anyone who will give her an exclusive. As for Francine, well, that all depends on who's coming." She emphasized the last word.

Marius chuckled. "Ah, yes," he said. "Yes, indeed."

Chapter 35

"Hello, luv. I'm calling from Miami. It's bleedin' hot down here. I saw a bird that reminded me of you - its feathers were brilliant red, gold and green. Beautiful, like you. (pause) Oh, well. I miss you. I wish I could catch you at home. (pause) Hey, nice article on Hard Wire! You're on your way to the big time. (chuckle) I haven't forgotten that you owe me dinner. Well, I'd better get ready for the show. You take care. I miss you, Kris. (pause) I said that already. Right. Okay. Good bye."

Kris sat rigid on the couch, letting the call play out, steeling herself against the urge to pick up the phone. He truly sounded as though he missed her, but what did she know?

She reached out to erase the message, but couldn't. She rewound and played it again, chiding herself for being so foolish.

Marty was a rock star.

Marty was a pervert.

Kris jabbed angrily at the "erase" button and wiped out his voice. Grabbing her notebook, she headed to the cafe, where she recounted the past weekend's activities at the Cat Eye show. Toni had insisted she wear her new outfit, but Kris didn't think the band warranted it. She wore a pair of faded jeans, a t-shirt a friend had sent her from California, bearing the logo of a punk band called Black Flag, and her new leather jacket. She swore Toni had cringed when she'd spotted Kris. Whatever.

They had run into Annie inside. She'd tried, unsuccessfully, to interview the band before the show, and she was furious.

"Do they know who they fucking turned down?" she fumed. "I smell BAD REVIEW!" She tossed back a shot of whisky and slammed the glass down. Her eyes narrowed as she spotted movement from the backstage area. Kris followed her gaze and saw a plain looking woman saunter out. She had brown hair with frosted highlights, and wore a ripped t-shirt, striped spandex tights and flat leather boots with fringe down the back.

"Who's that?" she asked Toni, as Annie's face darkened with fury.

"Her? That's Charley," Toni replied, dismissively. "She must have gotten here early to do them first. Too bad for you, Annie."

Annie snapped her fingers at the bartender, who quickly set another shot in front of her. She downed it, then spat, "She's not even a whore. She's just a hole." She stormed off, swaying slightly.

Toni raised her eyebrows at Kris. "Annie doesn't take rejection very well, and she absolutely hate it if Charley beats her to the punch."

Kris had recoiled in shock when Toni had identified that woman as Charley. She felt an overwhelming urge to get a closer look at the woman who'd haunted her thoughts for the past two weeks. Toni's voice popped into her head. *"Marty likes the back door now, because of Charley."*

Kris tracked Charley's movements through the club, and when she saw her entire the ladies room, she waited a beat before following. She pretended to reapply her lipstick until Charley emerged from a stall. Charley walked as though she had no backbone, hips swaying wildly with every lazy step. She stopped at the sink next to Kris and vigorously washed her hands.

Up close, Charley looked haggard. Her makeup didn't hide the lines around her eyes and mouth. Her eyeliner was smudged, creating dark shadows around her brown eyes, which held no trace of humor.

"Um... cool show," said Kris, trying to make conversation.

Charley turned slowly toward Kris, drying her hands absently with a couple of paper towels.

"You talkin' to me?" she asked, her voice low and raspy.

Kris smiled, pretending to play dumb. "I've never seen you here before."

"Then you don't hang around much, do you?"

Charley pulled two more paper towels from her purse and tucked them into her purse as she stared at Kris.

"You hang with Peroxide Bitch," she remarked.

"Who?" asked Kris, puzzled.

"Bimbette Toni, the lightweight."

"She doesn't seem very lightweight to me," Kris said wryly.

Charley looked her up and down. "Then you must be a fucking virgin." She left the bathroom, leaving Kris to ponder her words.

The rest of the show had gone uneventfully. Cat Eye sounded like several other bands that were making the rounds. The singer had a whiny voice that grew annoying after two songs, and the guitarists couldn't seem to play a note unless they were rocking back and forth in tandem, flinging their long blonde hair back and forth. Even their outfits were boring. Everyone wore the same black spandex tights, black Converse sneakers and ripped t-shirts in different colors. The singer's shirt boldly proclaimed WE SUCK! And featured a drawing of a woman on her knees, performing oral sex on a man with a wide grin on his face.

After the third song, Kris moved away from her spot next to Toni in front of the huge stack of amplifiers and dropped back to the bar. Tired of watching the band, she started watching the crowd instead. There weren't too many people in the club, and Kris noticed there were more men than women. The women she did see were more interested in the band than the guys standing next to them.

Movement by the front door distracted her. She saw the doorman arguing with someone, and as he moved, she noticed he was arguing with Rusty. He finally shook his head and let her in. Looking very flustered, Rusty hobbled into the club and made a beeline for Toni. The two got into a very heated discussion and moved away from the Marshall stack and into a corner.

As Kris watched, Toni grew very angry. She yelled something at Rusty, who burst into tears and ran to the bathroom. Toni glared after her, smoothed her hair, and turned back toward the stage.

Kris raced to the ladies room and pushed her way in. She heard sobbing from the stall at the far end of the bathroom. Stopping in front of it, she said gently, "Rusty, are you all right?"

The sobs subsided into hiccups. "Kris? I - I didn't see you out there." Rusty's voice was muffled.

"I got tired of standing in front of the stage, so I was hanging out by the bar."

Kris stepped back as she heard the latch on the stall door move, and a second later, Rusty stumbled out. Her makeup was a mess and her new short hairdo was mussed up. Rusty tottered to the mirror and made a face.

"I look like shit! No wonder Paulie didn't want to let me in!"

Kris pulled out several paper towels and held them under cold water. Squeezing out the excess, she handed the wet towels to Rusty, who smiled wanly and patted her face.

"What happened," Kris asked?

"Oh, I was... er... running for Toni and got mixed up," Rusty answered, an evasive tone in here voice. "It's nothing. I must be PMS'ing to be so upset." She wiped smudges from under her eyes, slathered on some lip gloss and re-spiked her hair with her fingers. Flashing a bright smile at Kris, she asked, "So, have you heard from Marty again?"

The question, and Rusty's quick turnaround, took Kris by surprise.

"Well, he did call and leave a message from Miami, but I just can't get over all the stuff Toni said about him," Kris answered, truthfully.

Rusty looked concerned.

"He seemed like the real deal to me, Kris," she said somberly. "I'm sure he's changed. You should give him a shot. Don't believe everything you hear about him."

Kris smiled, sadly. "He said the same thing."

"Believe him, Kris!" Rusty grabbed her hands. "I know he truly cares about you!"

"How do you know?"

"I just do," Rusty said, fervently. "I can't wait until I meet my rick rock star," she sighed. "I'm already tired of this other shit."

"What other shit?" Kris asked, sharply.

Rusty looked evasive again. "Never mind," she said, after an uncomfortable pause. "C'mon, let's go get a drink." She pulled the door open and practically sprinted to the bar. Kris followed, frowning. What wasn't Rusty telling her?

She was almost to the bar when she felt someone watching her. Glancing around the club, she spotted a tall man leaning against a wall at the far end of the cavernous room, shrouded in darkness. He raised a glass to her, smiling. She couldn't see him very well - he was dressed head to toe in black. He unnerved her so much, she didn't watch where she was going and walked right into someone.

"Sorry!" she cried, grabbing the woman's arm before she fell.

"Hey, s'no problem," the woman slurred, flashing Kris a watery, unfocused smile.

Kris waited until she'd reached the bar before chancing another glance in the tall man's direction. He was gone.

Why had he been staring at her? Or had he been? Maybe he hadn't been watching her at all. Their eyes had probably met by accident as they both scanned the crowd, and he had raised his glass as a friendly gesture. Kris put him out of her mind and accepted the drink Rusty handed her.

Rusty had stayed long enough to finish her drink, hugging Kris and leaving the club without watching the band. Backstage after the show, Kris watched Toni trying to chat up the guitarist, but he didn't seem interested. The drummer tried to catch her eye, but Toni ignored him. After a few frustrating moments, she stormed over to Kris and snapped, "Let's go. These guys are completely lame!"

They passed Charley as they left the dressing room. Toni stared icily at her, but Charley just grinned.

"Leaving so soon?" she rasped. "Or didn't they bite?" She clicked her teeth together and smirked. "Maybe they know what's not worth their time."

Toni stopped. Her face was white with anger, but when she spoke, her voice was syrupy sweet.

"Well, how would they know quality? They've already played in the junkyard!" Pivoting on her heel, she strode away.

Kris stared from Toni's retreating back to Charley, who didn't seem the least bit upset by Toni's barb. She grinned at Kris, said, "Watch it, girlie, or you'll end up painted with the same brush as her," and closed the dressing room door in Kris' face.

Kris paused in her writing, thinking again about Charley's words. Quickly, she jotted, "What does Charley mean by Toni being a lightweight? Is it because Toni only gives blow jobs when she can help it, while Charley goes all out? That Charley will travel with a band and sleep with all the members, while Toni stays in NYC and is selective?" Once again, the image of Marty, Charley, and a jar of Vaseline popped into her head. Her stomach clenched. "Don't even think about that," she admonished herself, slamming the notebook shut.

Chapter 36

Marius grinned as he leaned back into the plush leather seat of his limo. He'd enjoyed the look of surprised on her face as he'd raised his glass to her. What a natural beauty! So untouched by the sleaze of the scene. Seeing her tonight had cemented his desire for her.

He had ordered Toni to keep her fresh and untouched. In his dreams, Kris was still a virgin and he, her first and only lover. Realistically, he knew she wasn't a virgin, but he could tell by watching her that she had not had many experiences.

Marius pulled open the mini-fridge and pulled out a bottle of sparkling water. The whiskey he'd drunk inside L'Amour was terrible; cheap stuff that left a bad taste in his mouth. Squeezing a freshly-cut lemon into a glass, he poured the water and drank with gusto.

Soon, Kris Lindsey would be his. He swelled at the thought and grinned again. Luckily, he never traveled alone. A robed figure seated across from him noticed the growing bulge in his pants and quickly shed her robe before kneeling in front of him.

Marius leaned farther back into the plush leather and let her work her charms, imagining Kris' rosebud lips wrapped around him, sliding back and forth. He closed his eyes and groaned, knowing he wouldn't last much longer.

Chapter 37

Toni sighed and cut the engine of her Camaro. Rusty was turning out to be quite a handful. Her need for cocaine was nearly insatiable. Not for the first time in the last week, Toni regretted ever turning her onto the drug.

She pulled the keys out of the ignition and got out, making sure the door was locked before slamming it shut. Toni straightened her black leather miniskirt - it always twisted when she drove. Her black leather jacket was zipped up to her collarbone, and with good reason. She was naked underneath it. She looked down and checked her stockings, making sure the seams were straight down the back of her legs, and the tops of the stockings and garter belt snap were visible.

Toni walked briskly up the steps to the brownstone. The door wasn't as fancy as the one on Marius' brownstone, but this man did quite well for himself. He must have a lot of customers to afford this neighborhood. She rang the bell, heard scurrying footsteps, and braced herself. An eye appeared in the peephole, then the door swung open, revealing a short, skinny man with a ferret-like face. His nose even seemed to twitch. His watery blue eyes were magnified behind a pair of ridiculously thick glasses, and Toni knew he was very excited, even though she couldn't see his erection through his very baggy pants.

"Hiya, Eddie," she purred, forcing her way into the hall and closing the door firmly behind her.

Eddie scurried back a few steps, rumpling his dishwater blonde hair with one nervous hand. The other hand snaked its way to his crotch and he squeezed himself, almost absently.

"Unzip," he begged, his voice a squeak,

Toni held out her hand. "Payment first," she said, in a bored tone.

"Unzip a little... please?"

Toni took hold of her zipper and made as if to tug it down. Eddie let out another squeak and massaged his crotch more frantically.

"Uh-uh, Eddie. Get your hand away from your dick and pay me."

He turned and fumbled with a cabinet in the hallway, unlocking it with a key he pulled from his pocket. He grabbed a plastic sandwich bag stuffed with folded pieces of white paper and held it out to her, shivering.

"Half a gram in each packet," he said. "There's twenty packets in this baggie. For that, I - I want the works."

Toni took the bag from his trembling hand and stashed it in his purse with one hand; the other, unzipping her jacket all the way. It swung open to reveal her breasts, the pink nipples dusted with a bronze powder and already puckering in the cool air.

Eddie squeaked again and ran down the hall, waving for her to follow. Toni unzipped her leather miniskirt as she walked; her steps deliberate, heels clacking loudly on the parquet floor. By the time she reached the living room. Eddie was naked, his erection barely noticeable. Toni always felt a stab of pity whenever she saw his dick. It was tiny, like a little boy's.

She slid a sensual smile on her face and let the miniskirt drop to the floor; now completely nude except for her jacket, black stockings, garter belt and heels. She slowly peeled the jacket off her shoulders and let it drop to the floor, as Eddie lay back on his black leather couch, trembling with anticipation.

Toni took her time, knowing from experience that he would come as soon as she touched him. She'd be done and on her way home in ten minutes, tops. Not bad work for ten grams of coke. Smiling again, she pulled Eddie's glasses off his face and lowered her lips to his.

Chapter 38

"Ah, Miss Lindsey, a package came for you today."

Henry held the door open for Kris, pointing to the mail alcove with his lined hand. Kris picked up the Federal Express envelope lying on the counter. She could feel a small box inside. Funny, she didn't remember ordering anything, and she'd never pay to have anything shipped Federal Express. It was way too expensive. She looked for a return address and saw it was a hotel in North Carolina, in the same city where Black Gallows had played the night before.

Kris carried the package and the rest of her mail up to her apartment and opened it, saving the package for last. Inside was a small box and a folded note. The note read: *Please don't believe everything you hear about me and please don't judge me until you've heard my side. You have my heart. ~ M*

She reread the note, then set it down and picked up the box. It contained a small jewelry box. She pulled it opened and gasped at the fiery opal pendant necklace that lay inside. She lifted the necklace out by its chain. The opal swung and glowed before her eyes. Gently, she laid it back in the box and closed it, blinking back tears. The story about Charley and the Vaseline didn't sound made up and she couldn't get past it. Pulling a drawer open, she stashed the necklace and threw the note away.

Kris was eating dinner in front of the TV when the phone rang. She debated letting the machine pick up, then raced across the room, snatching it up at the last second.

"Hello," she said, breathlessly.

"Did I interrupt something?" Marty's voice sounded surprised.

"Uh... no," Kris replied. "I was just eating dinner and raced for the phone."

There was a pause.

"Do you have company?"

The question irritated her.

"For your information, I'm alone. Not that it's any of your business," she said, coolly.

"What the bloody hell's that supposed to mean?" His voice held a mixture of confusion and defiance.

She paused, debating how much to say, then burst out, "When you called from Buffalo, you had a girl in your room. I heard her laughing!"

"What?" Marty sounded even more confused. Then, he laughed. "Oh, I remember now. I called you from Billy's room. He and his girlfriend were drunk. She was giggling and he kept trying to shush her so I could leave my message."

Kris was quiet. He sounded so believable.

She cleared her throat.

"Well, I don't own you," she said, trying to sound unconcerned.

"Did you get my package?" His tone was husky.

"Yes," she whispered. "It's beautiful." She blinked hard to keep the tears at bay, and willed her stomach to stop churning.

"I meant what I wrote in that note, Kris." His voice filled with emotion. "You have my heart. I don't know how it happened, but you do."

Unbidden, Charley's image flashed in her mind. She had to know.

"Marty, I need to ask you something."

"Anything, luv."

"And will you answer honestly?"

"As honestly as I can."

"Do you know a girl named Charley?"

There was a long silence.

"Marty?" Kris knew she sounded slightly panicked, and mentally kicked herself for being so vulnerable.

He cleared his throat.

"Do you?" Kris persisted.

"Erm... yeah, I do."

"Okay," she said quietly.

"What did they tell you?" he demanded.

"Nothing I can repeat." Kris paused. "Please tell me where I can return the necklace."

"It's a gift. For you." Marty sounded angry and sad.

"I can't wear it."

"Oh, come on, Kris!" he burst out. "Please don't judge me by my past actions! Ask Linda! I really want to try with you. I've been on my best behavior this tour! I'll give you the number to her hotel room. She'll vouch for me!"

Pain stabbed at her.

"Oh, Marty!" she cried. "I can't handle this! I'm not in your league. I'm confused about everything. You tell me one thing. Toni tells me something else. I can't get past that."

Kris drew a ragged breath then continued more calmly. "My sister calls me a prude and maybe I am. I'm not that experience and I'm not very open-minded. You shouldn't be a monk for me. It's not your style and I'm not worth it."

Without giving him a chance to respond, she said softly, "Good-bye, Marty," and hung up.

Then, she let the tears fall.

Chapter 39

Marty listened to the dial tone buzzing in his ear, then slammed the phone down so hard, he thought he'd broken it. Why the HELL did he have to get involved with her? She was ripping his guts inside out? Why couldn't she have just gone with him when he'd asked her at Radio City? Then, he could have fucked her and forgotten her. As it was, he'd barely kissed her and she was making him feeling like a horny schoolboy. He couldn't stop thinking about her, couldn't stop imagining how she would feel wrapped around him; how it would feel to be deep inside her.

Marty stopped. He knew his feelings ran deeper than that. He didn't just want to fuck her, he wanted to be with her; to share his hopes and fears, no matter how daft they seemed. This time, he wanted more than a lay; he wanted a relationship.

Marty paused in front of the mirror and eyed his reflection critically. At 36, he was still in good shape, thanks to regular workouts and a mostly healthy diet. His stomach was still flat, his chest and arms, muscular. He didn't drink much and didn't do drugs anymore. Not since… he forced his mind away from that terrible memory; back to the present, where it was safer.

Or was it?

Marius Man had hinted he might air Marty's very dirty laundry if he didn't stop seeing Kris. Marty frowned at his reflection, his warm brown eyes suddenly chilly. He just couldn't do it. He couldn't leave Kris alone. He'd never felt this way about any woman, and he wasn't stupid enough to let her pass him by. He knew he could win her over, no matter what shit Toni fed her. With that thought, Marty pulled on a t-shirt and went looking for Linda and Brian.

Chapter 40

Toni sauntered backstage at a tiny nightclub on Staten Island, Rusty by her side. The club is so small, the owners didn't even bother naming it, but they'd installed a good sound system and it was a great place for up and coming bands to hone their sound and stage presence.

Hot Cat was playing tonight and Rusty was going to hone her skills and move up to the next tier. Hot Cat's singer, Brad, was more than willing to give Rusty an audition. He barred Toni's way at the backstage door and pulled her so close, she could tell that the simple act of hugging her had given him a massive erection. Not caring who was watching, Brad slid his hand up under Toni's lace blouse and cupped her breast, then pinched her nipple, hard.

She slid out from under his arm, digging her elbow into his side as she did. He was an animal and she hated him, but she smiled sweetly as she drew Rusty into the room and introduced her. Rusty smiled and held out her hand, but he shoved it down, pulling her close for a hug, trapping her hand over his erection. Toni saw Rusty's eyes widen at the contact and gave her a bawdy wink behind his back.

She gently pulled Rusty away from Brad and arranged for the two to meet after the show. Waving at him, she steered Rusty out of the backstage room and into the club.

The stage looked cramped and didn't stand very high off the floor. People standing in front of the stage would be nearly eye-to-eye with the band. A few tables scattered the sides of the small room and several dimly-lit booths in the back allowed amorous couples a bit of privacy. A small but fully-stocked bar split the dance floor in half.

As they reached the bar, Rusty asked breathlessly, "Is that the guy who wants to meet me?"

Toni laughed humorlessly.

"This guy isn't even close to rock star status and he definitely does not have the money to keep you in the clothes that you're wearing."

Rusty looked confused.

"So, why am I going with him tonight? I thought I was done with that stuff."

Toni ordered two Mai Tais and turned to face Rusty.

"I've got to be honest, Rusty. The man who wants to meet you wants someone with a bit more 'experience' than you've got right now. If he's gonna take care of all your needs, you've got to take care of all his needs, especially his special needs."

"He's got special needs?" Rusty was trying to take it in, but Toni could see her eyes moving back and forth. She must be hopped up on coke tonight.

"He's got some… quirks… and Brad can help train you to take care of those quirks," Toni replied casually.

Rusty took a long sip and pondered Toni's words. Her face cleared.

"Okay, I get it. I'm ready!" She grinned so happily, Toni felt a twinge of regret. If Rusty only knew what she was in for. Instead, she said, "That's the spirit!" and the two leaned back against the bar, waiting for the show to begin.

During the show, Toni spotted Marius sitting in a back booth. She wondered when he'd come in, then realized she hadn't seen him before because he was draped in women.

She told Rusty she was going to the ladies room, then made her way over to him. As she drew nearer, she saw two women crouched under the table and knew exactly what they were doing. Marius sat facing her, a woman on either side. By the way they were squirming, Toni could figure out just where his hands were. She was amazed that he could focus on her enough to smile and nod approvingly.

"She looks very nice," he said, his deep voice husky. "Is she ready to perform tonight?"

Toni nodded, keeping her expression neutral.

"And does our Rusty know just what she's in for?"

Toni smiled slightly. "I thought it better that she didn't know right now."

Marius nodded again, his eyes half closed. Toni knew he was close. She waited as his eyes unfocused and his body jerked. The women on either side of him shuddered, too. Toni was unimpressed. She knew they were damn good actresses.

Marius' eyes refocused and his expression turned unreadable.

"Make sure Rusty exceeds expectations."

"Don't you want to know about Kris?" Toni asked, surprised.

He smiled. "I don't need an update on Kris. I have very special plans for her myself." He turned and kissed the woman on his left.

Toni knew she had been dismissed, and headed back to the bar. She had nearly reached it when she stopped, staring in dismay at the scene in front of her. Rusty was falling-down drunk. She was barely hanging onto the counter.

Toni stormed over and hissed at the bartender, "What the fuck happened?"

The bartender shrugged. "I gave her one. Some dude bought her one." He paused, looking at the ceiling. "Oh, and she did a shot of tequila."

Toni fumed. Rusty was barely standing. Toni nudged a guy standing next to them and commanded, "Help me get her backstage, and for God's sake, don't let it look like she's fucked up!"

The guy snapped to attention and together, they made their way backstage, Rusty managing to put one foot in front of the other.

Brad didn't seem disappointed at the scene. In fact, he said gleefully that Rusty would offer up less resistance this way.

"I have a bondage getup I really want to try," he said, rubbing his hands together. He helped Toni half carry, half drag Rusty to her car. As they reached it, Rusty vomited all over Brad's feet, slurring, "Oops! Sorry!"

"That's okay, sweetie," Brad crooned. "Brad's gonna spank you good for that later."

Rusty smiled wanly, not taking in a word he'd said. They got her into the front seat and brad climbed in back. Toni rolled down the window, in case Rusty had to vomit again, and sped to Manhattan. She doubled-parked outside Brad's apartment and helped him get Rusty into the elevator. He said he could handle it from there. Toni handed him several packets of cocaine, saying, "This may help a little."

He pocketed the coke with a grin and before she could stop him, pinched her nipple again, before waving cheerily as the elevator doors closed. Toni headed back to her car, hoping Rusty wouldn't remember too much of this night.

Chapter 41

Kris was assigned two more stories for Metal Countdown. One was a profile of a German band called Juggernaut; the other, an interview with the lead singer of Kimba, a band making a mark on the local scene.

Juggernaut turned out to be five very down-to-earth guys whose only expectation was a fun interview session. She met them at a German restaurant on the Upper East Side and spent three very enjoyable hours talking about music and laughing at the funny stories they told about themselves and the bands they'd toured with.

Hans, the singer, recounted how he and Marty had stolen a motor scooter and driven through the streets of Paris, yelling French obscenities at everyone they passed. The others laughed as Hans explained how they'd lost their shoes and nearly lost their pants to a group of gypsies, who ended up tossing them into the Seine River.

"Ach… it still brings me to tears," said Hans, wiping his eyes. "We were so… how you say… pissed…. Drinking too much beer. And Marty was thinking he can communicate, but all he can say is 'croissant.' And so they threw croissants to us in exchange for our shoes."

Kris tried to imagine Marty riding around on a motor scooter yelling "croissant." Pain stabbed her heart, but she managed a wan smile. She could picture him, sitting behind Hans on the scooter, his long brown hair wet from the dip in the Seine.

She ended up getting six cassette tapes' worth of interviews, more than enough for a three-page article. She enjoyed the banter and camaraderie between the band members and left the interview laden with Juggernaut cassettes and t-shirts for herself and her sister Kim.

The interview with the singer from Kimba went just as well. Walter Smith was charming hand handsome, with hazel eyes and a mane of light, curly brown hair that reached halfway down his back. He talked easily about growing up in Flatbush, Brooklyn and working odd jobs while he tried to get Kimba off the ground. Kris asked him why he chose to name the band after a Japanese cartoon lion and he grinned.

"It was my favorite cartoon," he said amiably, shaking curls out of his eyes. "I thought Kimba ruled the jungle, man, even though he was just a little dude. I guess I want us to do the same." He laughed. "Pretty big dreams, huh? But I guess it doesn't hurt to aim high."

Walter gave Kris a Kimba cassette so she could get a sense of their music for the article. She listened to it when she got home and was impressed. She liked the tight guitar rhythms and the singing. Walter had a clear, powerful voice that caressed the notes as he sang. This band definitely had a future, she thought.

Kris spent the weekend working on both articles, leaving her apartment only to go to the café. Marty called twice but she let the answering machine pick up. She could hear a slight note of desperation in his voice, but forced herself to erase both messages without listening to them again.

When she finally sent the articles off to David, she did so with a great sense of accomplishment and decided to celebrate by going out to dinner. She called Rusty and invited her to the German restaurant where she had interviewed Juggernaut.

Rusty was waiting when Kris arrived and it was all Kris could do to keep her face from registering shock. Rusty was way too thin for her tall frame and seemed to be filled with a restless energy Kris had never seen in her friend. Rusty had always been chatty, but she now dominated the conversation, sometimes speaking so quickly, Kris had to ask her to repeat herself. When Kris asked how much weight she'd lost, Rusty stuck out her chest and said proudly, "Forty pounds!" She turned to the side so Kris could see her profile and boasted, "Look, chiseled cheekbones!"

They ordered their meals and settled back. Rusty asked about Kris' articles and seemed genuinely happy for Kris' burgeoning success. When the food arrived, Rusty picked at her schnitzel, pushing most of her food around her plate and gulping glass after glass of iced water.

"So, do you know who your mystery rock star is yet?" Kris asked, to break an awkward silence punctuated by sniffles from Rusty.

Rusty shook her head. "No, I'm preparing myself for him, though. Toni said it should happen soon. I can't wait! I'm going to be perfect for him. He won't want to dump me for anyone else!"

Kris frowned. "How are you 'preparing' yourself for him?"

Rusty looked away, then back down at her plate and said, almost too casually, "Oh, you know, the usual. Clothes, makeup, stuff. Hey, did you see the dessert case when we came in? Everything looks so yummy!"

Kris' frown deepened. She truly liked Rusty, so she knew she had to speak her mind.

"Rusty, you are such a beautiful and lively woman. ANY man should thank his lucky stars that you're his. You don't have to 'prepare' yourself for anyone! You're perfect the way you are! I wish you could see that!"

Rusty smiled sadly. "Thanks for saying that. I wish I could believe it, but I know it's not true. I know a rock star wants me, but he's a little 'different,' so I need extra preparation. I can't wait till I meet him. It's the only way I'll get out of this rut."

Kris shook her head. "It's not the only way. Trust me. Find in your heart what you want to do – and I know you can find a way to make it happen. I'll help you!"

"But that's just it, Kris," said Rusty earnestly. "My heart's desire is to be a rich rock star's girlfriend. That's all I want to do. I don't want to be a journalist like you or Annie. I don't want to be a dental receptionist. I don't want to model or act. I don't even want to be a groupie. I just want to be a rock star's girlfriend. I don't even need to marry him, as long as he takes care of me."

She put her fork down and gazed into space. "I've always imagined it. Me, on a rock star's arm, people 'oohing' and 'aahing' over me. Women wanting to trade places with me, but my guy has eyes only for me."

Rusty picked up her fork and speared a roast potato. "I wish I could make you see that this isn't useless. It sounds simple and stupid, but it means the world to me."

Kris looked across the table at her friend, trying to wrap her mind around what Rusty had just said.

"I can't fault your dreams, Rusty," she said. "If that's what's truly in your heart, I hope you get it. You deserve every happiness."

Rusty beamed and raised her wine glass.

"To happiness."

They toasted and drank, then Rusty excused herself and went to the bathroom. When she returned, she was more lively, but sniffled a lot more. Kris wondered whether Rusty had allergies, but didn't ask.

They enjoyed the rest of their dinner and hugged warmly before parting. Kris spent the taxi ride home pondering Rusty's words and actions. Her dreams seemed so farfetched, but someone else might say Kris' were just has remote. Although, she thought, leaning back in the seat and smiling slightly, she was on her way.

Thanks to Marty, said a small voice in her head. She ignored it and wondered what David's next assignment would be. But her mind kept intruding, flashing images of Marty's liquid brown eyes, his baby-soft hair, his tantalizing lips, the soft urgency of his kiss, the press of his body against hers. She shook her head forcefully. She could not forget Charley.

When Kris got home, her answering machine was blinking with messages. Two from Marty. One included a phone number. With a stab of pain in her heart, she erased both.

Chapter 42

Kris ventured to L'Amour on her own Saturday night. A local battle of the bands was taking place. None of the bands were very well known, but that suited her fine. She wanted to find Charley, but wondered if these bands were too low for even Charley's scale. Her question was answered a few minutes later, when she spotted Charley hanging out by the end of the bar.

Seeing Charley gave Kris another jolt of pain and another unwelcome image of Marty. Kris decided she didn't want to approach her tonight. Fate seemed to have other plans, when Kris came face to face with Charley in the ladies room.

"Hey, it's writer girl," drawled Charley, a cigarette hanging from the corner of her mouth, smoke curling toward the ceiling.

"How do you know who I am?" asked Kris, surprised.

"I make it a point to know about new blood that wanders into my territory." Charley replied, shrewdly, looking Kris up and down. "Weird, though. You don't look like the type to hang out with Peroxide Bitch and her gang."

Kris stared back. "And what do I have to look like?"

Charley shrugged, dragged on the cigarette, then tossed it into the sink, where it hissed as it hit a pool of water.

"Peroxide Toni likes to pretend she's better than the rest of us because she's got class. She wears spandex and lace and shit." Charley snorted. "Class, my ample ass! She's just got a big bankroll paying her to recruit naïve young girls, give them big dreams about true love with rock stars, then..." she stopped abruptly.

"Then what?" Kris demanded.

"Nothing. Forget it." Charley pulled the bathroom door open, then stopped. "The wrapping don't mean shit," she said cryptically, then left, the door swinging shut behind her with a loud, drawn out squeal.

Kris' mind raced. She pushed her way into a stall and sat on the toilet, pulling her notebook out of her jacket pocket. She wrote down the entire conversation, before she forgot anything Charley had said. She left only when she heard strains of a band on stage. The band sounded terrible; the singer growled and the guitarist was out of tune.

Kris splurged on a taxi to take her home. She gazed out the window as pitch-black Brooklyn streets flew past, then opened to reveal the breathtaking skyline of lower Manhattan, the twin towers of the World Trade Center glittering like jewels; the majestic Statue of Liberty casting a welcoming glow over the harbor. Kris caught her breath at the image of the lights so stark against the black velvet of the night sky.

When she reached her apartment, she found a large box in front of her door. There was no return address, no postmark; just her name and apartment number written in block letters. She picked up the box and carried it inside. When she opened it, she gasped. Inside lay the white dress, stockings and red pumps she had tried on at Charlotte's Harlots. There was no note.

Kris called Charlotte the next day to see who had sent the dress, but Charlotte claimed to not remember.

"I'm just glad you have it," she gushed. "The dress was made for you!"

Kris hung up, confused. Had Toni sent the dress? She had been annoyed when Kris has passed it up.

Deciding to put it out of her mind for the time being, Kris spent the evening the café, adding the following lines to her notes:

Peroxide Bitch.

Lightweight.

Big bankroll.

Recruiting naïve girls.

Kris chewed the tip of her pen, thinking hard. Where did Toni get the money for the fancy clothes and concert tickets? She owned a record store. Okay, a record store may get concert tickets now and then. Kris guessed Toni also got free tickets from musicians she serviced. But what about the rest of the time? A record store may do decent business, but good enough to keep her in the style in which she was accustomed? Kris jotted another line:

Benefactor = Rich Rock Star?

Chapter 43

Marius sounded pleased with Rusty's progress.

"I've picked a date for the party," he told Toni on the phone, his voice silky. "It will coincide with the Dark Disciple concert."

Toni was impressed. Dark Disciple was the biggest metal band out there. They were selling out arenas in minutes and they were touring with two opening bands – Lizard Lust and a guest band every several cities. Her breath quickened as she thought of Don Lyden. Marius heard and chuckled.

"Yes, very soon, my feisty little fox. You'll get your claws on your dreamy Don Lyden. I will help you, if you do your part to deliver Kris."

Toni believed Marius could deliver Don. He had a well-earned reputation for being connected to all aspects of the music industry. He had been the drummer for one of the premiere rock bands of the 60's and 70's, but had quickly become better known for his crazy parties and wild bouts of debauchery, than for his drumming skills. A leg injury had ended his drumming career, but by then, Marius Man had built himself up as *the* party planner, and anyone lucky enough to be invited to one of his parties knew they were headed to paradise. Nothing was off limits. Established rock stars with unusual tastes or quirks could get them fulfilled, no problem, no questions asked. Nothing was too weird, dirty or gross to Marius Man. Of course, he learned quite a few secrets, too; secrets he used to keep those stars at his beck and call.

Toni wondered what plans Marius had for Kris. She knew he had it bad for her, but didn't know how he planned to get Kris to fall for him. She'd never seen him show so much interest in a woman. He'd sampled other girls Toni had offered up, but let her control their style and schedules. Kris, he'd wanted left as she was, and saved only for him. His only instruction had been to send her the white lace dress she'd tried on at Charlotte's Harlots. Charlotte had apparently told him how well it had fit and how nice Kris had looked.

Marius had also told Toni that Kris and Marty had not done the nasty. This news didn't surprise her. That night at Radio City, when Kris had come to the hotel lobby hand in hand with Marty, she hadn't looked as though she'd had a marathon session with someone of Marty's caliber.

Marius *had* been very angry that Marty was still giving Kris so much attention. Toni told him about Marty calling Kris from every concert stop, but that Kris was not returning his calls.

"If he doesn't watch out," Marius had said in a cold, quiet voice, "he'll find himself out of work and locked up in jail."

Toni wondered what he'd meant by that, but Marius did not elaborate and she didn't dare ask.

She smiled and looked up from the albums she'd been cataloging in the store. Even though she'd never had Marty, she knew all about his quirks. Kris' innocent act might intrigue him for a while, but a letch never changed his spots and Marty would be pining for more adventure sooner or later. Sooner, Toni guessed. Much sooner.

She glanced at the clock and saw it was already seven. She left the pile of albums where they lay and stretched, working the kinks out of her back. Grabbing her purse from behind the counter, she turned off the stereo and lights. Flipping the sign to read CLOSED, she locked the door, pulled the security gate down and locked it, too. She hated owning and running a record store, but Marius had insisted, saying the store would be a great place to find and recruit girls. He'd been right. She met Maria and Annie at the store, and Kris, too. Okay, so Maria had turned into a complete loser, but Annie was gangbusters and recruited girls from God knew where. Toni had seen a few of them the last time she'd visited Marius' brownstone. They all looked like supermodels. She had no clue where Annie found them or how she lured them to Marius. She'd always thought Annie looked like a little dyke.

Toni stopped at home to change her clothes. Thank God her parents weren't home. Her dad never missed an opportunity to give her shit about the way she dressed. He didn't understand how it was; didn't understand she had a well-earned reputation to keep up. When it came to the scene, she was so good, she was known only by her first name. She doubted anyone even knew her full name. She was just Toni, or The Magic Tongue. She had made her own way, pulled her own weight, built up her own name. Marius' money and connections helped, but he hadn't made Toni. She'd made herself.

She had first pick of any up and coming band that came to town. Nearly everyone who knew the scene knew what an honor it was to be chosen by Toni. Many of the more established bands knew her, too, and the guys she'd dallied with usually stayed loyal, choosing her when they came back to town, instead of checking out new blood. When she sensed they'd begun itching to wander, she'd set them up with someone she knew would fulfill their needs. This kept them happy and loyal to her. They knew she was quality and would always deliver, one way or another.

Some guys who turned out to have tastes Toni couldn't fulfill, passed her on to other band members who did want what she had to offer. She had one strict rule: her ass was off limits! She considered anal sex gross and degrading. She'd do pretty much anything else: two on one, orgies; she'd even performed with Annie at a few parties. She didn't care to be with other women, but if Marius or one of his select clients wanted it, then they got it.

Once dressed, Toni clattered downstairs to the kitchen to see what was in the fridge. There'd been no leftovers from dinner, she noticed, so she unwrapped a slice of cheese and ate it, ignoring the rumble of hunger from her stomach. This snack would have to do.

She was lost in thought, and didn't hear footsteps enter the kitchen. Only when she heard her sister's voice did she look up, stepping away from the refrigerator. Angie looked as though she had just gotten home, yet her midnight blue power suit and cream silk blouse looked flawless; not one wrinkle in sight. That's how she thought of her sister; flawless. She truly was proud of Angie's successful legal career, but a wedge between them had been driven so deep, she didn't know how to reach out.

Angie didn't acknowledge Toni, or even give any sign her sister was in the room. Toni opened her mouth to say something, then changed her mind. She didn't know what to say. Toni turned and left the kitchen, heading toward the front door.

Toni picked Rusty up and drove her to a small party at an apartment down in Greenwich Village. The party was so small, it consisted of Rusty, Toni, and a high-ranking record company executive who liked to play house. Rusty knew what was expected of her. She stood nervously next to Toni as they rode the elevator up to his apartment. Toni could see sweat stains forming on the underarms of Rusty's silk blouse and wondered whether she'd thought to use deodorant. Too late now.

Outside the executive's door, Toni inspected Rusty's makeup, then pulled some breath spray from her purse.

"Open," she commanded, and Rusty obediently opened her mouth. Toni gave her a dose of spray, then spritzed some into her own mouth, and rang the doorbell.

The record company executive, a fit man in his late 50's with a shock of gray hair and a very recognizable mustache, opened the door, wearing nothing but an apron. Toni could see his erection pushing his apron out a bit. She smiled warmly and walked in, pushing him ahead of her. Rusty closed the door and they got down to business.

Chapter 44

Marty would not give up. He had called every day, always leaving a message and callback number. Kris had not responded to any of his messages, but he was giving her pause for thought. Why was he being so persistent? She thought he'd have forgotten about her by now and moved on to more willing partners. This was so unlike anything she'd heard about him.

She was reading her article about Kimba in the latest issue of Metal Countdown when the phone rang again. Thinking it was Marty, she let the machine pick up and jumped when she heard Linda's voice instead.

"Kris, pick up the phone if you're there."

Kris picked up the phone.

"Hi, Linda."

"So... you're just not home for certain blockheaded singers." Kris heard the smile in Linda's voice.

"He's not a blockhead," she replied. "He's just not for me. We're from two different worlds."

Linda laughed softly. "You're more alike than you think. Are you being put off by all the stories you're hearing from the girls?"

"Well, yes," Kris admitted. "I just can't get past some of the wilder stories."

Linda laughed again, but this time, there was no humor in the sound.

"Kris, the boys are coming back to New York to play one show with Dark Disciple by special invitation. It'll mean huge exposure for Black Gallows. They're playing Madison Square Garden – along with Lizard Lust." She paused. "I'd like to have dinner with you when we get to town. We can talk and maybe I can help you understand Marty. He obviously can't explain himself very well. After all, he *is* a bloke," she added, chuckling.

Kris laughed with Linda and agreed to meet for dinner. She marked the date on the calendar, noticing the show was just two weeks away. Her stomach jumped. Two weeks until she saw Marty again. If he was calling her every day, she knew he'd make every effort to see her just once. She wished Linda a good trip and they rang off.

Kris paced her living room, filled with nervous energy, then grabbed her notebook and headed out the door. Instead of stopping at her usual café, she hopped the subway down to Greenwich Village, thinking she'd drop by Charlotte's Harlots and find out who'd sent that dress. She knew there were several cafes in the area where she could have a coffee and write.

When Kris reached the shop, the door was locked and a big CLOSED sign hung in the window. Disappointed, she wandered down to Bleecker Street and found a café called Le Figaro; an interesting place whose walls were covered with pages from the actual French newspaper for which it was named. Finding a corner table, she ordered a coffee and opened her notebook.

Kris jotted down some notes about her conversation with Linda. She wrote Marty's name down and drew several large question marks after it. She had to be honest with herself; she did have feelings for him – strong feelings. His kiss melted her insides, his touch made her tremble and ache for more intimate contact. Even the sound of his voice sent a thrill coursing through her. But could she sleep with him? Just knowing the story about Charley disgusted her. Kris knew there'd been countless other women. Who knew what kinds of things he'd done with them?

Kris drew another question mark next to Marty's name and closed the book. Her coffee had turned as cold as her insides. She suddenly felt very unsure of herself.

Chapter 45

Toni smiled as she slid the shiny gold envelope open, her name scrawled on it in bold, black ink. She knew what lay inside, but couldn't wait to see it anyway. The invitation was the classiest she'd seen by far. The heavy gold card had the following words embossed in black ink:

"The honor of your presence is requested at THE gala event of 1985. Celebrate the triumphant return of DARK DISCIPLE to New York City!

Opening for DARK DISCIPLE at Madison Square Garden are LIZARD LUST and BLACK GALLOWS.

This invitation includes tickets to the SOLD-OUT show, plus a VIP party afterward.

Please RSVP at least 48 hours prior to the performance date."

Toni turned the envelope upside down. Two concert tickets and a small card embossed with the words VIP PARTY fell out. She felt a thrill of excitement. She was so close to Don Lyden, she could almost taste him.

The phone rang and she snatched it up.

"Hello?"

"Toni! I just got the most unbelievable invitation!" Rusty cried gleefully in her ear.

Toni smirked into the phone. "Unbelievable" was right, she thought, now that she knew exactly what Marius had planned for Rusty.

Aloud, she said, "I got one, too. Sounds fabulous, doesn't it?"

Rusty begged Toni to meet her at Charlotte's Harlots to pick out a suitable outfit. As much as Toni hated hanging out with Rusty, she needed a new outfit herself, so she agreed.

As she grabbed her purse and opened her bedroom door, the phone rang again. Thinking it was Rusty, she snatched up the phone and snapped, "What now?"

"Tsk, tsk. That's no way to greet a friend who's about to make your horny little dreams come true." Marius Man's baritone filled her ear.

"Oh, sorry," Toni said, flustered. "I thought you were someone else."

"Obviously," he replied silkily. "Did you get your invitation?"

"Oh, yes! You've outdone yourself! Dark Disciple, Lizard Lust and Black Gallows on the same bill!"

"I'm glad you think so." He laughed softly. "Now, do your part and Don Lyden is as good as yours. You make sure Kris goes to the party. I'll take her from there." Without saying goodbye, he hung up.

Toni hesitated, then called Kris. The answering machine picked up, so she left a message.

"Hey, Kris, it's Toni. Did you get your invitation to the biggest show and party of the year? I'm meeting Rusty at Charlotte's Harlots to pick out an outfit for the show. If you get this message before 7, meet us down there. If not, then call me later."

Toni hung up and smiled. Grabbing her purse again, she raced out the door.

Chapter 46

Kris listened to the message and glanced at the clock. Toni's call had come through just fifteen minutes ago, while Kris had been walking home from work. She decided to meet them downtown and splurged on a taxi to get there more quickly.

Her cab hit all green lights and slid to a stop outside Charlotte's Harlots in no time. Toni and Rusty and just arrived – traffic from Queens had been heavier. Charlotte appeared to be beside herself with excitement.

"This is even better than a fairy tale!" she gushed. Her excitement spread to Rusty, who wriggled in anticipation, eyes lining like a child let loose in a candy store where every price tag read: FREE.

Charlotte hurried from rack to rack, pulling out pieces of clothing. As she assembled outfits on hooks, the door jingled open and Francine and Annie walked in. Charlotte took this in stride, pausing only to turn on the stereo. The eerie, wailing sound of Dark Disciple's music pealed from the speakers.

Within minutes, Charlotte had assembled outfits for everyone but Kris. To her, Charlotte said, "You must wear that white dress."

Kris asked if she could remember who'd sent it. Charlotte looked reflexively at Toni, who said smoothly, "I did."

At Kris' surprised look, she continued, "I know it's a bit much, but you truly looked fantastic in it and I wanted you to have it."

Toni smiled at Charlotte. "Char gave me a great price because I'm such a great customer."

Charlotte looked uncertain for a moment, then nodded.

"Glad to help," she said hurriedly. "You really must wear that dress, Kris, dear. And come over here." She beckoned Kris to the jewelry case. "Let's find something sparkly to go with it."

As Kris eyed the necklaces, earrings and bracelets, she asked, "Are you guys taking anyone to the show?"

Toni and Francine were taking girlfriends. Annie didn't answer. Rusty asked Kris who she was taking. When Kris told them she was bringing her sister, Toni and Annie exchanged looks.

"How old is your sister?" Toni asked, keenly.

"Fifteen, but she looks older."

Toni looked shrewdly at Kris. "Does she look like you?"

Kris pondered this.

"A bit," she said. "She has brown hair and amber eyes. She's also taller and a bit more developed than I am," Kris finished, blushing slightly.

"Does she liked bands?" This from Annie.

"Oh, yes! Kim loves Lizard Lust and Black Gallows.

Toni grinned. "Bring her! She may just end up having the time of her life!"

Annie snorted and hastily turned away from Kris to study a rack of bustiers.

Francine opened her mouth to say something, but Toni shut her up with a sharp look. To Kris, she said, warmly, "Why don't you find your sister a cute outfit to wear? Char's got stuff that's not so revealing."

Charlotte, who'd been standing in stunned silence, sprang forward, smiling nervously. Asking Kris her sister's size, she set about pulling clothing off racks. In moments, the store was filled with sounds of zippers, snaps, and women's voices calling to each other over the wail of guitars and the plaintive but powerful screams of Dark Disciple's singer, The Monk.

"Ooh, I love that!"

"You need to show a bit more cleavage!"

Kris couldn't help but get caught up in the excitement. She chose a frothy peasant blouse in peach and a pair of black jeans with flared legs for Kim. From the jewelry case, she chose a necklace with a small, demure heart pendant with matching earrings.

Kris surveyed her choices. Mom would not be outraged over these clothes. She decided to splurge and buy Kim a leather jacket, too. Her sister would be surprised and happy when Kris sprang all this on her – a concert, party, *and* new clothes! She mentally lined up the interviews she could do, now that she was a bit better known from her articles for Metal Countdown. Kris smiled to herself. If everything worked out, maybe she could interview Lizard Lust and introduce Kim to Don Lyden. Maybe she could introduce her to Marty. She caught Toni looking at her quizzically and shrugged, turning back to the counter where Charlotte was tallying up her purchases.

Declining their dinner invitation, Kris waved at the others and left the store. She stopped at Le Figaro for coffee and jotted more notes. Could David help set up and interview with Lizard Lust, or were they still too big a band for her to cover? So far, the biggest band she'd interviewed had been Juggernaut, but that interview had gone well, hadn't it? She made a mental note to ask David.

Toni would be jealous if Kris did get to talk to Lizard Lust. Kris thought about introducing Don Lyden to Toni, then quickly changed her mind. She didn't think introducing Don to a woman like Toni was smart. Toni was a barracuda with very sharp teeth and she'd been longing to sink those teeth into Don for so long, who knew what she'd do if she came face to face with him. Kris allowed herself a small smile. Truth be told, she did want to dally with one certain rock star. She thought about her upcoming dinner with Linda and wondered what she could say that would ease the pain in Kris' heart.

Chapter 47

Four days before the show, Kris found a surprise waiting outside her apartment door. As she rounded the corner from the elevator, Marty stood and faced her, grinning sheepishly.

"You should set a chair out here for me," he said. Marty sounded genial, but his body gave away his nervousness. He shifted from one foot to the other, hands jammed into the front pockets of his jeans. His curtain of long brown hair partially obscured his face. He swung his hair back and smiled again.

Kris remained where she was.

"I didn't know you were in town already," she stammered, trying to regain her composure.

"I'm here early." He nodded toward the door. "Can we please go inside?" His tone was still casual, but she could see the strain on his face.

She unlocked the door and let him in. Without asking if he wanted any, she started to make a pot of coffee. She needed to do something with her hands. He had completely unnerved her by showing up like this. Her apartment suddenly seemed too small – his presence filled every room. He leaned against the counter, watching her measure coffee and water.

Kris could barely breathe; he was so close, powerful and compact in a pair of faded jeans, arms crossed over a barrel chest that strained against his t-shirt. His liquid brown eyes were warm on her face; his generous lips, curved into a gentle smile.

She reached up to pull two coffee mugs out of the cabinet and dropped one. His hand shot out and caught it before it hit the floor.

"Thanks," she said as he handed it to her. His sudden movement had knocked the breath out of her. Her hand shook slightly as she took the mug, and she cursed herself for being so weak.

Before she could pour any coffee, his hands closed over hers and he pulled her to face him. His lips were on hers before she could move or protest. His kissed her softly, still holding her hands. Her heart raced as he deepened the kiss, but as her body began responding, he pulled away, leaving her flushed from their brief contact. She could see the kiss had affected him as well.

Kris gazed at him, wordlessly.

"I had to see," he said, huskily. "And I do."

"See what?" she croaked.

"If what I feel is real or just in my head."

"And one kiss can tell you?"

"Oh, yes."

Marty smiled and traced her chin with his thumb, then turned away to pour the coffee. He carried the mugs into the living room, set them on the table, and sat on the couch, patting the spot next to him. Kris perched on the edge, waiting for him to speak.

He cleared his throat.

"Linda wanted to talk to you, woman to woman, but this is something I have to do myself," he said, his tone serious.

He took her hand and stroked it.

"As you know, I've had a pretty wild past. I've done things I'm not proud of. I've done things I haven't thought twice about. Being a rock band opens doors you've never dreamed existed. Being in a successful rock band gets you even more."

He stood and paced her small living room, tension pouring off his body as he walked.

"I've been with so many women, I've lost count. I've been to parties that defy imagination. I've never had a girlfriend, not even in school. When I hit it big, all the attention went to my head and I wanted to be free to sample anything and everything that was offered to me.

Marty stopped in front of the TV, then turned to look at her.

"Toni and the girls. Well, you can imagine how many girls like them there are around the world. All they want is five minutes. Some want even less. Many will do anything you want. Anything. When you're young, suddenly wildly famous and attractive to every woman who sees you, it's the headiest aphrodisiac around. You're like a god; every whim fulfilled with the snap of fingers, a nod, a wink of an eye."

Marty moved restlessly, then sat next to Kris again.

"I made friends with a rock legend. He played drums for the Wild Boys in the late 1960s and early 70s."

"Oh, I know who he is," said Kris. "He calls himself Mr. Man, doesn't he?"

"That's the bloke," Marty agreed. "Well, when he stopped playing, he developed quite a reputation as being the go-to guy for all your wildest needs. I fell in with him at a time of great experimentation in my life."

He paused and looked down at his hands.

"I was dabbling with LSD. I liked the way it freed my mind and expanded my creativity. I used to tape record all my trips and listen to them later for inspiration in writing songs. One night, a young lady and I were tripping together and as usual, the tape recorder was running. We were having fun, then it turned bad. We had been making up a type of mythology that existed in our heads, when she imagined a demon she made up was real. She grabbed a knife to fight it off. To this day, I don't know how she got a hold of the bloody thing."

Marty's voice cracked and he stopped, his breathing ragged. He stood and turned his back to Kris, before forcing himself to continue.

"I tried to get the knife away from her, but only half-heartedly. I imagined the demon would come after me if she didn't kill it. She started screaming that the demon was inside her body and started hacking away at herself."

He stopped, unable to continue.

Kris stared at him, horrified.

"What happened?" she whispered, already knowing the answer.

"She… she didn't make it," he said quietly, his eyes swimming with tears. "Marius took care of things. He hushed it up. It never made the news. He told me it had been an accident and my career needn't suffer because of it. He even made the tape recording disappear."

Marty started pacing again and Kris worked to digest the news.

"Why are you telling me this?" she asked, tremulously.

He stopped in front of her and grabbed her hands.

"I want no secrets between us," he said, his voice intense. "I don't know what'd going on but I have feelings for you I've never had for anyone. It's important that you

204

know everything about me." He paused, then repeated, "everything."

Kris pulled her hands away.

"What happened to that girl's family? Did they ever find out?"

Marty shook his head. "Marius said the girl had no family. She was living at his house when she... when it happened. She was part of his harem."

"Harem? Mr. Man has a harem?"

He looked at her in wonder. "You don't know?"

"Know what?"

"Toni, Annie, Francine. They're all his girls."

Kris was stunned.

"What?"

"They service bands and recruit new girls to work with them. That's why I've been trying to keep you away from them. I could see they were trying to get you in with them and you're not like them at all. I didn't want you to get hurt."

It was Kris' turn to pace the room. She swung around.

"Toni was trying to recruit me? All those shows we went to? The backstage jaunts? The offers to get my stories published?"

He nodded.

Kris paced some more, then stopped suddenly.

"She mentioned something once about me 'pulling my weight,' but I had no clue what she meant, and she never brought it up again. Instead, she focused all her attention on Rusty."

"That's because Marius wants you kept as you are."

She stared at him. "What did you say?"

He looked down for a second, then back at her.

"I overheard Toni and Annie at the hotel the night Toni called with the offer to get your story published. They're his top girls. Marius is personally interested in you. That's one of the reasons I got involved. I wanted him to think you were with me and back off. He's very bad news."

Kris looked at him, apprehension in her emerald eyes.

"Did it work?"

"I'm not sure. The last time I talked to him, he tried to warn me off, but I told him no way, that you're the only one for me and I'm not giving you up. Since then, I've gotten weird calls where all I hear is Melody hacking away at herself and screaming bloody murder." He frowned. "I know they're from him, but he's not going to threaten me. I've never fought for anything in my life, but I'm not giving you up without a fight." He stood and faced her.

"This is the truth, Kris. There's no one else for me. I know I've laid a lot on you tonight. Please, whatever you do, don't hate me. I don't think I could take it if you hate me."

Kris' head was spinning. She searched his face, saw the pain and love etched in every line. She reached out and stroked his cheek.

"I can't hate you," she whispered. "I don't know what I feel, but I can't hate you."

"That's all I can ask for," he said, huskily. "I can build on that."

Chapter 48

"She hasn't responded to the invitation."

Toni heard a definite note of anger in Marius' voice and threw him a surprised look.

"She said she was going. She even talked about bringing her younger sister."

"She has a sister?' Marius' voice perked up slightly. "How charming. How young?"

"Fifteen, but Kris says she looks older. She bought her sister an outfit to wear to the show. A little too demure for my taste, but she is fifteen, after all."

"Well, well, well."

He chuckled, pushing her down on her hands and knees and positioning himself behind her.

"This makes me very happy. Can you feel how happy this makes me?"

He nudged his erection against her and smiled, reaching for the jar of Vaseline.

"Now, just close your eyes and imagine I'm Don Lyden."

Toni gritted her teeth. She knew what was coming next.

Chapter 49

"So, he told you everything." Linda's eyes were kind and concerned.

Kris nodded. The two were sharing coffee and the café near her apartment. Linda had insisted on seeing Kris as soon as she and Brian had gotten into town. Linda knew Marty had already been by. Now, he was at the hotel, giving Kris time to think.

Kris was happy to see Linda. She felt an affinity to his gentle woman, who lived the life of a rock star's wife, yet carried herself like a woman you'd meet at the neighborhood grocery store. Kris admired Linda's calm self-confidence in the face of all the glitz, flash, and flesh that surrounded her husband and his band mates, night after night. Linda felt no need to join in the dance. Her grip on her handsome husband was very solid.

The two talked about the tour after it had left New York City. Kris asked about groupies in other cities around the world.

"Are they the same as they are here?"

Linda pondered the question.

"There are groupies everywhere we go, but I have to say the boldest and flashiest are here in New York and out in Los Angeles. The groupies in Europe blend in more with the crowds, but American women, it seems, will do anything to stand out."

Linda gave a harsh laugh. "They're like peacocks, aren't they?" she mused. "The pretty peacocks are male, but that's what these groupies remind me of, strutting around and flashing their feathers. I guess they are a bit like men, too, aren't they? Going after what they want and damn the consequences!"

Kris had to agree. Everything she'd seen of Toni, Annie, even Charley, fit that description. They took aim at whichever guy they wanted and Heaven help anyone who got in their way. She told Linda she'd been thinking of writing a book about groupies. This idea amused Linda greatly.

"Oh, lass! It's sure to be a bestseller!" she laughed, then winked. "Especially if you include all the naughty bits!"

Kris blushed. "That's the hard part," she confessed.

Linda laughed again. "Just let your imagination wander. I doubt there's anything you can think of that hasn't been tried at least once."

She glanced at her watch and jumped up.

"I've got to run! Brian'll be wanting dinner soon."

She hugged Kris and insisted on paying the bill. With a promise to meet for the show, she dashed out the door.

Kris wandered up to her apartment, lost in thought. She'd had a lot of time to think about what Marty had said. In fact, she'd been thinking about Marty so much, she'd nearly made a critical error in a brief she'd typed up for her boss. Luckily, her friend Rose had caught it and brought it to her attention before she'd turned it in.

Linda had confirmed that Marty hadn't strayed, not once, since the band had left New York. He'd kept calling, even though she hadn't picked up the phone or called him back. His messages had been cheerful and upbeat. He'd shown up at her door, even after she'd told him to leave her alone. He'd bared his soul, telling her all about his past; sparing no painful detail.

Kris locked her door and sagged against it, struck by the realization that she didn't care who he'd been with; didn't care about his past. The only think she knew for certain was that she wanted to be with him – needed to be with him.

She collapsed on the couch, trembling. She didn't know how this would end, but she knew she couldn't go another minute without him. Slowly, she reached for the phone.

Ten breathless minutes later, the buzzer sounded and she paused, willing her heart to stop pounding so wildly. She deliberately took her time answering the door, pulling it open slowly. Marty stood there, hands in his pockets, eyes intense as they searched her face.

Kris reached out and pulled him into the apartment, closing the door behind him. His face was somber; his eyes, wary. He waited for her to speak. Instead, she stepped up, framed his face with her hands and pulled him toward her. Her eyes closed as their lips met, and her heartbeat quickened as she opened her mouth, deepening the kiss.

She wrapped her arms around him and pressed against him, her breath catching as she felt the extent of his arousal. He slid his hands down her back and pulled her even closer. Their tongues intertwined, making her head swim.

Marty suddenly broke the kiss and asked, raggedly, "Are you sure about this?"

She nodded, whispered, "yes," and led him to her bedroom.

He was as gentle as he was passionate, and when she finally cried out, his covered her mouth with his and stroked her until she stopped shaking, before quickening the pace to take his own release.

Afterward, he lay beside her, his arms and legs wrapped around her.

"That was worth waiting for," he said softly, kissing her ear, then her neck.

Kris snuggled closer to Marty, her face resting on his chest. He threaded his fingers through her hair.

"You're quiet, luv. Is everything all right?"

She sighed.

"Yes," she answered, kissing his chest. "Everything is definitely all right."

She felt him smile. "Just 'all right?'" he teased.

She smiled back. "You know what I mean," she retorted, poking him in the ribs.

Marty wined and grabbed her hands.

"I haven't the foggiest idea what you're talking about," he said, rolling on top of her. He pinned her hands on either side of her head and lowered his face to hers.

"Methinks another demonstration is in order," he murmured, claiming her mouth.

Kris gasped for air. She was drowning in a whirlpool of sensation. His hands and mouth seemed to be everywhere at once, leaving her unable to move. When he finally entered her, she came almost immediately, that whirlpool sweeping her right over the edge. She could feel every movement Marty made inside her, knew he was close, even as he moved faster, before collapsing on top of her with a strangled cry.

He remained inside her, holding her tightly, not wanting to release any part of her.

Kris must have fallen asleep. When she opened her eyes, sunlight was streaming into her bedroom. She reached out and felt an empty space where Marty had lain.

She frowned and sat up quickly, heart pounding. Had he left her?

She heard him humming in the kitchen and relaxed, snuggling back into her pillows and remembering their incredible night. Throwing back the covers, she leaped out of bed and pulled on his t-shirt, breathing in his scent on the material – sandalwood and musk.

Marty was popping bagels into the toaster as she walked in. Coffee brewed merrily in the pot, releasing its heavenly aroma into the air. He grinned at her, eyes twinkling.

"Ah, the lady awakens," he sang, leaning over to kiss her. "That shirt looks better on you than it does on me," he added, cupping her breasts through the thin fabric. "It doesn't make *me* look like a beautiful lass who just woke up after a night of glorious sex with a handsome bloke."

She laughed and reached for the coffee pot.

"So, Master Chef, what's for breakfast?"

Marty pulled her against him, wrapping his arms around her.

"Well," he said, into her neck. "I was going to make some eggs, but you seem to be fresh out." He kissed her neck and continued. "Then, I was going to make some cereal, but you're fresh out of that, too." He spun her around to face him. "In fact," he murmured against her lips. "Your cupboard and fridge are woefully bare."

He slid his ands under the t-shirt and caressed her bare skin. Her knees buckled and she held onto him for support as they made their way back to her bedroom; the bagels and coffee forgotten.

Chapter 50

Toni stretched luxuriously in the chair while Joey flitted around her, painting highlights into her hair. The only sound was that of foil crinkling as he wrapped each drenched strand. Two more days and Don Lyden was all hers! Toni closed her eyes and imagined the magical moment when he pulled her into his arms. Years of waiting, planning, and plotting, finally over. They would soon be face to face, skin to skin.

She would have to dress carefully. Marius had told her Don liked women who looked and acted demure on the surface, before revealing their naughty selves between the sheets. She could be innocent, Toni thought. Innocently naughty! She grinned wickedly, her blue eyes flashing. Joey grinned back, brush in hand.

"What's going on in that pretty head of yours?" he asked.

"Oh, just thinking about how all my dreams are about to come true!' she said, gaily.

"Good for you!" he encouraged. "You go and grab that golden ring!"

"Oh, I intend to grab more than that," she replied, slyly.

An hour later, her hair freshly highlighted, she swaggered down to Charlotte's Harlots. She found Charlotte lounging behind the counter, reading a trashy romance novel. She glanced up as the bell over the door tinkled, and smiled at Toni.

"Love your hair!" she gushed.

"Thanks," Toni replied airily, strolling over to the rack of lace tops.

Charlotte turned back to her book. She knew Toni liked to browse on her own and didn't need help putting outfits together. So, she was surprised when Toni called her over a few minutes later.

"Char, I need help choosing an outfit that makes me look a bit... demure."

Charlotte gave her a sharp look. "Demure? Now, why would the world's sexiest rock goddess want to look 'demure'?"

"I just need to," Toni snapped, suddenly irritated. She flung an arm out at the row of lace tops. "What's demure here?"

Charlotte led her away from the lace, over to a row of peasant blouses.

"You want to avoid lace, spandex, rubber. Stick to simple lines. Hide the goods, but not the femininity."

She pulled a blouse off the rack. Toni eyed it dubiously. It was made of gauzy material in a cotton candy pink color. Charlotte pulled a pair of jeans in soft blue denim off another rack and handed both to Toni.

"Try these on," she said briskly.

Toni grabbed the clothes and stepped behind the curtain. She emerged several minutes later, feeling very awkward. She caught Charlotte's stare and spun to face the mirror.

She gasped. She looked ten years younger than her 33 years. The blouse clung where it should and fell away where it should. The neckline gave an illusion of revealing more than it did.

Toni lifted the shirt to see the jeans. They fit like a glove, but didn't look obscene. She let the shirt drop and checked her reflection again. On a whim, she pulled her hair back. The effect made her look even younger, especially with wispy bangs clinging to her forehead.

Charlotte stared at Toni as though she'd lost her mind.

"I don't know what you're up to, but the change is amazing," she remarked.

Toni whirled to face her. "You think so?"

Charlotte nodded, still looking at Toni as though she'd gone around the bend.

"Great," said Toni. "I'll take these."

She stepped back behind the curtain and changed back into her leather pants and red spandex vest. Five minutes later, she was strolling down Bleecker Street, swinging her shopping bag idly as she tried to figure out where to get the demure undergarments Marius suggested she buy. Don apparently like women to wear simple white cotton panties, like the kind schoolgirls wore. Where the hell would she find those in Manhattan? She decided a department store would be her best bet. She left her car parked where it was and took the uptown subway. Macy's should have what she needed, and parking in Midtown was a bitch.

Toni found what she was looking for at Macy's, paid and quickly made her way back downtown to meet Annie and Marius. Forgoing the subway, she took a cab to the diner they'd chosen, and sighed with relief as she spotted Annie sitting in a back booth. Marius hadn't arrived yet. He hated anyone being late to a meeting with him.

She slid into the booth opposite Annie and stashed her bags. Her friend glanced curiously at them but didn't ask, and Toni didn't volunteer any information. She could see

Annie was irritated about something. The dark-haired woman kept tapping her fingers impatiently on the tabletop.

"Where the hell is he?" Annie growled, lighting a cigarette and ignoring the disapproving looks from the people at the next table. "I've got a lot to do before the show."

Toni shrugged and gulped the coffee the waitress set before her. The diner door swung open and Marius strolled in. He filled the restaurant with his presence, but he seemed unaware of the attention he was getting from the other diners. The owner scurried over to help him, but Marius waved him off and made his way over to where Toni and Annie sat. He squeezed in next to Annie, giving her a stern look. Guiltily, she stubbed out her cigarette.

"A filthy habit," he chided. "I thought I'd asked you to quit."

He looked across the table at Toni.

"And coffee…" he murmured.

She opened her purse and took out her breath spray, but he shook his head.

"Coffee needs a toothbrush," he said quietly. "You both need toothbrushes."

He sat and sipped his own coffee while they did his bidding. When they returned to the table, he smiled benignly at them. They hung their heads slightly, like two wayward children caught in some misdeed.

"Much better, he said approvingly. "Now, ladies, we have some plans to make."

Chapter 51

*Marius leaned back in his deep leather armchair, fingers steepled under his chin, fuming. Marty was not backing off the filly! He'd just told Marius that Kris knew all about his dark, sordid past. Knew, and accepted Marty anyway. The little prick had warned **him** to keep his hands off!*

His hands clenched into fists, then relaxed, as another plan came to mind. He knew just how to separate them and he didn't need Toni's help. The bitch had been useless about this from the start.

Marius' lip curled as he thought about her. Poor Toni. Her one great, unfulfilled desire – Don Lyden – could care less about her. This one already had his randy eye on Kris' sister. The fifteen-year-old. The jail bait. He had called before going onstage, asking Marius to set up a "meeting." Marius chuckled. Oh, if the world only knew Don Lyden's dirty little secret.

Marius looked up as the door opened and two naked women walked in. Their skin glistened with oil; their hair framed their faces silkily. The women stopped, bowed to him, to each other, then began wrestling, their limbs blending as their bodies intertwined.

He tried to focus on the erotic sight, but couldn't stop thinking about Kris and that little prick. He knew he had a foolproof plan to get Kris for himself, but felt an overwhelming urge to punish the bastard who had sullied her; ruined her virginal image for him.

Marius heaved himself out of his chair and snapped his fingers at the women. They stopped writhing and turned their faces toward him, still on their knees.

"You're both lovely, but it's not working," he rumbled. "Go bathe and perfume yourselves, and prepare for the arrival of our guests."

Stepping around them, he pulled the door open to his secret office. Once inside, he opened a file cabinet drawer and flicked through several folders. He found the one he wanted and pulled it out. Smiling grimly, he said, "Marty's past is about to bite his balls off."

Chuckling again, he left the office and went to check on the party preparations.

Chapter 52

In the lull between Lizard Lust and Dark Disciple, Kris, Kim and Linda stayed in their seats and chatted. Linda was in the midst of recounting a funny encounter with a Customs agent in Budapest when the lights suddenly went out. The crowd lapsed into an expectant silence, as though it had drawn a collective breath and held it.

Somewhere on stage, a deep purple light began to throb. An over-modulated bass guitar kept time with it, each note sending vibrations through the packed arena. The purple light flashed on and off several times. Then, as it held, a high, quavering guitar note pierced the air. That sound faded, then picked up again. This time, it wasn't a guitar, but a voice – high, strong and clear. It held and held, the bass guitar building up a rhythm. As the note broke off, the drums crashed to life and the stage flared with light, revealing the band – two guitarists, bassist, drummer and The Monk.

He was unnaturally tall and thin, dressed in a brown, hooded robe held closed by a belt made of large, wooden rosary beads. His voice pierced the air again and this time, as it trailed away, the robe fell off, revealing a figure dressed entirely in black leather. The Monk Ripped the microphone off the stand, and the band kicked into action.

The show was unlike any Kris had ever seen. The band used different colored mist, lasers and a giant crystal ball with a huge eye glinting from its center. The music; dark and throbbing, contained a mystical quality that enthralled the crowd. Where Marty had jumped and gyrated across every inch of the stage, The Monk's presence filled the entire arena as he stood still, the audience mesmerized by his commanding wail.

Dark Disciple played two encores before the lights came up on a spent and breathless crowd. The same security guard who'd shown them to their seats turned up to lead them backstage. The backstage area was a state of controlled chaos. Linda led them expertly through the sea of bodies to the refreshment table, where they helped themselves to bottles of water and settled into seats near the back wall, watching the action ebb and flow around them.

They spotted Don Lyden, surrounded by a group of beautiful women. He seemed both amused and bored by the attention. He chuckled at something the scantily-clad redhead next to him said, then gently disentangled himself from their groping hands. He looked around, spotted them and walked purposely toward them, waving cheerfully.

"Hullo, ladies!" He called out. "How did you like the show?" He smiled warmly at Kim, who blushed and smiled back.

"We enjoyed it, as usual," said Linda, as Kris and Kim nodded. Don's answering grin faded to a grimace as he noticed a gaggle of women heading his way. With a quick, "Excuse me," he took off in the opposite direction.

Kris, Kim and Linda shared a laugh over Don's dilemma, and spent the next few minutes talking about the show and the assorted men and women wandering backstage. They spotted Brian and Marty weaving through the crowd in their direction, stopping every now and then to shake a hand, sign an autograph or pose for a photo. Kris' heart swelled as she watched Marty draw nearer. She could relive their passionate night just by closing her eyes. She opened them and caught Marty looking at her, a wicked grin on his face. He knew just what she'd been thinking.

It took Marty and Brian several minutes to reach the women, but they did so with kisses all around. Nate ambled up behind them, balancing bottles of beer for Marty and Brian.

"Oh, hey, Marty," he said. "Billy's looking for you. Says he's got a message."

Marty looked puzzled, but said amiably, "I'd better go look for him, then."

He kissed Kris and told the group to go to the party without him; he'd catch a ride with Billy. With a wave, he walked off. The rest of the group collected their things and piled into taxis for the drive uptown.

The party was at a brownstone on the Upper West Side. A valet helped them out of their cabs and directed them up a set of stone steps ending at a shiny black door, which swung open before they reached the top step. A tall, slender woman dressed in a robe of shimmering gold stood at the entrance. Silky black hair framed her oval face, and almond shaped brown eyes sparkled as she smiled in welcome. She waved them in with an elegant sweep of one arm.

The entry way emptied into a high-ceilinged room; bare except for a heavy round table laden with flutes of champagne. They each picked up a glass and made their way into another, more cavernous room. Sheets billowed from the high ceilings, reflecting of lights that changed color in time with the music pumping in through speakers built into the walls. People milled about, drinking and chatting.

A petite woman with red hair, also dressed in a golden robe, stepped forward and beckoned them toward an archway. They followed her and found themselves in a room decorated entirely in shades of red: red walls, red couches and deep, red velvet cushions. They found Billy's girlfriend lunching on one couch, looking bored and sulky. She brightened a little as they walked in.

"Is Billy with you?" she asked.

"He had to talk to Marty," Nate replied, plopping down next to her. "They should be here soon."

She seemed pacified by this news, drained her champagne and looked around for another. At that moment, two robed women wandered into the room. One balanced a tray of cocktails, while the other carried a tray laden with finger foods. Everyone helped themselves to egg rolls and more champagne, then comfortably settled themselves on a couch and chatted, as the room slowly filled with guests.

Billy showed up half an hour later, looking uncomfortable and a little drunk. When Kris asked him where Marty was, he didn't answer and wouldn't meet her eyes.

When she pressed him, he mumbled, "He's here."

"Here where?" Kris persisted.

"Yes, where?" Linda echoed, brows drawing together in a frown.

Billy looked at his feet. Then, in a low voice, he said, "I saw him with… Charley."

The news hit Kris like a punch in the stomach. She couldn't speak.

Linda looked outraged. "What's he doing with *her*?" she demanded.

Billy shrugged, eyes still glued to the floor. "Dunno. I went looking for him after the show and saw him stagger out with her. I thought maybe he and Kris had a row and he was looking to get laid. When I got out of the cab a few minutes ago, I saw them heading upstairs."

He pulled his girlfriend to her feet. Still not meeting Kris' eye, he mumbled, "Sorry," and led his girlfriend out of the room.

Kris tried to catch her breath. She willed herself not to throw up in front of the others. The champagne churned in her stomach like a vile acid. She set her glass down and noticed her hand was shaking.

"I've got to find a bathroom," she said, and walked jerkily from the room; the others staring worriedly after her. She spotted a robed woman ahead of her and tapped her on the shoulder, asking for a restroom. The woman regarded her for a moment, then said, "Follow me."

She led Kris through another archway, up a flight of stairs and down a maze of hallways. Kris wondered abstractedly how all this could fit into one brownstone, before realizing the building spanned an entire block.

The woman stopped in front of a door.

"Here you go," she said softly, before turning and swiftly walking away.

Kris turned the handle and pushed the door open. With the part of her mind that still functioned, she marveled at the beauty of the room. At its center was a square, black marble tub that looked large enough to comfortably hold ten people. A double sink in the same black marble took up one wall. The gleaming marble was offset by gold fixtures and towel racks held hand towels that looked to be made of spun gold.

Kris lurched to the sink and twisted the cold-water tap. She ran her wrists under the tap and splashed water on her face. She sat on the edge of the tub and tried to imagine what could have driven Marty to Charley. Something about this just didn't reel right. The lurching feeling in her stomach eased as her mind cleared. She needed to find out exactly what was going on. She dried her hands and left the bathroom.

Looking up and down the hallway, Kris tried to remember which way she'd come. She heard voices drifting from a nearby room. The door was slightly open and one of the voices sounded familiar. She moved closer and heard the voices again. One was Marty. She also recognized the other, husky female voice.

Kris reached out a trembling hand and pushed the door open. Marty was sprawled, naked, on a massive bed covered with black satin sheets. His head lolled from side to side as he mumbled incoherently. Straddling him and moving furiously up and down was Charley.

Kris backed away, but not in time. Charley swung her head around, spotted Kris, and smiled lewdly.

Marty grunted. Charley turned back to face him and leaned down, her breasts swinging in his face.

"What's that?" she crooned. "You're coming? Oh, so am I, baby! So am I!" She made panting noises, shuddered and collapsed on top of him.

Kris turned and ran blindly down the hallway, fighting the urge to vomit all over the carpet. She ran smack into a solid figure and fell back. Hands grabbed and steadied her.

"Hey," rumbled a deep, calm voice. "Where's the fire?"

"I've got to get out of here," gasped Kris, trying to wrench away.

"There, there," said the voice soothingly. "Let's get you somewhere to sit down, and a drink to calm your nerves."

The hands steered Kris through a door. Dimly, she registered that she was in a study. She was guided to a deep leather armchair. Seconds later, a small glass was pressed into her trembling hands.

"Brandy," said the voice. "Very calming. Drink up."

Kris took a sip. The liquid burned a trail down to her stomach and she grimaced. The room came more clearly into view, as did the man standing in front of her. He was very talk, with coarse black hair and shining, dark eye, which looked kind and concerned.

"Finish the brandy," he said gently, and she obediently brought the glass to her lips and sipped again.

"Good," said the man, taking the glass from her. He kneeled in front of her. "Now, tell me what's upset you. I don't like having unhappy guests at my gatherings."

Kris stared at him.

"This is your house?"

"Yes, this is my humble little abode. Allow me to introduce myself. My name is Marius Man. You may call me Marius."

"Mr. M-Man?" Kris stammered.

"It's Marius," he repeated softly. "And I know who you are. It's a pleasure to meet you, Miss Kris Lindsey, the budding journalist."

He stood, pulled another chair over, and lowered himself into it.

"So, Miss Lindsey, tell me what's upset you so greatly." He patted her hand, his large fingers dwarfing her own. She resisted the urge to snatch her hand away.

"I... nothing," she replied. Her head had started spinning. She blinked hard to remain focused.

"Nothing? Come now. What happened? Did you... see something, by any chance?"

Kris stared at him, but there seemed to be two faces smiling back at her. His fingers were now tracing a path up her arm. This time, she did try to pull away, but her arm wouldn't cooperate.

"What are you doing?" She fought to get the words out.

"I'm trying to help calm you. Perhaps it was the sight of our illustrious Mr. Brinkman taking advantage of our charming Miss Charley that sent you running so blindly into my arms? Hmmm?"

Somehow, he was behind her now, massaging her shoulders with his large hands. She tried to tell him to stop, but could not speak. Her head fell back. She couldn't think anymore. She just wanted to sleep. Her eyes closed.

Chapter 54

Toni entered the brownstone with Rusty. Rusty had been shocked by Toni's appearance. Everyone had. Toni felt uncomfortable in the peasant blouse and jeans, but she reminded herself that Don was worth it.

They picked up their glasses of champagne and wandered from room to room. Toni spotted Kris' sister sitting with Linda, Brian and Nate. There was no sign of Kris or Marty. She wondered whether Marius had put his plan into action yet.

She watched a golden-robed woman approach Kris' sister and speak into her ear. The teen nodded and followed the woman toward the stairs Toni knew led up to the special bedrooms. Now, where would that woman be leading the girl?

She started as someone tapped her shoulder and turned to see Rusty standing next to her again, beaming with excitement. She'd learned the identity of the rich rock star who wanted to meet her. She was on her way to a rendezvous with The Monk.

"Have a great time," Toni said. "I promise you'll have a night you never forget."

Rusty stared at her, nonplussed. "Have you already been with him?" she asked, self-consciously.

"Oh, good God, no!" spat Toni. "I've just... heard a lot about him."

227

She pushed Rusty toward the stairs. "You go and have a great time."

As Rusty tottered away, Toni thought, "He'll either break Rusty or turn her into one hell of an ice queen." The Monk was not normal when it came to sex. Not normal at all.

She weaved through the throngs of people now gathered in the cavernous front room, keeping an eye out for Don Lyden. Marius had promised to keep him for her. She spotted Don a few minutes later and started to walk toward him, when she saw the robed woman who had come for Kris' sister approach Don. He leaned down as she spoke in his ear, then grinned and nodded, motioning for her to lead the way. They headed toward the same stairs the woman had led Kim to a short time earlier.

Eyes narrowing in suspicion, Toni followed them, making sure to keep far enough away that they wouldn't notice her. The woman led Don down a far hallway then stopped in front of a door. He smiled and said something to her, then disappeared into the room.

Toni ducked into another room as the woman headed in her direction. She heard the woman pass, then slowly pulled the door open and stepped back into the hallway. She made her way up the hall to the room Don had entered.

She pressed her ear to the door and heard muffled conversation. A moment later, a female voice rose in pitch, sounding panicked. A male voice laughed. She heard a scuffle, then the female voice screamed, and the male voice called out in anger. The female voice screamed again, then Toni heard a scrabbling on the other side of the door.

She wrenched it open and Kris' sister fell into her arms, her shirt ripped in two, hair disheveled, and eyes wild with terror.

"Help me," she begged, throwing her arms around Toni. Toni stared over her head into the room. A naked Don Lyden was striding to the door, his long hair flowing around bare shoulders; his erection, huge. Toni stared from it to his face, which was scarlet with rage.

"What the fuck are you doing, bursting in here like that?" he screamed. He reached out for Kim, who shrank behind Toni.

"Don't leave me with him! Please!" she cried, hysterically.

Toni stared from Don to Kim.

"What the hell were you doing in here with him, then, if not to fuck him.?" She demanded.

"I didn't know he was coming in here!" Kim shrieked. "The lady told me my sister needed me. She brought me here to wait and said she'd bring Kris to me. She said Kris was sick."

Kim stared fearfully at Don.

"Then... he came in here. First, he said he wanted to talk until Kris got here. Then, he told me how pretty I was, and how young and fresh I was. He asked me to kiss him. Then... he ripped my shirt off... and..." She broke down and sobbed. "I told him I was only fifteen, but he said he liked his girls young. He said..." She choked. "He said he liked to teach them!" She threw her arms around Toni. "Please don't make me go back in there!" she begged.

Toni stared from Kim to Don, comprehension slowly dawning on her face. Don didn't like his women to *look* young. He liked them young, period.

Rage welled up inside her; rage at Marius for letting her believe she had a chance with Don, known all the while that he was a pervert; rage at Don Lyden for preferring younger girls; rage at herself and the depths to which she had let herself sink, for the chance to fuck this bastard.

She turned to Kim and pointed to a stairway.

"Those stairs take you to the main party room – the one with the sheets. You should be able to find the red room, where Linda and the others are."

Kim stared at her, then asked, "What about Kris? Is she okay?"

"I don't know," Toni answered grimly. "But I'm going to find out."

She gently pushed Kim toward the stairs.

"Go. Linda will take care of you."

Kim stumbled down the hall, trying to hold the ripped edges of her blouse together.

Toni swung around and marched into the room, slamming the door behind her.

Don, who had quietly watched the exchange between Kim and Toni, now spoke.

"I swear, I didn't know she was fifteen," he said. "She looks older, even you have to admit that."

Toni didn't answer. She seethed with anger and revulsion.

He took a step toward her. "You're very pretty, too, and sweet looking." His erection, which had drooped slightly, perked up again.

She noticed and said, icily, "Oh, so you want to play with *me* now?

A slow smile spread across his face.

"I just want a little resistance. Act like it's your first time. You know, a little role playing. That's what I was trying to do with Kim, until she freaked out on me. She thought I really wanted to rape her!" He laughed nervously, then flashed a charming smile at Toni, who looked at him scornfully.

"You expect me to believe that shit?"

He stepped toward her. "It's the truth. I swear it! We can have a good time. You look the part, nice and innocent."

He grabbed her arm. "Let me force you a little. It makes things more fun."

For some reason, the image of Billy bending her over the boxes in the hotel storage room flashed in Toni's mind as Don reached out, grabbed her by the hair and pulled her head back to he could kiss her. As he forced his tongue into her mouth, she bit down, hard.

He leaped back with a howl of pain.

"You bitch!" he shouted thickly, blood seeping through his lips and down his chin.

"I thought you said you wanted me to resist you," she said sweetly. "You know, a little 'role playing.'"

Toni sidestepped him as he tried to slap her. She kicked him hard, between the legs. He crumbled in agony. She kicked him again, tears blurring her vision, her guttural scream a mixture of fury and anguish.

Leaving Don writhing on the floor, she wrenched the door open and stormed out of the room, straight into Marty Brinkman. His eyes were slightly unfocused and he was naked, except for a towel he clutched around his waist.

"Hey, watchit," he slurred, steadying himself against the wall.

Toni glared at him. "Where the hell are your clothes?"

He shook his head, looking foggy. "Dunno. Had a horrible dream. Woke up naked in a bed."

Toni peered at him closely. He'd obviously been drugged.

"Where's Kris?" she demanded.

"Kris? Haven't seen her." He shook his head, like a dog shaking off excess water. "Dreamed about her, too. Bad one."

Toni led him to the bathroom. She stuck his head under the cold water tap and turned it on full blast. He helped and tried to back away, but she held his head firmly, letting the icy water run over his face.

"Okay! Okay!" he spluttered. "I'm better!"

She released her grip and he came up for air. Water dripped down his face. Holding the towel around his waist with one hand, he grabbed a hand towel with the other hand and wiped his face. She noticed his vision had cleared.

"Where's Kris?" he asked.

"That's what I just asked you," she replied. "I just saved her sister from Don Lyden. From the looks of things, a few minutes longer and he would have succeeded in raping her."

Marty looked alarmed. "Kim? Don Lyden?"

"Oh, yes," she said bitterly. "Fucking pervert."

The alarm on Marty's face turned to panic. "Kris. He said he'd leave her alone."

Toni laughed harshly. "He's had his eye on her since he first saw her. I'm sure he's got her under lock and key somewhere."

Marty strode to the bathroom door and jerked it open.

"I've got to find her," he said urgently.

"Not like that, you're not."

He tucked the towel firmly around his waist and stepped into the hallway. With a sigh, Toni followed him.

They heard a commotion on the stairs, then Nate and Brian appeared. They spotted Marty and Toni, and hurried toward them.

"What the hell is going on?" Brian demanded, eyeing Marty's getup and looking from him to Toni.

"Kim's in a right state. Says Lyden tried to rape her. Linda's taken her to Kris' place."

He looked around. "Where's Kris? Where are your trousers? And what's this about you being with Charley?"

"Dunno, mate," Marty replied. "Woke up starkers. I think I was drugged. I don't even remember Charley." He turned incredulous eyes to Brian. "I was with *Charley*?"

"That's what Billy told us," said Nate.

Marty looked confused. "I remember Billy giving me a beer, then waking up in a bed. I did have a bad dream, though. I dreamed that Kris walked in on my having sex with Charley."

He shook his head. "But I'd never be with Charley! Not after last time!"

"Well, she came up these stairs," said Brian. "She was looking for a bathroom, after Billy told her about you and Charley. No one's seen her come back down."

Marty turned to Toni. "Does this hallway have another exit?"

Toni shook her head. "This is the hallway with the special bedrooms," she explained. "There's only one way to get here, and it's by using those stairs." She pointed to the stairs Brian and Nate had just climbed.

"Well, then, she's got to be here somewhere," Marty said grimly. He marched up the hall, throwing doors open as he went. The first three rooms were empty. In the fourth, they found Rusty, tied spread-eagled to the bed, The Monk leaning over her. There were angry red welts all over Rusty's body. She looked at them, her mouth gagged, eyes wide in fear.

Marty did a double-take.

"Are you okay?"

Tremulously, Rusty nodded.

The Monk glared at them.

"She's perfectly okay," he snapped, in a clipped tone.

"Are you sure, luv?" Nate asked gently.

Rusty nodded again.

"Okay, then. Sorry we bothered you." Marty made to pull the door closed, when Toni caught the look on Rusty's face. Rusty was glaring at her, eyes filled with hate.

Toni felt a stab of guilt. She should have warned Rusty just what she was getting herself into with The Monk. It was too late now.

The rest of the rooms were empty, except for the last, which was locked. Marty pounded on it.

"Open up!" he yelled. There was no answer for several minutes, then the door swung open quietly and Marius stepped out, pulling it closed behind him.

"What is all this racket?" he said coldly, his glittering black eyes sweeping over them. "I have guests who require privacy and discretion."

"Where's Kris?" Marty demanded.

Marius looked at Marty with amusement. "The question I would ask is, where are your clothes?"

"Fuck you," spat Toni. "Just answer his fucking question."

Marius turned his gaze to her.

"Very innocent," he said approvingly. "Why aren't you sharing your wares with Mr. Lyden?"

Taking in her look of rage and revulsion, he nodded understandingly.

"Ah, you learned you were a little too, how shall we say it, 'mature' for his tastes, perhaps?"

He smiled. "I'm afraid some men do prefer their meat fresh, not spoiled past their expiration date. But, come. I'm sure I can find someone who will have you."

He made to walk down the hall, when Marty, Nate and Brian blocked his way.

"You're not going anywhere," Marty growled, crossing his arms across his chest.

Marius' brows rose in surprise.

"Are you threatening me, Marty? After all we've been through?"

His gaze swept the rest of them, then his voice grew cold.

"I think it's best that you leave now, before I'm forced to call security."

Turning his back on them, he placed a hand on the doorknob and turned it. In that split second, Marty pushed past him into the room, Nate and Brian on his heels.

The room was dark, lit only by candles on a nightstand next to the bed. They spotted a form huddled on the bed, dressed in white.

Marty rushed over and saw Kris curled up, wearing a white lace dress, sheer white stocking, and red, high heeled pumps. Her auburn hair fanned out on the pillow, framing her face. Her eyes were closed and she appeared to be asleep.

Marty heard Toni mutter behind him, "Oh, my God, you had Charlotte get you another dress, in case she didn't wear hers to the show tonight."

Marty turned back to the bed. Stepping up, he shook Kris gently.

"Wake up, luv," he said. She didn't move.

He shook her again, more insistently.

"Kris, please wake up."

She stirred slightly, then mumbled, "Marty?"

"Yes, luv, it's Marty. Come on, wake up, so we can get you out of here."

"Go 'way," she mumbled, frowning, her eyes still closed. "Saw you… Charley."

"What?" He looked over at Marius. Saw the smile of satisfaction on his face.

Marius stepped around the group to the other side of the bed. Laying a hand on Kris' head, he said, "You heard the lady. She doesn't want you here. Go back to Charley and whatever you were doing. She's staying right here."

"Like Hell!"

Marty shoved Marius aside and tried to gather Kris in his arms. His towel slipped and fell to the floor. She struggled weakly against him.

"No… don't want you."

Nate strode forward and took Kris from Marty.

"Shh…" he said softly. "Here's Nate, your friend. I've got you."

"Nate?" Kris murmured, eyelids fluttering.

"Yes, it's good old Nate," he said. Her head fell against his shoulder.

"Nate… saw Marty… Charley… it was horrible." Her eyes closed again.

"Been drugged, she has!" said Brian angrily, as Nate left the room carrying Kris.

Marty picked up the towel and wrapped it around his waist. He turned toward Marius, anger coursing through his veins.

"You son of a bitch! You'll never get your filthy hands on her again! I'll kill you first!"

Marius eyed Marty with hatred. "You'll pay for this, Brinkman," he muttered. "My revenge is already in the works. Enjoy your final days of freedom."

Marty glared at him. "Bring it on," he retorted. "You tell my secrets, I'll tell yours. Either way, you won't get Kris."

He pushed roughly past Marius and into the hallway, the others right behind him.

Chapter 55

Toni helped the others get Kris home. She and Linda helped Kris into the shower and turned on the cold water. After a few minutes, Kris began shivering, looking wildly at Toni and Linda.

"Where am I? What are you doing here?" She looked down at her clothes. "Why am I wearing this dress?"

"You're home," Linda replied gently. "We brought you home."

Kris blanched. "Marty?"

"He's outside, luv."

The memory of him and Charley flooded into her mind. Bile rose in her throat.

"Gonna be sick," she said, then vomited over herself.

Linda helped her wash as Toni searched for clean clothes. When she returned, Kris looked at her, teeth chattering.

"What are you doing here?" she asked.

"Long story," said Toni shortly. She paused. "Look. What you saw with Marty."

Kris shook her head. "I don't want to talk about it."

"Marius set it up. Marty was drugged."

"No. I saw him. He was enjoying himself."

"Of course he was!" snapped Toni. "He was doped up. Out of his mind. I know, I ran into him later, wandering the hall naked."

"He was drugged?"

"Yes, and so were you," said Linda brusquely, helping Kris step into a pair of sweatpants. Kris' legs felt like jelly and she grabbed Linda's shoulders for support.

Linda slowly led Kris out of the bathroom and into her bedroom. Toni pulled back the covers as Linda helped Kris into bed.

"Thank you," said Kris, weakly, sinking into the pillows, then suddenly sitting back up.

"Kim!" she cried.

"She's okay," said Linda, shaking her head warningly at Toni over Kris' head. "She's outside with the rest. Now, you sleep," she said firmly, pulling the covers up.

Kris closed her eyes. When she awoke, sunlight was streaming in the window. Marty was sleeping on a chair next to the bed.

"Marty," she croaked. Her throat felt dry and scratchy.

His eyes flew open and he sat up.

"How are you feeling, luv?" he asked gently.

"Horrible headache. Throat hurts."

He picked up a glass of water from the bedside table and held it to her lips. She drank deeply and leaned back into her pillows.

"What happened?" she asked.

"Seems old Marius had plans for all of us," he said grimly.

"All of us?" She looked confused.

"He drugged me and set you up to mind me engaged what he hoped you'd see as mind blowing sex with Charley. Then, he stepped in to mend your broken heart."

"He seemed so nice, at first," she remembered. "So concerned. He gave me brandy." She grew quiet. "But, he seemed creepy at the same time. He kept touching me."

Marty made a convulsive gesture.

"That 'nice' man laced your brandy with a drug to knock you out," he said. "He'd planned for me to be out for a while. Charley was supposed to give me a second dose after her little act, but she forgot. Toni found me wandering the hall wearing nothing but a towel."

"You said 'all of us' – who else was he after?" She dreaded the answer.

"Well..." Marty paused. "He had designs for your sister. Not for him, but for Don Lyden. Seems he's got a thing for young girls."

Kris gasped and sat up. Marty gently eased her back onto the pillows.

"She's fine. Toni saved her before Don could do anything. Good set of lungs your sister's got. Toni heard her screaming through the door."

"Toni – she must be so angry. She's wanted Don Lyden for as long as I've known her."

"From what I heard, she beat the crap out of him. Nearly bit his tongue in two."

Marty smiled. "Kim's fine, luv. In fact, I'd better get her."

He leaned forward and kissed her softly. "I don't want to lose you," he said, his voice ragged. He cupped her face in his hands, his eyes searching hers. She could see pain in the liquid brown depths. He pressed his lips to here again, then pulled away. Her heart filled with pain as he left the room.

Kim burst in seconds later. The sisters hugged hard, both crying.

Kris saw the hurt in Kim's eyes; the loss of innocence. Kim caught her looking and smiled through her tears.

"I'm okay," she said. "I'll be okay. Nothing happened. Toni got there in time."

She hugged Kris again and said, "I'm so glad they got there in time for you, too!"

Kris threw back the covers and got out of bed. She found she could stand, without having the room spin around her. Kim helped her dress. They found Marty in the kitchen, making coffee. Kris looked at Kim, who nodded and left the room.

Kris took the steaming mug from him and set it on the counter, moving away as he held his arms out to pull her to him.

Taking a steadying breath, she said, "Marty, we can't go on. I want you to leave."

He looked stunned. "What do you mean?"

She took another deep breath. "Last night was... horrible. I don't want to go through anything like that again."

His brown eyes bored into hers, intense. "You won't," he said fervently. "I promise." He tried to take her hands, but she pulled them away.

"My sister was nearly raped. I was drugged. This is too much to handle."

His eyes were now pleading. "I explained. It won't happen again."

"It's not enough." It took all her strength to turn away from him. "Please go."

He was silent for a moment, then said, in a quiet voice, "If that's what you want."

She kept her back to him as she nodded.

"Okay, luv. I'm sorry." Quietly, he left the kitchen. Seconds later, she heard the front door open and close.

Kim rushed into the kitchen.

"What happened?" she cried.

"I sent him away."

"He's coming back, though, right?"

Kris shook her head, tears spilling from her eyes.

Kim looked at her incredulously. "He saved you from that man!" she said. "How could you send him away?"

"It's because I was with him that I got into that predicament in the first place," Kris said, swiping at her tears with the palm of her hand. "You, too. You could have been raped. I can't live with that."

"That's not fair," said Kim. "He loves you. I know he does. And I know you love him, too."

"It's not enough," cried Kris, holding back a fresh flood of tears. "I'm not cut out for this kind of life!"

Kim looked at her without speaking. Then, she said, softly, "Maybe you're not."

Chapter 56

Kim wanted to stay with Kris for a few more days, but Kris insisted her sister return home to the Jersey shore. In truth, Kris wanted Kim as far away from New York City as possible. As much as Kim insisted she was all right, Kris knew her sister had her own healing to do.

She stayed inside her apartment, curtains closed against the light. She let the answering machine pick up the calls, picking up only when Kim called to say she'd gotten home safely. Linda called twice, concern evident in her voice, but Kris didn't have the energy to talk to her.

Linda's third call got her attention.

"Kris, luv, it's Linda. Please pick up if you're home. (pause) Oh well, I guess I've missed you, then. I so hoped to see you before we left, but I understand. (pause) Well, I'll try to ring you when we get home to England. You take care, luv."

Kris listened to the message dully. So, they were leaving. She'd never see Marty again. Grimly, she told herself it was for the best.

David MacGregor called, wanting her to interview a thrash band called Puppet Master. She called him back and asked him to find someone else. Her heart just wasn't in it anymore.

He listened silently, then said, in an unusually quiet voice, "Don't be angry, but Marty told me what happened. It's terrible, but then again, Marius Man is a terrible, filthy man. And he is NOT representative of everyone in the music industry. Yes, there are shitty bands and shitty people out there, but there are good bands, too, and a helluva lot of good people. You're a damn good writer, Kris. Don't throw it away because some piece of shite like Marius."

When she didn't respond, he said gently, "Just say you'll consider it. They don't get into town until next week. They're a great bunch of guys. I know you'll do a great story."

She promised to think about it and hung up.

Kris sat and stared blankly at the walls around her. She remembered making love with Marty on this couch, remembered the pleasure they'd given each other; how he'd made her tremble and moan, right here on the floor. There wasn't a room in the apartment that didn't hold a memory of Marty and the passion they'd shared.

She jumped up, stuffed her feet into sneakers, grabbed her keys and left the apartment. She walked aimlessly, then found herself outside the café. Not ready to go home yet, she stepped inside and ordered a cappuccino, only to leave it untouched as she stared into space.

The bartender's voice cut into her reverie. "Hey, I think that guy is trying to get your attention. He keeps walking past the window." He pointed to the plate glass window running the length of the café. Marty stood outside, gazing in at her, pain in his eyes. He reached up and touched the glass. Tears welled up as she looked at him. Slowly, she shook her head and looked down, her tears splashing onto the table. When she looked up again, Marty was gone.

Chapter 57

Toni stood behind the counter, watching customers browse throughs tacks of albums. Her mind replayed the night over the party over and over again. Don with Kris' sister. Don, the fucking pervert. Marius had known all along. She felt sick with disgust.

She had fantasized for months about a monster – a monster who liked to force young girls to have sex with him. And Marius had known what Don really was, all along. Her stomach churned with acid and she felt the urge to smash things; felt the urge to rush Marius and unleash her fury on his mocking face.

She hadn't heard from Rusty since the party, either. She hoped Rusty had survived her night with The Monk, without too many scars.

Her thoughts turned to Kris, who'd called and left a message thanking her for saving Kim. But, she hadn't seen Kris around lately, either. She usually came into the record store about once a week. She hoped Kris had survived her ordeal. She and Marty were probably shacked up, she thought, and felt a sudden twinge of jealousy.

"Hey, gorgeous!"

Bobby's voice brought her back to reality. The Hardwire singer was standing on the other side of the counter, grinning at her, blue eyes twinkling merrily.

"What are you doing here?" she asked.

"Hadn't seen you in a while," he replied, "so I figured I'd come find you."

"Well, you've wasted your time," she said, coldly.

His smile faltered. "That's not why I'm here."

She stared at him. "Of course, that's why you're here!" she snapped. "Why else would you be here? To ask me on a date?'

He shifted uncomfortably, then said, "Well, that was the idea."

Her look of annoyance turned to one of disbelief.

"You're asking me out on a date?"

He looked down, then straightened, meeting her gaze steadily. "Yes," he said. "Yes, I am."

"Why do you want to date me? I'm nothing but a quick blowjob backstage."

He held her gaze. "I guess I just liked seeing you. Not just the fooling around, but I liked seeing you. And I guess I'd like to get to know you—really get to know you."

"You… and me… on a date," she repeated.

He flushed with anger. "Is that so damn hard to imagine?" he said, hotly.

She grew quiet and studied him thoughtfully. Slowly, she answered, "No… I guess not."

"Does that mean you'll go out with me?" he asked, hopefully.

"What about your girlfriend?"

He waved, dismissively. "We're finished. We've been finished since the second time I saw you."

She studied him again, then nodded. "Okay."

His smile lit the room.

Chapter 58

The messages kept piling up. Toni called twice, and Kris detected actual concern in her voice the second time. A couple of hang ups. Linda calling from England, sounding scratchy and far away. Her boss, Steve, asking how much time she needed to take, and wondering whether he needed to hire a temp to fill in.

Since her one foray to the café, Kris had not left her apartment. Seeing Marty had been too painful. She thought he had returned to England with the rest of the band, but what if he hadn't? She couldn't bear to see him again. She couldn't stop thinking about him; his warm brown eyes, his ready smile, the passion that flared so easily between them.

Three days passed. She slept, watched TV, slept some more. She felt so tired all the time. Linda called again. Kim. Two more hang-ups. Then, David, asking her to call with a decision on the Puppet Master interview.

"Come on, Kris. Show me the backbone I know you have." His tone was gruff, his Scottish brogue, pronounced. "Pick up the bleeding phone!"

Kris picked up the phone. Without realizing what she was saying, she told him she'd do the interview.

"Good!" he boomed. "You'll be glad you did." Promising to call her back with contact information, he rang off.

She stared at the phone in surprise. She couldn't believe she had just agreed to do the story. But even as the thought crossed her mind, she realized she felt better. Her head felt a little clearer.

Kris called Kim to tell her she was okay. She phoned Linda in England to tell her the same thing. They talked for several minutes, neither mentioning Marty.

David called back with Puppet Master's contact information and she called to set up the interview. She jotted the information in her notebook, realizing it was nearly filled with writing. Flipping through the pages, she read months of notes she'd taken about the groupie scene. Kris pulled her battered typewriter out of the closet and banged it onto the table. She had moped long enough. It was time to write about it. About ALL of it.

Chapter 59

Toni found Bobby surprisingly kind and funny. He took her to dinner, to the movies, to Coney Island. He even won her a stuffed animal, throwing balls at milk cans. He'd looked silly doing it, too – his long, curly blonde hair whipping in the wind, his leather jacket hampering his throw. He hadn't seemed to care, though. He'd just wanted to see her smile.

She went to several Hardwire shows. Backstage, he didn't give other girls a second glance. He showered, signed a few autographs, then made a beeline for her. The other girls had stared at him in surprise, at her in shock. Gone was the rock goddess they all strived to emulate. To say Toni had toned down her look was a vast understatement. She had traded her spandex and leather for jeans, gaudy makeup for more subtle colors and tones. She'd even dyed her hair closure to her natural brown color. She found she didn't need the brilliant plumage anymore.

Marius had called a week after the party disaster, demanding to know where she'd been.

"I don't answer to you," she said, coolly.

He laughed harshly. "You think not?" he asked, silkily. She didn't reply. He tried a different tact.

"Don Lyden's been asking about you. Wants to see the fiery woman who kicked his ass. I daresay, he actually enjoyed your abuse."

The thought of Don Lyden sickened her. She could still see his state of excitement as he'd chased Kim and tried to rape her. If he had enjoyed the beating she'd given him he was even sicker than she thought.

"I'm well through with Don Lyden, thank you very much." She kept her voice cool and steady.

Marius chuckled. "I thought he was the one you had to conquer."

"I don't do perverts."

"Funny, I thought you did everyone." His tone was less silky.

"Fuck you," she spat.

"You have, my dear, many times, many ways." He paused. "Well, good thing I've got a new top girl then." He laughed softly. "You trained her well, my dear."

Toni didn't know or care who he was talking about.

"See you around." He chuckled again.

"Not if I can help it," she said, and hung up the phone.

Toni had stayed busy re-thinking her life. Having Bobby around had helped. He did seem to like her for herself, and didn't put any stock into her past activities. She hadn't believed she could care for a man, but he had helped her uncover long-buried feelings. Their lovemaking, while passionate, was less frenzied than backstage trysts. She had even cried after one session, unable to handle the flood of emotion that had accompanied her shattering orgasm. Bobby had held her, stroking her hair and letting her cry. Somehow, he had understood. Slowly, she allowed herself to relax, to feel, to love.

Her mother and sister noticed the change in Toni. She could tell they wanted to know what had happened, but neither asked, and she didn't volunteer any information. Not just yet, she told herself. Her father was oblivious.

The weekend after Marius' phone call, Toni stood backstage at the club in Staten Island, waiting for Bobby. Hardwire had just finished their set. She had been staring aimlessly into space, when she heard someone call her name. Looking up, she saw Rusty making her way over. Rusty stopped in front of her and looked at her, coldly.

"Well, well, well," she drawled. Toni started in surprise. This didn't sound like the old Rusty. Gone was the breathless excitement. She sounded hard.

"Hey," Toni said.

Rusty looked her up and down, critically. "My, aren't we dressed down tonight?" Her blue eyes were chips of ice.

Toni shrugged, trying not to look confused by Rusty's attitude. "What have you been up to? I haven't seen you since the party." She tried to sound conversational.

Rusty's smile didn't reach her eyes. "Oh, I've been busy," she replied. "Very busy." She looked at Toni with dislike. "I've become very popular. And I guess I have *you* to thank for that."

Toni stared back. "For what?"

"For this!" Rusty spread her arms. "For making me think I could have a rosy future with a rich rock star, if I 'practiced' with guys like this. For letting me think someone cared about me enough to buy me cool clothes and pay for my hair and makeup, then letting me find out the hard way that there was no one. Just Marius Man and his perverted friends."

Her eyes narrowed. "For turning me into... YOU!"

Toni met her glare without flinching. "No one is making you do this."

"No?" Rusty raised one perfectly penciled eyebrow. 'Don't I have to work to pay for these nice clothes and nice hair and nice makeup?" She gave a harsh laugh. "Besides,

251

I've discovered I'm good at this. Good at pretending I like giving head, being fucked in the ass, being tortured. And I have you to thank for my *glamorous* life."

Toni flared with anger. "You *wanted* to be me. Now you are. So stop whining about it!"

Rusty drew herself up to her full height. "I wanted a rich rock star to take care of me! I didn't want to be a fucking groupie! I didn't want to feel like a heavy metal hooker!"

She laughed again. "But that's the hand I've been dealt. In time, I'll make people forget about the great Toni. Your reign is over. Mine is just beginning."

Toni flashed her a dismissive look. "Knock yourself out."

Bobby came around the corner then. Rusty smiled brightly when she spotted him, running her hands seductively down her spandex-clad hips.

"Hi Bobby," she purred, moving to his side. "Remember me?" She traced a long, red-tipped fingernail up and down his arm. "We had a good time at L'Amour."

He looked uncomfortable. "Uh… hi," he said, looking from Rusty to Toni. Toni ignored Rusty. She took Bobby's arm and asked, "Are you ready to go?"

"Uh, yes," he stammered. He said, "See you around" to Rusty and walked away, leaving the tall, blonde woman standing alone at the bar, oblivious to the men who were giving her their undivided attention.

Chapter 60

The Puppet Master interview went well. The four band members were down to earth. No pretense. They swore heartily throughout the interview and spent a good bit of time bashing what they called "lame-fuck hair bands." They gave Kris one of their cassettes and a ticket to that night's show at L'Amour. She listened to the tape when she got home. It had a hard pounding sound with frantically fast guitars and low, guttural singing. She loved it.

That night at L'Amour, she saw much of the same crowd that usually packed the club for shows. They seemed to be into the band as well. When Puppet Master finished their set, she headed backstage to check out the scene. The room was filled with groupies, but the guys didn't seem to notice. They stood around, chatting with the handful of guys who were there. Kris glanced around and spotted Rusty, primped and made up like the rest of the women. The open friendliness was gone from her face. Her eyes glittered with a hardness Kris had never seen.

She made her way across the room and tapped Rusty on the arm. Rusty spun around, her face relaxing as she recognized Kris.

"Hiya, honey!" Rusty exclaimed as she hugged Kris. "I haven't seen you in ages!" A genuine smile lit Rusty's face. She held Kris at arm's length and studied her.

"You've lost weight," she remarked. "How's Marty?"

"I don't know," Kris replied. "I haven't seen him since the party."

Rusty didn't look surprised. "Ah, too bad," she said, airily. "That's how it goes with rock stars."

She looked past Kris and spotted Puppet Master's bassist standing along.

"Gotta run." Rusty hugged Kris again, then sauntered over to the bassist. A moment later, they disappeared into the bathroom. Shaking her head sadly, Kris left.

A few days later, she stopped at the record store to visit Toni. What she saw surprised her. Toni was wearing jeans, her makeup was more toned down, and her hair was several shades darker than her trademark peroxide white. She looked more natural and it suited her. Toni smiled when she saw Kris.

"Nice to see you," she said, coming around the counter. The hug she gave Kris was awkward, but Kris appreciated the gesture.

Toni studied Kris critically. "You've lost weight," she remarked. "And you don't need to lose weight."

Kris shrugged. "I hadn't really noticed."

Toni led her behind the counter and pointed to a chair. Kris sat as Toni chose a tape from a stack of cassettes and popped it into the stereo. A second later, the rapid-fire sound of Puppet Master filled the store. Toni looked at Kris and grinned. "The next big thing," she shouted over the music. "I can't stand it, but I've got to play it."

"I just interviewed them," said Kris. "Nice guys. I saw Rusty at their show."

Toni snorted, then looked abashed. "I saw her, too, at a Hardwire show." She looked as though she wanted to say something more, then stopped. She and Kris sat silently, listening to Puppet Master's music hammering the store's stereo system.

Finally, Kris spoke. "There's something I want to know."

Toni looked at her. "What?"

"Did you have anything to do with Marty being with Charley at the party?"

Toni met her gaze evenly. "No." She sighed. "I know Marius had the hots for you," she admitted. "He had me buy that dress for you, after Charlotte told him how great it looked on you. He must have had her send him another dress, because you were wearing it when we found you that night."

Toni sighed again. "I was too wrapped up in my fantasy of getting together with Don Lyden to realize the extent of Marius' obsession with you." She snorted. "Little did I know what Don was into, either."

Kate smiled sadly. "Your desire for Don saved my sister," she said, touching Toni's arm.

"Thank God for small favors," Toni spat, with a grim smile. "I beat the shit out of him. Would you believe the fucker enjoyed it? At least, that's what I heard."

"Well, what have we her?"

They jumped at the sound of Marius' silky, deep voice. They'd been so engrossed in their conversation, neither had noticed him walk in.

Kris stood next to Toni and they both turned cold glances on Marius. He was dressed head to toe in his trademark black, complete with black cowboy boots. His black eyes glinted as he smiled at them.

"Ladies, don't you know how to greet an old friend?" He took Toni's hand and bent to kiss it, but she snatched it away angrily.

"You're no friend of ours," she snapped. "What the hell are you doing here?"

He kept smiling. "A man cannot live without the sweet sounds of music," he said smoothly, his long fingers trailing along the stack of cassettes arranged on the counter. Kris looked at him with loathing.

He turned his attention to Toni. "You haven't been to see me. I've missed you and our... fun times."

Toni's gaze grew glacial. "I told you. I'm through with you."

His smiled widened. "Ah, but is one ever really truly done?" he mused. He eased a cassette out of the stack and laid it on the counter. 'I'll take this," he said, pushing it toward Toni. She picked it up, her eyes narrowing when she saw it was Hardwire's latest. Kris noticed the sudden, tense look cross Toni's face.

Toni slammed the cassette down on the counter and snarled, "You can't threaten me! You would live to regret it.

Marius let out a bark of laughter. "Threat? Who's threatening anything? I just thought I'd take in Mr. Bobby Bright's dulcet tones. He's quite the... performer, I hear." He pulled out his wallet and removed a one-hundred-dollar bill. Sliding it across the counter, he said, "Keep the change, doll face. You've earned it."

Pocketing his wallet and cassette, he turned to Kris and murmured, "I regret never having had the chance to savor your... beauty." His eyes slid down Kris' body, making her feel slimy and dirty. "Ah, pity, Mr. Brinkman won't be savoring much longer, either. His past is about to catch up with him, I fear. The past never dies, you know, even if people die." With a jaunty wave, Marius strolled across the store and out the door.

Toni said heavily, her hands shaking uncontrollably.

"What is it?' Kris asked, worriedly.

Toni sat rigidly, as through trying to compose herself. "Nothing," she said, finally.

"That's BS," said Kris. "Tell me. Maybe I can help. I do owe you."

Toni glanced around the store, saw it was empty, and slumped back into her seat. After a few moments' silence, she told Kris about Bobby and the time they'd been spending together.

"And now," she finished, "it's as though Marius is threatening that. Why else would he come in here, buy a Hardwire cassette and talk about Bobby like that?"

Kris had to agree. She suddenly remembered Marius' comment about Marty. "Marty! He's done something to get Marty in trouble."

Toni looked concerned. "He knows something that could get Marty arrested?" She looked wildly around the store. 'I don't' know where he is, though. I don't' even know if he's still in town."

"You could try calling Linda," Toni suggested.

Kris felt her heartbeat slow a little. "Yes, that's what I'll do."

She started to gather here things, then burst out, "I hate that man! I wish we could do something to get him out of our lives for good!"

Toni didn't answer.

Chapter 61

Toni walked Kris to the door and was hugging her goodbye when Bobby showed up. He greeted Kris warmly, but she barely noticed him as she ran out the door.

Once outside, she tried to hail a taxi, but every one that drove by was occupied, so she began walking briskly uptown toward her apartment. Wave after wave of rage at Marius washed over her, leaving her insides boiling with hate. She felt impotent to do anything about him. He was just too powerful. She walked on, envisioning horrible things happening to him.

Kris hadn't been paying attention to her surroundings and was surprised to find herself outside the hotel where Marty had stayed until he'd moved into her apartment for those few blissful days. Tears welled up as Kris remembered their time together.

The tears spilled out before she could stop them. She squeezed her eyes shut as sobs wracked her body. She could smell his scent, the heady mixture of sandalwood and musk. She could even feel his arms around her.

Then it registered: someone *did* have his arms around her! Her eyes flew open and she found herself staring into a pair of liquid brown eyes.

"What?" she said, but he pulled her closer.

"Shh…" he said. She wound her arms around his neck and relaxed against him. Burying her head in his shoulder, she let the tears flow freely. He held her as the crowd swarmed around them; a life buoy in a roiling sea of bodies. She felt his lips on her forehead, her temple, her check. She lifted her face and his lips found hers. She closed her eyes and savored the kiss, her mouth opening under his. The crowd disappeared. There was only him.

She broke away suddenly, as Marius' words flashed in her brain.

"Marty!" she said wildly. "Marius says he's done something to get back at you! Something to get you arrested!"

Marty stroked her hair, unconcerned. "There's nothing he can do to me now. David and I have taken care of it. He can't get me. All he can do is drum up bad publicity."

His eyes found hers and he tightened his grip on her. "But, as long as I have you, I don't care about anything else."

She didn't remember him hailing a taxi. She sat in the backseat, curled in his embrace, not speaking. His hands moved endlessly, stroking her arms, her hair, her face. Henry helped them out of the cab and greeted Marty happily.

"We've missed you, young man," he said, shaking Marty's hand and glancing pointedly at Kris.

Marty grinned and said, "I'm back to stay," before leading Kris to her apartment. Once inside, he closed the door and turned to face her. She saw the pain and need in his eyes.

"Please don't send me away again," he pleaded.

Mutely, she looked at him and shook her head. That was all the answer he needed. His lips crushed hers, the contact taking her breath away. Somehow, they made it to her bedroom, clothes falling off along the way. Then, they were on her bed and he was above her, inside her, and the tidal wave of passion was building again. She cried out, surrendering to the emotion that overwhelmed her. She looked at his face; saw tears in his eyes as he moved closer to release. He kept her pinned under him, not taking his eyes off her face. She didn't trust herself to speak. Framing her face with his hands, he kissed her softly and said, "I would give *everything* up for you."

Chapter 62

Kris felt more alive than she had in weeks. As it turned out, Marty had never left New York. He had camped at his hotel, biding his time.

"I knew you cared for me," he said, stroking her hair. "I hoped I would get the chance to make you see we belong together." He turned on his side and studied her face. "But you never left your apartment, except that one time you went to the café."

She looked at him in surprise. "How do you know I never left my apartment?"

He smiled. "I watched for you. That bloke at the café must think I'm some sort of nutter. I walked past that place every day."

"Did you have David MacGregor call me?" she asked, rolling onto her stomach and propping herself up on her elbows.

He nodded. "I didn't have to prod him much. He really does like your writing." He trailed a finger down her spine. She shivered. "I knew you had to get back out there. I went to the Puppet Master show and watched you."

She looked at him sharply. "I didn't see you there."

"Well, I stayed out of sight, didn't I?" He chuckled, then his eyes darkened. "You have a beautiful back," he murmured, bending to plant soft kisses down her spine. Her entire body reacted to his touch. Gently, he turned her onto her back and lowered his mouth to her breast. She sucked in her breath and closed her eyes, feeling the passion build again.

"Oh, what you do to me!" he groaned, rolling on top of her.

Chapter 63

Marius paced his study, furious over the latest turn of events. That prick Brinkman had thwarted his attempt at revenge. He must have had that MacGregor fuck help him doctor the files. He knew David MacGregor had lots of connections in the press and within the police. The shithead's uncle was some high mucky-muck who would do anything to help his favorite nephew.

He stopped, picked up a glass and tossed back its contents. The whiskey burned a fiery trail to his stomach, where it continued to burn. He closed his eyes, savoring the pain. His ulcer was growing, but he didn't care. The pain kept his head clear.

Marius began pacing again, thinking of the best way to put his plan into action. He smiled grimly. Eager-to-please Rusty had turned out to be better than he'd hoped. She had balls, this one, even though she fucked more like a machine than a woman.

There was a soft knock, and Rusty's platinum blonde head appeared around the door.

"They're here," she said. "Shall I get them started?"

'Yes, you know what to do." Marius turned his back on her and heard the door close softly. He strode over to the bar and poured more whiskey.

He was sipping it when the door opened again. Without turning around, he said, with a bite in his voice, "I thought I told you to get things started."

He felt the silky softness of the robe all his women wore brush up against his back and felt two hands slide around to stroke him, and he stiffened despite his annoyance. He closed his eyes as fingers eased his zipper down and pulled his penis out; the touch feather-light. He was throbbing in earnest now. He tried to turn, but a voice whispered, "Shh… give yourself up to the sensation."

Marius remained where he was, savoring every stroke of the hand, which was coated with oil and sliding smoothly up and down at his painful erection. He knew he wasn't going to last much longer. His hazy mind tried to figure out who was standing behind him; the touch felt familiar. But, his orgasm was building and his mind was going foggy.

The hand squeezed tightly and moved faster. He groaned as he bucked with the force of his orgasm. It seemed to go on and on. Only one woman could make him cum like this, and she couldn't be here.

"Toni," he groaned, as the hooded figure moved around to face him. He reached out to pull back the hood, when a needle pricked his arm. He felt the sting and the rush of liquid into his veins. He grabbed at the hood again, but she jerked out of reach. Hazily, he saw her wiping the syringe with her robe, but something was wrong with her. Her hair was jet black and she wore sunglasses.

"Toni," he groaned again, falling to his knees. His heart was beating way too fast. "Help me."

She smiled coldly at him. "Help will be here soon," she said softly, settling into his leather armchair.

Marius fell onto his face, powerless to move. His brain worked furiously, even has his heart pounded like a jackhammer. She sat, smiling coldly at him, sipping from his glass of whiskey.

"You always gave the best…" he croaked, before his body gave a final jerk, then lay still.

Chapter 64

Rusty was heading back to Marius' office to see what was taking him so long, when the door opened and a golden-robed figure slipped out and hurried down the hall. Curious, Rusty waited until the figure turned the corner, before letting herself into Marius' study. She stopped short as she took in the sight of him lying sprawled on the floor, his pants down around his knees. Without checking his pulse, she knew he was dead.

Rusty sniffed the air. She recognized the scent as the cloying perfume Toni wore. So... Toni had come here tonight and killed Marius. For what? To protect her little love affair with Bobby?

Quietly, she shut the door and locked it. She had never been inside Marius' study alone. Time to see what he kept inside those locked drawers. She bent and searched his pants pockets for his keys. Pulling them out, she turned her back on his prone body and made her way to his filing cabinets. It didn't take long to find the key that unlocked Marius' secrets.

Sinking into the chair behind his desk, Rusty opened a file and began reading. An hour later, she had all the information she needed to take over Marius' empire, and begin planning her revenge.

Chapter 65

The news bulletin woke Kris. Marty must have fallen asleep with the TV on. The breathless newscaster announced, "Breaking news: infamous musician and industry bigwig Marius Man has been found dead inside his Upper West Side mansion. Preliminary reports indicate Man died from a massive overdose of cocaine and heroin. Several witnesses say the 52-year-old ingested a large amount of both drugs and was drinking heavily when he collapsed. We have a crew at the scene and will bring you more developments as they come in."

Kris sat up in bed, staring transfixed at the TV. Marty stirred beside her.

"What is it, luv?" he asked, sleepily.

"Marius. He's dead," she replied, stunned.

His eyes flew open. "What?"

"They just said on the TV." She pointed as another Breaking News update come on.

"This is Amy Graham with this Breaking News update. I am outside the palatial Upper West Side mansion of Marius Man, former drummer for the 60's and 70's rock band Wild Boys. We've learned Man has been found dead from an apparent overdose of cocaine and heroin. Witnesses say he was hosting a party for a well-known rock band and ingested large amounts of both drugs. Police won't name the rock band. Several women at the party say Man collapsed and died without regaining consciousness.

The question now is, who inherits his empire? Marius Man controlled a successful entertainment company. His mansion runs the length of the block. He also owns an apartment in SoHo and a summer home in East Hampton."

The reporter turned as police officers led several women clad in golden robes out the front door, to waiting patrol cars. She moved toward them, calling, "Excuse me, can you tell me what you saw inside?"

The women buried their faces in their robes. Two sobbed uncontrollably.

Kris' eyes widened as another figure came out the door. "Look!" she said, grabbing Marty's hand. "It's Rusty!"

Rusty, dressed in a severe black suit with a very short skirt, shut the door and made her way down the stairs in dangerously high heels. Her makeup was stark against her pale face, her white blonde hair standing up in short spikes. The reporter rushed up to her, but Rusty muttered a brisk, "No comment" and stepped into a waiting patrol car, flashing her long legs as she slid into the back seat.

The news of Marius Man's death spread like wildfire. The preliminary autopsy confirmed he died of a massive drug overdose. Marty told Kris that something about this didn't ring true.

"In all the time I spent with him, the most I ever saw him do was drink a glass of whiskey or brandy. I never saw him do drugs." He shrugged and pulled Kris close. "Ah, what do I know, anyway? He's gone and we move on."

His words stayed with Kris. Had someone killed Marius Man? If so, why? She didn't have to think hard to come up with several reasons. He had manipulated so many lives for so many years. Now, he'd never hurt anyone again. She resolved to put him out of her mind.

Chapter 66

Toni watched the news with grim satisfaction. So, they thought the fucker died accidentally. Good. And good riddance, she thought, fiercely. She looked down at the golden robe lying on her bed. She'd covered all her bases, even worn a wig. She doubted anyone had recognized her. There had been so many women at the party, it had been easy to get lost in the crowd. She'd even come face to face with Don Lyden, who barely glanced at her. He had been with a girl who looked about 13. She saw one of the robed women pour something into a soft drink and hand it to the girl.

With a sound of disgust, Toni tore her mind away from that image. Instead, she focused on Marius' face when he realized he was dying, just as she brought him to orgasm.

"Coming and going at the same time," she thought smugly, stuffing the robe, wig and syringe into a black garbage bag.

She finished packing and hauled boxes downstairs to the back door. Bobby would be arriving shortly to help her move to his apartment.

Toni sat at the kitchen table and looked around the room. She felt a pang of loss, thinking about the happy times her family had enjoyed in this kitchen, so many years ago. Before high school. Before Toni chose the path that severed her relationship with her sister, and turned her into a pariah in her father's eyes. Only her mother had continued to love her unconditionally.

Unexpected tears welled up in her eyes. Hearing someone coming down the stairs, she hastily wiped her eyes and attempted an expression of indifference. Her sister came into the kitchen, stopping when she saw Toni. Her eyes moved to the boxes by the back door.

"So, you're really moving out," Angela remarked, opening the fridge and taking out a soda. She popped the top and joined Toni at the table.

There was an awkward silence. Then, both sisters began to talk at the same time.

"You first," said Toni.

Angela played with a tendril of hair that had escaped her neat ponytail. She seemed at a loss for words.

"Okay, then, I'll go first." Toni took a deep breath, and said, "Things haven't been the same between us since high school, when you saw me... well, when you saw me that day. I hate that you saw it.

I was never smart, like you. I didn't know what I wanted to do with my life, but I knew I didn't want to be invisible. I wanted to be someone, and those boys made me feel powerful. It was amazing, having guys worship me, guys in multi-platinum selling bands. It was amazing, having women look up to me, wanting to *be* me.

It wasn't until Marius' party when I realized just how much I really hated this life; how blind I'd been to the way I was using others, to attain my own goals. It made me sick."

She stood and moved to the sink. "Then, having Bobby care about me, as a person, not a groupie, made me realize just how much I'd been looking for the approval I wasn't getting here at home. I don't know whether I deserve this happiness, or even how long will last. I'm glad to have the chance to try a normal life."

Tears filled her eyes as she looked at her sister. "I don't know how to get back what we've lost. I just wish you happiness in your own life."

She turned her back on her sister and hunched over the sink, wiping at her tears. She heard the chair scrape as it was pushed back, and thought Angela had left the room. The thought made her shoulders shake, with sobs she could no longer hold back. Then, arms encircled her, and she heard her sister's voice.

"I'm so sorry I judged you for so long. Believe it or not, part of me was jealous of what I considered your free-living ways." Toni snorted in disbelief. "It's true," Angela insisted. "I was so straight laced, always following the rules, always being the good girl. I wished I could have just a little of your independence. I never realized you were hurting as much as I was."

Toni turned and hugged her sister fiercely. They were both crying now. Neither spoke. No other words needed to be said.

They were sitting at the table drinking coffee when Bobby arrived with several friends to move her things to his apartment. He greeted Angela warmly, and invited her to visit them once they were settled. When the last box was loaded, Bobby told Toni he'd wait for her in the truck, then left her alone with her sister.

Toni smiled at Angela. "I'm terrified I'm going to fuck this up," she confessed, but Angie shook her head.

"This is the best thing that could have happened to you. Bobby looks like he really cares about you."

Angela saw the black garbage bag sitting by the door, and offered to toss it in the trash, but Toni grabbed the bag and said she'd take care of it. Seeing the curious look in Angie's eyes, she smiled reassuringly. "This is just stuff I no longer need, from my... past life." With a wave, she opened the kitchen door and went to join Bobby.

Chapter 67

Kris worked steadily on her book about groupies. She wasn't sure whether to include the incidents with Marius, but Marty urged her to.

"Make a clean break," he said. "Get it out into the open." So, she'd added him but changed his name, as she had done with the others.

When she typed out the last page, Marty had a surprise. He and David had secretly shopped her book and lined up several agents for her to meet. Bemused, but touched by their support, she set up appointments.

The first two agents were businesslike. They seemed very busy and promised to look things over and get back to her, before ushering her out of their plush offices.

Trying to quell her disappointment, she called the third agent, hoping things would go better.

Kris liked Lisa Teague right away. Lisa was tall and solidly built, with spiky black hair, very red lips and a direct gaze framed by heavy, black-rimmed glasses. Her handshake was firm.

As they sat down in Linda's office, an assistant came in with a coffee tray. Lisa waited while Kris added cream and sugar to hers before getting down to business.

"I loved your manuscript," she said. "The only thing I would do, if I were you, is change a few descriptions. It's easy to recognize the real people behind some of the characters. I have an excellent editor who can help you there. But, all in all, I'm confident I can get you a great publishing deal." She leaned back in her chair and sipped coffee.

Kris was stunned. "You like it as it is?"

"Why wouldn't I?" Lisa smiled at the look on Kris' face. "Look, I know David MacGregor. He told me you were an excellent writer. I trust Davo. And he's right. Once I started reading your manuscript, I couldn't put it down."

Kris liked this woman even more. She felt she could trust her. She smiled back at Lisa and said, "I trust David MacGregor, too. And he recommended you highly."

Lisa grinned. "Sounds like we have ourselves a deal."

She held out her hand and they shook. "I'll have Sally draw up a contract and have Emi Clarke, the editor, call you about the changes."

Kris left the office, exhilarated. She found a pay phone and called Marty to tell him the news.

The publishing offers came in the following week. Lisa excitedly told Kris that three companies were involved in a bidding war. "All three are good, reputable companies, so you'll get a great deal no matter who wins."

Kris worked with Emi to complete the changes. She liked the editor, who always had a smile on her face, making her half-Japanese face look more Asian. They finished the changes as the bidding war ended.

When Lisa told her to final price, Kris nearly fainted.

"And that's not counting royalties," said Lisa smugly. "Of course, there's the cut for Emi and me," she added, in an offhanded voice.

Kris laughed in disbelief. "That still leaves me with a fortune!" she exclaimed. "What will I do with all that money?"

Lisa hugged her fiercely. "Live, honey. LIVE."

Chapter 68

Metal Countdown threw Kris a launch party at L'Amour. Kimba and Hardwire played to a sold-out crowd of people from the publishing and recording industries, plus lots of friends, family and acquaintances. Kris was besieged by people wanting to say hello.

Marty remained by her side for most of the night, but moments before the toast, he told Kris he had to leave for a few minutes. When she asked where he was going, he kissed her and said, "It's a surprise."

Moments later, she saw Linda Hart making her way across the club, and rushed to greet her friend as David MacGregor's Scottish brogue boomed out from the stage.

"Here to play at special request, as we toast Kris Lindsey on what's sure to be a bestseller... Black Gallows!"

Kris' heart leapt as the curtains opened and the band launched into a scaled down version of its hard-rocking set. Her heart swelled as she watched Marty onstage, knowing nothing could tear them apart now.

Chapter 69

Toni was impressed by the turnout at Kris' party. She was glad that Kris and Davo had asked Hardwire to play. There were so many record company bigwigs here, they were sure to land a major label deal tonight.

She looked over to where Kris was standing with Marty, and smiled. Things could have turned out so differently for her. Toni was glad Kris had stood her ground and resisted Toni's efforts to groom her, and shuddered to think what would have happened had Marius' plan succeeded.

Kris caught her gaze and waved happily. Toni waved back, then headed to the ladies room. She stepped into a stall and ripped off some toilet paper. Closing the door, she sat on the toilet and dabbed at her eyes. She was so damned emotional lately.

She heard the door creak open and the clack of high heels on the tile floor. The feet stopped outside her stall and a hand tipped with long red fingernails slid a note under the door. The heels clacked again as the figure left the bathroom.

Toni bent and picked up the note. She unfolded it, and gasped at the two words written on it.

"I KNOW."

Chapter 70

Rusty stood in the crowded club, surveying the scene. She saw her girls mingling with the crowd, delivering invitations to a party at the brownstone alter that night. She smiled humorlessly. Marius' empire was hers now and she had every intention of keeping it a success.

She glanced dispassionately at Kris. Marty was hovering around her like a moth to a light bulb. Rusty felt a pang as she saw the happy smiles on their faces, and forced herself to turn away. She truly liked Kris, but there was no way she was going to sit on the information Marius left about Marty and his past. No, she had to put them out of her mind. She had a plan, and she had to put it into action. She didn't need a damn rock star to make her happy. She was now the most powerful woman; no, make that the most powerful *person* on the scene.

A movement near the ladies room caught her attention. She smiled smugly as she watched Toni stumble out of the bathroom, a panicked look on her face. Toni stared wildly around the club before her eyes met Rusty's.

Rusty raised a hand tipped with long red fingernails and waved cheerfully at Toni. Then, turning on her high heels, she sauntered out of the club.

She had work to do.

Acknowledgements and Thanks

Much love to my friends and family, who supported me through this challenging endeavor.

Thanks to a special group of people who read various incarnations of Steel Goddesses and offered priceless feedback: Andrea, Arleen, Carolyn, Dana, Ella, Jesse, Joanna, Julie, Karen V, Kate, Kris, Matt, Pat, Tiara, and Tonya.

Much appreciation to Iron Maiden, whose music fueled my frenzied writing sessions. This book is dedicated to you and other bands who helped shape the 80's metal scene in New York City, and to all the groupies who helped keep those bands going. I salute you.

About the Author

Ann Brandt is the alter-ego of a broadcast journalist living and working in the Pacific Northwest. She worked in the music industry in New York City in the 80's, spending her days as an administrative assistant at several major record labels, and her nights going to concerts and singing in heavy metal bands. And yes, she did spend some time backstage.

More information:

AnnCBrandt.Author@gmail.com

AnnBrandtWrites.wordpress.com

45582259R00173

Made in the USA
San Bernardino, CA
11 February 2017